TOWNE SQUARE

WHAT READERS ARE SAYING

Praise for *Main Street*

Winner of the 2017 Golden Leaf Best First Book award sponsored by the New Jersey Chapter of Romance Writers of America

Winner of the 2018 Carolyn Readers' Choice Award in the Romantic Suspense Category sponsored by the North Texas Chapter of Romance Writers of America

"I dropped my Kindle, threw my hands in the air yelling oh my god no freaking way! I totally did not see that coming! And that ending... I need the next book now!"
—Kelly, Amazon reviewer

"Characters you fall head over heels for, and at least one you turn pages for to see if karma steps in!"
—Dena Hawkins, Amazon reviewer

"The detail, the description, the visualization is solid and you, as a reader, can see everything that is being expressed."
—Harlan Bryan, author of *Wounded* & *Wildfire* novels

"The work flows from one scene to another flawlessly... The characters are memorable and entertaining with the type of personalities that make a story come to life."
—*The Cozy Review*

"I loved the characters; they were funny, exciting and sexy. The story was fast paced; the mystery was suspenseful."
—Tina C, Amazon reviewer

"This book keeps you hopping. I couldn't put it down."
—LRC, Top Amazon Contributor

"Intriguing, romantic, and funny... a perfect combination."
—Rebecca Dukett, Amazon reviewer

"...action, love, drama, and suspense... I didn't want the book to end."
—Joha D, Amazon reviewer

"Dianna Wilkes has created a masterpiece with *Main Street*. Romance and intrigue flow readily throughout the story."
—J Banda, Amazon reviewer

"There are plenty of twists and turns, both emotional and evil."
—*The Good, The Bad and The Unread*

"...full of mystery, suspense, romance, and balanced out with humorous real-life moments."
—Lea Kirk, *USA Today* Bestselling Author

ALSO BY DIANNA WILKES

Providence Island Series

Main Street, Book 1

Towne Square, Book 2

South Pointe, Book 3

Crossroads, Book 4 (coming soon)

TOWNE SQUARE

PROVIDENCE ISLAND, BOOK 2

DIANNA WILKES

Copyright © 2018 Dianna Wilkes
Excerpt from *South Pointe*, © 2018 Dianna Wilkes

All rights reserved.

ISBN-13 (print): 978-0-9983895-3-0
ISBN-13 (ebook): 978-0-9983895-2-3

Publisher's Note: The characters and events portrayed in this book are fictional and or are used fictitiously and solely the product of the author's imagination. Any similarity to real persons, living or dead, places, businesses, events or locales is purely coincidental.

Cover design: Karri Klawiter
www.artbykarri.com

Editing & print formatting:
Dana Delamar
By Your Side Self-Publishing
www.ByYourSideSelfPub.com

No part or the whole of this book may be reproduced, distributed, transmitted or utilized (other than for reading by the intended reader) in ANY form (now known or hereafter invented) without prior written permission by the author, except by a reviewer, who may quote brief passages in a review. The unauthorized reproduction or distribution of this copyrighted work is illegal, and punishable by law. Please purchase only authorized electronic editions. Your support of the author's rights is appreciated.

DEDICATION

In memory of Noah Holley

You were always there for me, Dad.

Chapter One

Damn it, Kate. Why couldn't you stay dead?

Erik McCall stormed across the second level of the downtown Providence Island parking garage. His footsteps echoed in sharp, steady beats, keeping pace with the pounding at his temples. Twenty-some years had passed, but it took less than three weeks for Kate to spin his world into chaos. Just like before, she was playing on Rhys's emotions, driving a wedge between father and son.

He heaved a deep breath, then detoured from his path to the stairwell and headed to the overlook instead. A bead of sweat trickled down the side of his face, and he wiped it away with an impatient sweep of one hand.

Barely the end of May, and summer's heat was already bitch-slapping spring into submission.

Calm down. Losing his temper wouldn't solve anything. Proof of that was lashing out at Rhys after his unreasonable defense of that woman. Not that it hadn't been deserved. Rhys allowed sympathy for Kate to sway his loyalty away from the one person who had been there for him all that time.

His father.

As justified as Erik's decision had been, he regretted it. He'd fallen right into Kate's trap. Losing his temper. Firing his own son from the family business.

His breathing slowed, his heart settling into a calmer cadence as he gazed out at PI's downtown streets. Nothing like looking out over his kingdom to put a shine on his day.

Down the block, one street over, the tip of McCall Construction's headquarters saluted him. He gave an approving nod before scanning the vista, north to south. Fitness center. Library. Courthouse. Bank. And so on and so on. From common laborers to seasoned craftsmen, each generation of McCalls had left its mark on PI.

His attention shifted to a two-story monstrosity with an art-deco façade. Kate's building. Yellow tape from the sheriff's department stretched across the front entrance. Word hadn't gotten around yet on what had happened, but obviously nothing good.

Biggest mistake of his life had been marrying that woman. A sham that wouldn't have happened if she hadn't gotten herself pregnant. When a two-car accident on the mainland had sent her off to the afterlife over two decades ago, she'd ceased to exist even as a memory.

So what if he hadn't watched her being planted six feet under? Dead was dead.

Except Kate hadn't died.

When the attorney for the other driver had ponied up a check with more zeros than Erik had seen in his lifetime and an offer to take care of Kate's burial, he'd taken the money. No questions asked. He'd returned to PI with Rhys, the four-year old son Kate had tried to keep from him.

End of story—until Kate showed up on his turf last week, calling herself Dana Canfield and claiming there had been a mix-up of identities between the two female drivers. Along with a case of amnesia that had erased her memories prior to the crash.

As if he were to blame for that mess.

If anyone was at fault, it was the hospital for not catching the mistake in the beginning. Or James Canfield and his lawyer for allowing it to continue. Her fake husband could have corrected the mistake from the get-go.

Erik snorted. For all her considerable faults, Kate did have some serious talent between the sheets. Must have been good enough to keep Canfield satisfied all these years until a bullet sent him to the beyond and put Kate on a collision course back into his life.

Whatever had raised Rhys's suspicions that Dana Canfield was his long-thought-dead mother didn't matter. What mattered was his son failing to face him man-to-man and ask for an explanation. Instead, Rhys had turned his back on his own father for a woman he barely remembered.

Fire hotter than the morning sun charged through Erik's gut. His eyes misted, and he blinked away the unexpected, unwanted moisture.

You're my *son.*

The child he'd raised while dealing with his own father, a man who'd fought every change Erik had wanted to make for the business. Some days had been more than he could handle, and he'd often left Rhys in the care of Tom Carson's family to take much-needed breaks.

He swallowed down the lump in his throat. Was that why Rhys was so easily swayed by Kate?

I tried, son. Maybe it didn't feel that way to you, but I never abandoned you.

Erik's fingers tightened around the metal guardrail. He sucked in a deep breath, savoring the salty tang of the warm ocean air rushing into his lungs. Another deep breath, and his hands relaxed.

I can fix this. Mend fences with Rhys and offer him his job back. McCall Construction was *their* heritage. All Kate could offer Rhys were faded memories and false hopes.

You didn't beat me before, Kate. You won't win this time either.

Erik pushed away from the overlook and walked to the stairwell. With each step, he ticked off a mental list of the work waiting for him.

The flicker of a shadow as he entered the stairwell gave him a split-second's warning before a crowbar slammed onto his shoulder. His knees buckled, and bile surged into his throat. He stumbled down a few steps, grabbing at the handrail.

Erik reached blindly for the assailant's shirt. If he could pull the punk off-balance....

The punk retaliated with a hard shove.

The world spun in a sickening whirl of motion and color. Concrete and iron flashed in a series of strobing images as Erik tumbled down the remaining steps. His back slammed into the cement landing, pain ripping along his spine. A gray haze clouded his vision as he struggled to breathe.

He squinted up at the blurry figure standing at the top of the stairwell. A deep-throated chuckle filtered through the sound of his own labored breathing. He wasn't beaten yet. Let the punk come close enough for him to get in one shot. He blinked…

…the man was gone.

Fumbling for his cell phone, Erik swallowed back a scream of pain. He closed his eyes, but the world continued to spin. He sank back against the gritty concrete with one final thought before tumbling into darkness.

Kate was back, and so was trouble.

Jamie Danvers pulled her well-used Ford compact onto the circular driveway where her employer Dana Canfield resided. With the Canfield building designated a crime scene for the time being, their regular morning meeting had been moved to Dana's home.

Knowing her employer's love for art deco, Jamie was surprised that Dana had chosen a traditional Federal-style house. Brick with white clapboard siding and wrought iron railings that led to a wide front porch. A house too large for a woman alone, but perhaps that was the reason she'd selected it. After her husband's murder and her son Joshua's disappearance the previous year, maybe Dana needed that reassurance. A symbol of hope that one day she'd have a family again.

Finding a job the second day after Jamie had arrived on PI was more than she'd dared to hope, especially with less than two hundred dollars to her name. A dual art/marketing degree didn't count for much when the majority of her resume consisted of retail and restaurant jobs. When she'd applied for a job at Canfield Designs, she'd expected a polite refusal, but instead she'd received an interview for an administrative assistant position that same afternoon. Dana's enthusiasm for the current renovation project on Main Street had been contagious. By the time the session had ended, Jamie had wanted the job with a fierce desire. Not just for the financial opportunity, but for the creative challenge as well.

Having an encouraging employer like Dana was a blessing, and Jamie was determined to do everything in her power to help make Canfield Designs a success.

Knowing you, you'll find a way to mess it up.

A band of tension tightened around her temples. She shoved away memories of her mother's strident voice and a past that still tried to control her.

I won't. Not anymore.

Keys and purse in hand, she exited the car. The front door opened as she climbed the brick steps.

"I thought it was you when I heard the car pull in," Dana called from the open doorway. Dark curly hair tumbled in stylish disarray just above her shoulders, and her full lips curved in a welcoming smile. Her pink sweater set and gray trousers looked simple, but the cut and materials suggested a high-end purchase and conveyed a casual elegance that seemed effortless.

Jamie gave a silent sigh. Her plain black slacks and blue sweater were several years old but suitable for the present time. Other expenses had dibs on her first paycheck.

She stepped into the entry, noting the tension lingering in Dana's dark brown eyes. "I hope I didn't alarm you sitting there. I was…" *Wishing? Daydreaming?* "…admiring your house."

"I try not to jump at every noise." Dana's smile eased into something more natural as she pushed the door closed. "Remind me to take you on a tour before we leave. Though with all the boxes yet to be unpacked, the overall effect isn't very impressive."

A ding sounded from the back of the house.

Dana whirled and headed down the hallway. "Let's talk in the kitchen."

Morning light spilled through the windows that lined most of one wall, bathing the room in a soft golden glow. No boxes were in sight in this room. If Dana had accomplished nothing else, at least she'd set up the kitchen.

Dana slid a tin of blueberry muffins out of the oven and set them on an iron trivet. Jamie's stomach rumbled softly as she propped her forearms on the countertop. The golden-brown cakes glistened with a sprinkling of sugar. The tantalizing scent almost tempted her to risk a burned finger and pluck one from the tin.

She resisted the urge, asking, "What can I do to help?"

"Grab the juice out of the fridge. Milk too, if you prefer. Sorry if I seem disorganized. I didn't get home from Nick's until an hour ago."

"Oh, that's…" Jamie's voice trailed off.

"TMI?" Dana chuckled as she transferred the muffins to a cloth-lined basket. "I didn't mean to embarrass you. Although I'm sure Nick and I have given off sufficient vibes to indicate we're now a couple."

Dana's whirlwind courtship with handsome mechanic Nick Warden had been a surprise to no one. Their chemistry was off the charts, and Jamie suspected a wedding wouldn't be too far in the future. Despite the terror Dana had faced the prior day, she glowed with happiness.

"I'm happy for you. I think you and Nick are wonderful together."

Dana stretched an arm across the countertop, laying one hand on Jamie's. "Yesterday when Detective Lansing held that gun on me, someone with blonde hair passed by the window. I got only a quick glance, and I thought it might have been you."

Jamie's appetite disintegrated in a swift flood of acid. "I should have been there. I could have…"

"You could have been hurt. Because of me."

Jamie wrapped both hands around Dana's. "You're not to blame for anything that happened. Detective Lansing is the one who's responsible, and he paid for it."

"He certainly did. But whoever killed Lansing is still out there." Withdrawing her hand, Dana picked up the basket and walked toward the breakfast nook. "And we don't know if or when he'll strike again."

Jamie set the pitcher of juice on the table, noting the three place settings. "Is Rhys still joining us?"

Dana frowned as she seated herself. "He's at the hospital. His father had some sort of accident. I don't know any other details." Tight lines around her mouth contradicted her calm tone.

Jamie hadn't met Erik McCall, but based on comments made by her roommate Paige Carson, he seemed to be a hard, bitter man. "Do you hate Mr. McCall?" The question slipped out without warning. She clamped her lips together and lowered her eyes, waiting for a well-deserved rebuke.

"If you'd asked me that when I first learned of his part in my identity being switched with the other woman in the car crash, I would have said yes." Dana lifted a grape from the fruit tray, examined it, then popped it into her mouth.

Jamie let out the breath she'd been holding and selected a

muffin from the basket. She broke the pastry in half, releasing a fragrant wisp of blueberry-scented steam. "But not now?

"Oh, I still despise him. He claims he knew nothing about the identity switch. He even bragged that he wasn't the least bit sorry. But as Rhys pointed out, Erik believed what he was told because it suited him. He was rid of me and got full custody of our son."

"It wasn't right."

A shadow washed over Dana's delicate features. "My life changed because of Erik's selfishness. He left me with strangers, and our son grew up without his mother. He's responsible for not caring enough to do the right thing. But James—my supposed husband—knew, and he said *nothing*. All those years we had together... Why would he pretend I was his wife?"

Jamie stared down at her plate. She knew firsthand the sting of rejection from people she'd loved, heartbreaks that couldn't be healed, trust that couldn't be regained. Dana was a strong woman, but such strength had to have come with a price. "We haven't known each other very long, but I hope you feel you can talk to me."

Dana rubbed her left hand, the indentations from rings worn for many years still visible. Her gaze shifted to the window overlooking the patio, and her mouth curved into a brief smile. Outside, a colorful array of potted plants decorated the area. A surprise gift from Nick, with assistance from Jamie and Paige.

When Dana looked back in Jamie's direction, the smile vanished, and the shadows returned.

"Everyone, including James, told me my memories—ones I know now were of Rhys—had never happened. I couldn't remember basic facts about the man I was told was my husband. I had no memories of our child. I suffered from brain damage—"

"But you didn't!" Heat burned across Jamie's cheeks. "How could he have done that to you? To his own son?"

"I ask myself those same questions. All those years, I felt something in our lives was missing, and it was my responsibility to make it right. What hurts the most is how hard I tried to *be* Dana Canfield. I had to convince a scared little boy that I was his mother. I pushed away any thoughts of the things that seemed right and real because that was what I had to do for my family and my marriage." Her dark eyes shone with unshed tears. "Can you imagine what it's like to constantly feel as if you're inadequate?"

If there's a way to mess up.... Another wave of treacherous memories threatened Jamie's composure. She swallowed back the hurt and forced the tremor from her voice. "Yes, I can."

Dana shook her head, dark curls tumbling around her neck. "I need to keep reminding myself that I'm blessed. I found my son, and we're in business together. I have a handsome, sexy man in my life, an exciting project to keep me busy... and the world's best assistant." She smiled, then reached for her tablet and unfolded the cover. "Let's get to work. I want to hear about your website idea. I haven't had a chance to look over your email from yesterday. Is the purpose of the site to promote the Main Street renovations?"

Jamie pushed down the butterflies that swooped through her belly. If Dana didn't like her idea, it wouldn't be the end of the world. Right?

"PI has a municipal website with the usual governmental and tourist information, but it only lists the names of the stores and a short description about each one. From my conversations with Alison at the chamber of commerce yesterday, they only intend to highlight the restoration work."

Jamie paused, waiting for a comment, but Dana merely nodded. *Here goes.* "My suggestion is to create a Main Street merchants' website. We include a page on the renovation, but the primary focus is on the merchants. The history of the shops. Bios of the owners. Personalize the shopping experience to the potential customer. Sales, coupons, seasonal gift baskets. Even cross-promotions...." Her voice trailed off, the butterflies fluttering into stillness. "I'm totally off base, aren't I?"

Of course she was. Everything she'd said was out of scope. It wasn't part of the construction plan. It wasn't part of the design plan. It was her going off on a tangent that had nothing to do with the work she was paid to do. Heat rose up her chest and neck, and a light sweat broke out across her brow.

"Will the website increase sales?"

Dana's question snapped her attention back to the conversation.

Jamie reached for her juice glass. She took a sip as she regained her composure. "The potential is there. More than what the chamber's site would accomplish. The Merchants' Association would be responsible for the site. We can assist in the setup, making sure the site has been properly optimized for search engines with the right metadata and SEO keywords." She pushed her plate to one side. "I also thought we'd check on placing advertisements in travel magazines."

"Have you talked with anyone in the mayor's office? Will this duplicate anything they're doing?"

"Not at all. Their position is that the Merchants' Association is responsible for promoting their shops. I know this is outside the scope of the project—"

A dimple flashed in Dana's cheek. "I love it." She tapped on the tablet. "We need to regain goodwill with the merchants while they're dealing with the construction. If they agree, make sure they understand they're responsible for maintaining the site after the initial launch. Can you mock up some sample web pages we can use for visuals? Also, set up a meeting with Bart Caine. He's the president of the Merchants' Association."

Jamie swallowed the thread of acid that seeped into her throat. "It would have more impact coming from you."

"Keywords? Metadata? That's your specialty, my dear. Which reminds me—" Dana removed a card from the inside pocket of the tablet case and extended it across the table. "Give this a once-over before I have your business cards printed."

Jamie turned the card over in her hands. The letters were elegant and black, set off by Canfield's signature teal and gold design.

Canfield Designs
Jamie Danvers, Marketing and Communication

She read it once, then a second time, before looking up in confusion. "Dana, this isn't—"

Elbow on the table, Dana rested her chin in the palm of her hand. "I didn't think I had a chance in a million when Rhys interviewed me for this project. I was a one-woman company with little experience with commercial projects."

Jamie frowned. "I didn't know that."

"I did my homework. I made trips to PI and created sketches of how I envisioned Main Street. A slightly conceited move, considering Rhys had his own vision." She straightened, shrugging. "But it worked. He hired me on the spot. He loved what I said about merging art with science. My design skills with his architectural and construction knowledge."

Jamie looked down at the card, running her fingertips over the glossy surface. "When I saw the name on your building, I had no idea if you even had an opening. I walked past the door three times before I had the nerve to go in."

"I'm glad you did. When I read your resume, I realized what we were missing. You have a retail background and can connect with the merchants in a way that Rhys and I can't. Even though you didn't have the advantage of preparing for your interview, you were able to relate most of the questions I asked to something in your portfolio or your experience." Dana pushed the tablet case to one side. "Do you know what impressed me the most?"

Jamie shook her head. Dana thought her impressive?

"When you responded with 'I don't know the answer to that question.' You didn't try to make up something that had nothing to do with what I asked. It was refreshing and honest. What you don't know, you'll learn as we go along."

The title, the promotion, the card. All those outward symbols took a back seat to Dana's greatest gift. Her trust and respect.

Jamie forced the words past the lump in her throat. "Thank you. I won't let you down."

"I know you won't. You've more than earned it." Dana lifted her juice glass in toast. "By the way, I need you to help me start looking for a new admin."

"Yes, ma'am!" Jamie tapped the lip of her glass against Dana's, and they laughed as a musical note filled the air.

The doorbell rang as the clink of crystal faded.

"I'll answer it." Jamie hopped to her feet before Dana could move. "My job. Front line until we get a new admin."

She detoured through the living room with a skip in her step, faltering when she glanced out the front window. The sheriff's cruiser was parked behind her Ford. She rushed to the foyer and jerked the door open. Sherriff Sam Wallace stood on the porch, hand poised above the doorbell.

Jamie slipped past him, closing the door behind her. "What?"

The brusque greeting sent Sam's eyebrows soaring upward. Clad in a crisp uniform, he appeared nothing like the friendly guy who hung out with Rhys, Paige, and Jamie for weekly dinners at the Lighthouse Cantina. Today, the tall, broad-shouldered lawman was all about business. His square jaw tightened as he glared down at her. She lifted her chin and returned the stare.

"I'm here to see Mrs. Canfield."

"If this is bad news—"

He cut her off with a shake of his head. Snaking an arm around her, he opened the door and strode into the house.

Jamie's mouth dropped open. She raced in after him, sliding to a halt as Dana appeared in the entrance to the kitchen.

"Good morning, Sherriff." Dana's tone was nothing short of gracious, but the stiff set of her shoulders radiated tension.

Sam tipped his head in polite acknowledgement. "Mrs. Canfield. Sorry to intrude, but I have a few items to discuss with you."

"We were having a breakfast meeting. Have a seat, and you can join us while we talk." Without waiting for Sam's reply, Dana returned to the table. She stood beside her chair, gesturing to the place setting that been prepared for Rhys. "Please."

Jamie smirked as Sam reluctantly moved from the doorway to the table. *And that's the way you do it.* Within seconds, Dana had seized control and put Sam in his place.

"I don't have coffee prepared, but there's juice and milk. Help yourself."

"Juice is fine." He poured a glass of orange juice and, after one sip, set the tumbler aside. Pulling an object from his shirt pocket, he pushed it across the table to Dana.

"Your cell phone. It's been cleaned and sanitized. We pulled off the recording. I can give you a copy—"

Jamie stiffened. What was *wrong* with Sam? Did he actually think Dana would want a recording of Lansing threatening her at gunpoint?

"That's not necessary." The breathy, high-pitched response sounded nothing like Dana's usual elegant tones.

Sam nodded, his dark brown eyes warming several degrees in understanding. "I'll send a copy of the recording to Detective Cooper at the Sutton PD along with statements from you, Rhys, and Nick. Based on Lansing's statements on the recording, Cooper should be able to close the murder case on your husband. Before I submit my report, I need clarification about something you said—or didn't say."

"I thought we'd covered everything."

"On the recording, Lansing said something about files that your husband had concealed. You didn't mention that when we spoke."

Jamie stirred restlessly in her chair, her fingertips worrying the edge of the muffin. *This isn't right. Dana shouldn't have to keep reliving this horror.* The hot words brewing on her lips simmered as Dana shifted in her chair.

"My apologies for not remembering everything when you questioned me. When Detective Lansing said that, I was trying to avoid getting shot."

Her cool steady gaze met the sheriff's hard glare. Seconds passed in silence before Sam conceded the stare down.

"Fair enough. But now that you have been reminded, any guess what he meant?"

"It might be related to...." Her words trailed off. A gray pallor swept across her face. "That explains all the things that happened not long after James was killed."

Sam pawed a notebook and pen from his pocket. "What things?"

"A pipe burst, flooding his office at work. Most of his personal belongings were ruined before I could collect them. His car was stolen right after that and never recovered. Then a fire broke out at our home. The smoke alarm went off, but there was only minimal damage, mostly in his home office. I thought it was just a run of bad luck. There was no reason to suspect any connection to his death."

"I'll request a copy of those reports." He pulled a card from between the pages of the notebook. "We finished our investigation at your office. This is the number for a forensic cleaning company. You'll need to contact them about removing any compromised materials and sanitizing the area."

"I'll take care of it, Dana." Jamie extended her hand for the card. Her patience was waning. "Anything else, Sam?"

He shot another one of his intimidating stares across the table, then turned a softer focus back to Dana. "Have you spoken with Rhys?"

"He called from the hospital this morning. He didn't say much other than his father had been in an accident. Was it a car wreck?"

"He was attacked in the downtown parking garage."

Dana's shocked gasp mingled with Jamie's. "Are his injuries serious?"

Jamie held her breath as Sam flipped his notebook to a clean page. She knew exactly what he was thinking. Crumbs tumbled on her plate as her fist tightened around the uneaten muffin. *Don't you dare ask that question, Sam Wallace!*

"Mr. McCall received a number of injuries, but he's currently stabilized. Rhys can fill you in on that. What I need to ask is where you were between the hours of six-thirty and seven-thirty this morning."

"How *dare* you?" Jamie bolted to her feet, the legs of her chair screeching against the tiles. Dana had done nothing to deserve this inquisition. But Sam didn't care. Sam just did his job without regard to the fact that he'd pounded another nail into Dana's heart.

A gentle entreaty from Dana wasn't enough to stop her. Sam was on his feet now too, but Jamie was quicker. And her aim was true.

The muffin hit Sam right between the eyes.

Chapter Two

Rhys McCall stood by his father's bedside trying to reconcile the battered form lying there with the vital man he'd always known. If the worst day of his life had been yesterday when his mother's life was in jeopardy, today came close to tying it.

A bank teller on her way to work had found Erik McCall lying unconscious on the landing between floors at the downtown parking garage. His injuries were inconsistent with a mere fall. By the time Rhys arrived at Rollison Memorial Hospital, his father had been examined and diagnosed with a fractured collarbone and possible fractures of the T11 and T12 vertebrae. No indication of subdural hematoma—thank God.

For now, Erik McCall remained unconscious from a combination of shock and pain medication, and all Rhys could remember were the harsh words they'd exchanged when he'd learned that Dana was his long-thought-to-be dead mother.

"I'm telling you for the last time. As far as I knew, Catherine died in that automobile accident…"

"Even if you didn't care to find out for sure back then, you should have told me about the resemblance when Dana arrived."

"What good would that have done?" A smirk crossed his father's lips. "You even remember what she looked like? Nope, didn't think so."

Without a doubt, Dad hadn't grieved when he'd been told his wife had died in an automobile accident. He hadn't bothered to confirm it either. One thing Rhys could believe is that his father had accepted the news because it suited him. Still, it seemed the man he knew would have verified the information.

He rested one hand on his father's uninjured shoulder. *I don't understand the choices you made. Was it to protect me? Did you believe you were doing the right thing? I hate what you did...* He blinked a sudden rush of tears from his eyes. *...but I don't hate you. All I want now is for you to be okay.*

The ten minutes he was allowed was too brief. Not that he could have done anything by staying, even if he'd been permitted. Still, a touch on his father's hand, a quiet tone as he spoke might have filtered through, letting Dad know someone who cared was near.

Assured his father's condition had stabilized, he left the hospital for the daily Main Street project meeting.

Rhys hit the button to lower the windows in his SUV as he drove to Dana's house. Warm air, scented with pine, brushed across his face, and the pressure-cooker tension in his chest began to subside. He pushed back several strands of hair that tumbled onto his forehead, then gave up when they defiantly ignored his efforts.

The attack this morning had to be connected with the identity switch that had sent his mother into living another woman's life. Dad knew something. Something he wouldn't admit or didn't realize, and that knowledge now put him in danger.

Until Rhys could get answers, he had to keep his mind on work. Which meant returning to McCall Construction. Less than two weeks had passed since his father had fired him from the company business. He could have challenged that edict as he owned a minority share of the company. Could have fought to keep a hand in the business his father had once begged him to help save from bankruptcy. But considering both their moods at the time, staying would have changed nothing.

This morning though, everything had changed. His father was out of commission for an unknown length of time, leaving a newcomer named Kevin Davis in charge.

Not for long. Rhys had invested too much of his own sweat equity over the years to allow the company to falter again. And too many jobs depended on the continued success of McCall Construction.

As he approached the entrance to Dana's circular driveway, he eased his foot off the accelerator and flipped on the turn signal. At the sight of Jamie's car, his first smile of the day emerged.

The initial jolt of attraction that had hit him during their first meeting had been unlike anything he'd ever experienced. It was more than mere physical awareness. Jamie Danvers captivated him, and she intrigued him. At times, she hid behind a shyness that didn't seem natural. When that barrier fell away, she came alive. Her face glowed with an inner radiance, and her ocean-blue eyes sparkled. When ideas sparked in Jamie's creative mind, he could barely keep up with the flow that passed through her lips.

Tempting lips. Kissable lips.

The brief respite shattered as the sheriff's vehicle came into view. Rhys's fists tightened around the steering wheel.

No...

He bolted from the SUV and leaped up the steps to the front door of Dana's house. A wavy image in the cut glass of the front door reflected the panic sketched across his face. He threw open the door, and a roar of voices slammed him from the direction of the kitchen. He pushed the door shut and rushed down the hallway.

"Mom?"

He stopped short in the doorway, mouth dropping open. Sam and Jamie stood in a face-off. The lawman's hands rested on his hips while the gorgeous blonde waved her arms. Dana stood on the opposite side of the island, watching the exchange. Her right eyebrow lifted in a gentle arch, a warning that she was about to lay a Canfield down on someone.

"The next word I hear will be from the person volunteering to clean up that mess on the floor. After that, you can join Rhys and me at the table for a civilized breakfast." She turned a brilliant smile in his direction. "Good morning, sweetheart. Ready to eat?"

Silence reigned as Rhys's gaze dropped to the chunks and crumbs of what once appeared to be a blueberry muffin littering the tiles. He sidestepped the mess and walked over to Dana.

"Morning, Mom." He dropped a light kiss onto her uplifted cheek as she placed another setting on the table.

Sam scooped the larger pieces from the floor while Jamie wet a paper towel and cleaned up the remaining crumbs. After a quick washup at the sink, they returned to the table.

Rhys glanced from Jamie to Sam, then back to Dana. "What did I miss?"

Sam shot a fierce glare across the table. "Your girlfriend beaned me with one of Mrs. Canfield's muffins."

"I am *not* his girlfriend. And you deserved it for practically accusing Dana of attempted murder."

"What?" Irritated at Jamie's dismissal of any romantic interest, Rhys almost missed the remainder of her accusation. He half lifted out of his chair. "What do you mean—"

"Excuse me?" Dana barely lifted her voice, but it was enough to gather everyone's attention. Once again, silence fell. "That's better. Jamie, thank you for coming to my defense, but in fairness, the sheriff hadn't completed what he was saying before you threw that muffin."

A faint flush colored Jamie's cheeks, and she dipped her head in acknowledgement. "I'm sorry, Dana."

Sam cleared his throat. "And?"

Jamie lifted her head, shooting a blue-eyed glare in his direction. "And finish what you were saying so I can decide whether to bean you with something else."

"I'm sure that won't be necessary," Dana murmured, settling a napkin on her lap.

"Best not." Sam scowled a final warning before turning his attention to Rhys. "I delivered Mrs. Canfield's phone, asked her about one of Lansing's statements, advised her the barricade tapes are coming down today, and gave her a reference for a forensic cleaner. Also, updated her that I forwarded a copy of the report to Allen Cooper at the Sutton PD. They'll launch an investigation into Lansing's other cases. Unless there's other evidence, they'll close James Canfield's case with Lansing as the shooter."

Rhys poured the remainder of the juice into his glass. He set one of the two remaining muffins on his plate next to the fruit he'd selected, then reconsidered and added the second one. By now, everyone else should have had their fill. If not… too bad. "As for who shot Lansing?"

"Cooper's theory is Lansing probably was involved in a number of illegal deals. He made someone nervous, and they silenced him. If Lansing had been arrested, he would have rolled with everything he had to save his skin."

Rhys shrugged. "Maybe."

"That's the direction they're exploring. If they're satisfied with my report, Mrs. Canfield shouldn't be called in for any further questioning on her husband's or Lansing's cases."

Rhys swallowed the last piece of cantaloupe on his plate. He sent a quick glance at Jamie. "So why—"

"After unloading all that, Sam asked Dana where she was at the time of your father's attack."

"Standard procedure," Sam said. "A question for which I still need an answer."

"I don't have a problem answering that question." Dana tapped a napkin to her lips, then replaced it on her lap. "At the time you indicated, I was leaving Nick's apartment on my way back home. He followed me here and made sure the house was secure before leaving for Richmond." She looked across the table at Jamie. "He's picking up Megan from the airport."

A broad smile broke across Jamie's face. "That's wonderful! I know how much he's missed his daughter."

Rhys's eyes narrowed. "Wait a minute. When I left here yesterday, you were furious at him."

"We made up." Dana's lifted brow dared him to challenge her further.

Nope. Not going there. He turned his attention back to his breakfast.

Sam pushed back his chair and stood. "My cue to leave. Mrs. Canfield, thank you for what breakfast I did get to eat. If you remember anything more about those files, contact me."

Dana stood. "I'll walk you out."

Rhys glanced at the departing figures, then back at Jamie. "What's with the food fight I missed?"

A rosy flush crept across her face. "Sam is such a jerk! Dana finds out most of her life has been a lie and that she was betrayed by the person who was supposed to love and protect her. Then she was almost murdered yesterday. And then Sam storms in this morning and practically accuses her—"

"Whoa!" He held up both hands.

"Do *not* tell me 'Sam's just doing his job.'"

Those very words took a nose-dive down his throat. Sam was his friend, but he could fight his own battles. Rhys leaned back in his chair as the heightened color faded from Jamie's cheeks.

She heaved a deep sigh. "I'm sorry. I shouldn't have spoken that way to you. Especially after the morning you've had. How is your dad?"

He provided a brief recap of Erik's condition, concluding with a shrug. "Nothing else I could do there, so I came on over here."

Dana returned to the table and patted Rhys's shoulder. She laid a cell phone next to his plate as she passed. "Here's your phone. Sam returned mine."

He checked for any missed calls. Not as many as expected. "How about you, Mom? Any missed calls?"

"Several. All from Toddy. If he's heard the news about Detective Lansing, I'm sure he's worried." She gestured toward the living room. "I need to call him back."

The worry lines around the corners of her eyes negated the smile that was supposed to reassure him. He eased from the chair and moved to the doorway leading to the living room to watch. Dana walked to the love seat, curling one leg under her as she sat down. After a moment's hesitation, she tapped the phone.

The rattle of dishes drew his attention back to the kitchen.

"Who's Toddy?" Jamie asked, glancing over one shoulder as she loaded plates into the dishwasher.

"Canfield's godfather, eccentric uncle. Shirttail relative of some sort."

"They must be close if he's called several times."

"She mentioned he was supportive after her husband was killed." Dana's words echoed in his head. *...my anchor this past year... but he has to know...*

"And...?"

Jamie's frown was a sure sign he'd been less than subtle about his doubts. Had Toddy been a participant in the cover-up of Dana's real identify? Or had Canfield deceived a kindly old man and made him an unknowing ally? Before he could respond, Dana's voice filtered in from the next room.

"For Heaven's sake, Toddy, I can't believe you said that!"

In three swift strides, Rhys reached the doorway. Perched on the edge of the sofa, her slender body rigid, Dana held the cell phone in front of her.

"Oh, honey. You're off your meds again, aren't you?"

"Toddy...."

Jamie's fingertips grazed Rhys's forearm. "I don't like him."

Rhys didn't care much for the man either upon first impression, even if Toddy had been Dana's champion after James Canfield's death. Still, if Toddy had heard the news about Lansing's attack and spent the night unable to reach Dana, no wonder he sounded irritated.

"My phone was confiscated by the sheriff. It wasn't returned to me until this morning."

A deep and dramatic sigh followed. *"Sorry, dear. I must have missed that yours is the only phone on that little piece of real estate. I should be grateful you haven't forgotten me entirely."*

"Your emotional blackmail isn't amusing."

Laughter rippled over the line. *"But you love me."*

Rhys nudged Jamie and tipped his head toward the living room. Dana nodded as they settled into the chairs opposite the sofa.

"I need to see you. There's something we need discuss in person."

"You're coming home?" Another short silence was followed by a rush of words. *"You'll stay with me, of course. Have to, since you sold off the home place. Maybe we'll even take a short trip. Get away—"*

Dana shook her head, dark curls dancing around her cheeks. "There's too much work here for me to be gone very long. I thought we could meet halfway for lunch."

"Oh, well... then that's what we'll do."

The older man's disappointment was unmistakable. Whatever quirks Toddy had, he obviously held a deep affection for Dana.

"Tell you what. Let's meet in Sutton. I'll have Roger drive me down. Shorter trip for you. I'll make reservations at Callavicci's for the two us."

Rhys lifted his hand, capturing Dana's attention. He held up three fingers, and she nodded.

"Make that a reservation for three. There's someone I'd like to introduce to you. Thank you for offering to meet me closer to PI."

"Not a problem, dear. You don't need to be driving in your condition. I look forward to seeing you tomorrow."

Toddy ended the call before Dana could respond. She dropped the phone onto her lap, then clutched her hair with both hands.

Rhys exchanged a brief glance with Jamie. Her expression looked as suspicious as he felt. "Hope you didn't mind I invited myself to join your luncheon."

Dana lowered her arms and sank back on the couch. "Of course not. I'm glad you'll be there with me when I confront him."

Jamie stiffened. "Is he involved in what happened?"

"I honestly don't know. Toddy's been part of my life ever since the accident. I can't believe he's part of the cover-up." A poignant sadness swept across her face. "But I wouldn't have suspected that of James either."

Rhys considered that possibility and its alternative. If Toddy was guilty, that meant an additional source of danger to Dana. On the other hand, if he was innocent of any involvement, he could be at risk as well. Either answer meant additional heartbreak for Dana.

His phone buzzed, and he glanced down at the display.

Stacy Andrews, office manager for McCall Construction. No doubt calling about Dad. He punched the button to place the call on speaker.

"Hey, Stacy, it's Rhys."

"I will fulfill every erotic fantasy you've ever had if you will get your gorgeous self to the office ASAP."

His jaw dropped. "What—"

"Hold on."

A second later, Rhys heard her speaking to another person, her tone more formal.

"I have him on the line now. Yes, I'm giving him your message."

He heard a barely audible *"Good grief"* before Stacy resumed their conversation.

"Kevin would like to meet with you as soon as possible regarding the active McCall projects... Okay, he's gone. Get over here... now. Oh, and I'm serious about that fantasy offer."

The line went dead.

He juggled the phone in one hand. "You two should be there as well since Main Street is one of those projects."

"You don't need me for that." Jamie stood, gesturing toward the kitchen. "Dana, I'll stay here and work on the mock-ups for the merchant website."

Rhys blinked, stunned at Jamie's abrupt departure. What did she mean she wasn't needed? *He* needed her there. He bolted to his feet.

"Wait," Dana said.

He whirled around, irritated by the delay. Dana nodded at his phone. A second later, understanding shot through his male brain. Stacy's offer. Knowing the sexy redhead's proclivity for flirting, she might well have meant what she said. Jamie had mentioned once that she and Stacy had been college roommates for a short time. Meaning there might be some additional history there as well.

Bottom line, he had no intention of taking Stacy up on her offer. But did Jamie believe that he would?

"I'll leave a key for Jamie in case she needs to go out. I have a couple errands to run afterwards, so I'll follow you in my car." Dana squeezed his hand. "Nothing that can't be fixed, sweetheart."

He tugged her hand, pulling her into his arms for a quick hug. Despite years of separation, the bond between mother and child had merely been suspended, not destroyed. He was the one who now had to bend for that embrace, but it still felt good and *so* right.

"Got it. Mom knows best."

Dana flashed him a saucy wink before turning toward the kitchen. "Glad you remembered."

A chuckle exploded through his lips. Dana was exactly right. He could fix this.

Operation Jamie was officially underway.

Rhys halted as they reached the front steps of the McCall Construction building. Unlike the unique design of Dana's office, McCall's was a testament to tradition. Two stories, oxford white, and trimmed in dark vintage blue, with stone flowerboxes flanking the front entrance.

"Second thoughts?" Dana asked.

"About going back to work here?" He shrugged. "Yes. No."

"Makes sense."

He shifted his gaze to her, searching for any sarcasm that wasn't evident in her voice. She met his look with a gentle smile.

"It's natural to feel ambivalent. You have an ownership stake in the company and every right to protect the business."

"Circumstances—"

"Are what they are. I suspect Kevin won't oppose your return, and that's what generated the call from Stacy."

"Maybe. Then again, he may just want to pick my brains without me returning full-time."

"Not his decision, is it?"

"No, it sure isn't." With a grin, he nodded toward the steps. "So let's find out."

They entered the building and walked to the elevator, riding in silence to the second floor. Rhys exited first, holding the door for Dana. Behind him, a soft feminine body brushed against his back.

"Hello, handsome," Stacy purred. "You made good time getting here. Taking me up on my offer?" When Dana stepped into view, Stacy's tone switched to a more professional demeanor. "Oh, hello, Mrs. Canfield. I didn't know you were joining us."

"Rhys thought I could assist if there were any questions regarding Main Street."

"Can you let Kevin know we're here?" Rhys asked as they walked toward Stacy's desk.

"Good luck with that. He's been on a tear all morning. Especially since the hospital won't give out any information about Erik's condition."

"He hasn't heard of HIPPA?"

"That's what I told him." Stacy shrugged, irritation flashing across her face. "He's tied up right now on a call with a supplier."

Rhys frowned. "Don't you handle those calls?"

"I do, but this guy wanted to talk with"—Stacy made air quotes—"the man in charge. He may be a while."

Rhys bit the inside of his mouth, struggling to hold back a snort of laughter.

Dana came to his rescue. She gestured toward Stacy's desk. "Could you print out a copy of the Main Street status? Rhys and I will look over it for any updates while Kevin's on the phone."

Rhys nodded toward an open doorway on his right. "We can work in my old office."

He flipped on the light as he entered the room. The room was small, with a single window permitting natural light to infuse the area.

His gaze ran across the room, noting the diplomas and certificates on the wall and the coffee mug and notebook on the credenza. If he had taken those with him, all visible traces of his tenure at McCall would have been gone. He crossed the room and removed one of the diplomas from the wall. The slight shading where the frame had hung appeared ghost-like, a haunting reminder that a quick paint job would eradicate this faint evidence of his presence. He wiped a fingertip along the top of the frame and returned it to its original position.

Returning to his desk, he opened the bottom file drawer. A whoosh of air left his lips as he retrieved a thick folder from its depths. Walking out after being fired by his father without taking his personal belongings hadn't been the wisest course of action. The folder in his hands was one thing he never should have left behind.

I'm back now.

Dana entered the room, her dark brown eyes scanning the cramped quarters. "Oh, honey, this breaks my heart."

"Offends your designer sensibilities, huh?"

"I may have to sit down and catch my breath." She laughed, fanning her face with one hand. "This is…"

"Functional."

"At the least."

With a nod, he granted her point. "Did Stacy print the Main Street project plan?"

"She did, and I checked it over while I was at her desk. Everything is up-to-date."

He tapped the top of the folder he was holding. "Towne Square. Our next project… maybe."

Her eyes widened, and a gleam appeared in them. "Ooh, let's see."

He opened the folder and unfolded a drawing representing the front elevation of a large building.

Dana frowned as she studied the graphic. "This is the empty building that lines one side of Towne Square."

"At one time, it was Marcum's Department Store. Lunch counter and dry goods on the main floor. Clothing, books, home furnishings on the other four floors. This was back during my great-grandfather's time. The store downsized eventually to just the first floor, with everything from medical and dental offices to a dance studio occupying the other floors. John Marcum, the current owner, couldn't retain enough tenants to make it worth keeping the property open."

"Is there sufficient business interest to warrant renovating the building?"

"For businesses? No." His gaze met hers. She was more than interested in the building. He recognized her artist's desire to get her hands on what essentially was a blank—if somewhat broken—slate. "Condos."

A frown creased her brow. "You said 'maybe.' Is there a problem with permits or zoning?"

"No. I've run the concept past the mayor's office. There's no ordinance against residential property. There's an old statute still on the books from when homes used to be located in this area. We might get some pushback though because everything else in the area is commercial now. However, legally, we're fine."

"So...?"

"Finances."

"How much?"

"Dana, I'm not..."

She brushed away his protest with an impatient wave of her hand. "I know you're not asking. *I'm* asking."

He pulled another page from the file and extended it to Dana.

She looked down the list, murmuring, "Estimated value, estimated counteroffer, estimated down payment and closing costs, taxes..." Deep breath. "Operating expenses for demo and renovations." She looked up.

"Yeah." Rhys gestured to the paper. "At the bottom is the total I can finance, which is..."

"Well short of the mark."

"As I said, maybe. More like maybe not. I'd been toying with the idea since I came back to PI." He grinned. "When you came onboard for Main Street, I thought 'Dana would love to get her hands on this project.'"

"I certainly would."

That *look* bloomed across her face. The one he'd witnessed when they'd toured Main Street together for the first time. The one that had immediately convinced him that Dana was the right partner for the job.

"I can come up with a good portion of the balance," Rhys said. "If we can get the asking price reduced, it's..."

"We'll make it happen." Dana bounced on her toes. "Do you have time today so we can work up a preliminary plan?"

Dana's enthusiasm fed his own growing excitement. "I do. How about we go back to your house so we can spread out these papers? You run your errands while I talk with Kevin. Afterwards, I'll pick up lunch from Carson's, then meet you back at the house. Is an hour enough time?"

"Perfect. I'll call in the lunch order so it'll be ready when you get there." Dana picked up her tote bag and settled the strap across one shoulder. "Love you."

"Love you too."

Rhys replaced the sheet of paper in the folder. When a tap sounded on the doorframe, he looked up and suppressed a sigh.

"Hey, buddy." Kevin Davis sauntered into the room and settled into the guest chair across from the desk. Blond hair, blue eyes, and all-American features, Kevin fit the image of a young executive rising to success. With a Stanford MBA and a silver-spoon birthright, he seemed better suited to a career in a financial center of a major city rather than one at a small construction company off the shores of Virginia.

"Whew! Belmont wore me out, but I fixed the problem. I'll give Stacy some guidance so she can handle those types of calls in the future." The gleam in Kevin's eyes faded into something soft and compassionate. "How is Erik? The hospital wouldn't give me any details."

"His condition is stable, but with the extent of his injuries, he'll be out of commission for some time." Rhys paused a beat, waiting for any lingering doubts about his decision to return. Nope. Not a one. "I'm returning to work here."

A triad of emotions flickered across Kevin's face. Surprise and relief mixed with more than a touch of suspicion. "Great. I'll—"

"As acting CEO. You'll continue as CFO."

Kevin's expression cooled as he tapped his fingertips against the desktop. "Fair enough. Plenty to keep you busy. Coordinating work crews. Managing projects."

"I'll be in tomorrow morning after the Main Street meeting with Dana and Jamie. I also need to stop by the hospital to check on Dad. Schedule time in the afternoon for us to meet." When Kevin remained seated, he glanced across the desk. "Anything else?"

Kevin stretched out his legs, crossing one above the other at the ankle. A hint of wicked humor snaked through his thin smile. "I happened to be passing by your doorway and heard part of your conversation with Dana. You need financing for your next project." His all-American visage dissolved behind a shark-toothed smile. "And I have a trust fund burning a hole in my pocket."

Rhys bit back his first response. Kevin's offer was the last thing he'd expected. Talk about a deal with the devil. Kevin Davis had settled in too quickly and with more confidence than a new hire normally showed. McCall Construction might be the largest private employer on PI, but it was small potatoes for a guy like Davis. Best thing Rhys could do for the present was to keep an eye on the man.

He was tempted to throw Kevin's trust fund back in his pearly white teeth, but he wasn't ready to burn that bridge just yet. Until he could figure out the hows and whys, it might be beneficial to keep Davis on the hook.

He gave a brief nod. "I'll discuss it with Dana."

"What time's the meeting at her house?"

Rhys narrowed his eyes. "You heard quite a bit for 'passing by.'"

Kevin shrugged. "I *was* passing by, but hearing what I heard, I hung around for the full show." He pushed to his feet, a piratical gleam in his cool blue eyes. "With any luck, no one else will swoop in and purchase that building while you're considering my offer."

"Doesn't matter." Rhys leaned back, resting his head on linked fingers. "I have a first-refusal agreement with the owner."

"Well… good for you." An unspoken "and the horse you rode in on" hung in the air. "You've thought of everything."

"I certainly try." He couldn't hold back a grin as he bounced to his feet and rounded the desk. "Which reminds me. Even though I have an office at the Canfield building, I'll need more work space. I'll ask Stacy to pull the plans I had to renovate that vacant area on this floor. I'll need your sign-off along with mine on the work order."

Kevin paused at the doorway. Shoulders squared, jaw set, eyes narrowed. The picture of a man totally pissed off restored a considerable measure of Rhys's good humor.

"I'll look it over," he said as he stepped into the hallway, "and let you know."

Rhys grinned. "Thanks, buddy."

That didn't go the way I planned.

Kevin paced the width of his office, fuming at the results of his conversation with Rhys McCall. An arrogant sense of entitlement and a clear case of boss's son syndrome. No wonder Erik had served Rhys his walking papers once Kevin was onboard. But Erik wasn't here, and Kevin needed Rhys's knowledge of the business. The last thing he wanted was to fail Erik. Besides, it might prove amusing if the prodigal son got handed his walking papers a second time after Erik returned.

But, it was more than that. There was that strange exchange when Dana had left.

Love you.

Love you too.

A bit much for business partners, especially on such a short acquaintance. If it was just a cougar/cub situation, that would be strictly their business. But there was a familiarity between the two of them that hinted at a deeper relationship. Had they known one another during the time Rhys had worked on the mainland? And was his return to McCall less about stepping in to help or more about using the company to drive his own personal projects?

Having Rhys back in the company fold would provide the perfect opportunity to learn more about that connection.

And if it had anything to do with Erik's assault.

Chapter Three

Seated at the table in Dana's breakfast nook, Jamie entered the last update on the Main Street project plan and saved the file to the extra laptop Dana had provided. Her glance fell on her cell phone lying next to the computer. She scrolled through the call list, finger pausing over one name.

Do it. Get it over with. Maybe this time she'll…

Jamie pressed the call button.

"Yes? What is it?"

"Hi, Mom. It's Jamie."

"I saw your name on the display. Why are you calling?"

Curt tone, cold words. Why had she expected anything different?

"I want to let you know about my new job."

A sniff came over the line. *"I hope this one lasts longer than your other ones. Hold on…."*

Several other voices mingled with that of her mother. A burst of laughter reached her ears, and Jamie bit her lip.

"You're on speaker. Your sisters are here. Don't take long. We have plans."

"Hey, Jay," Beth said. *"Which is it this time? Big box store or call center?"*

Lana's voice broke in. *"My guess is minimum wage plus tips."*

Jamie's hand tightened around the phone, a lump thickening in her throat. She sucked in a deep breath, forcing the tremble from her voice.

"I'm working for Canfield Designs, handling the marketing—"

"Jamie, we have salon reservations and have to leave. This can wait for another time. Try not to lose this job."

The line went dead. Conversation over, and she only had herself to blame. No one had made her call. She'd chosen that action, knowing the risk of further rejection. Yes, she'd held more than a few jobs, many of which were entry level, but she'd never been fired. Each job she'd left had been due to a lay-off or for a better position elsewhere.

Reality though didn't win against false perceptions, and a dreamer had no place in Janette Danvers's tidy world.

Jamie set the phone on the table and walked to the sink. She gazed out the window while cool water splashed over her wrists, relaxing the tension that raged inside her. The morning sunlight had moved on, leaving a shaded patio that beckoned her to take her laptop and work outside.

She could do exactly that. She even had Dana's blessing: *Don't glue yourself to this table. Take a walk. Work from home if you want. Just call or text me if you decide to go elsewhere.*

"I am *so* lucky to have a boss like you, Dana."

There was no way she was going to let down the woman who'd given her more encouragement in the past two weeks than her own mother had during Jamie's entire life. She walked back to the table, searching through her briefcase for the flash drive containing the initial mock-up and notes for the merchant website. Not there.

"Where—"

In the center drawer of her desk at Dana's office. *Perfect. Just perfect.* She shoved both hands in her hair, sending the shoulder-length tresses into disarray.

Why didn't I take it with me when I left the office? Or at least upload the files to the cloud site?

Her focus had been on meeting Alison for a final test ride on the trolley from the terminal to the Main Street drop-off rather than on finishing what she'd started. She had no excuse. No time either to re-create everything and have it ready for Dana's review this afternoon.

Jamie drew a deep breath, willing herself to calm down. She dropped back into the chair and flexed her hands over the keyboard.

If I could just get back into the office—

She could. The building had been cleared by the sheriff's department as far as the investigation was concerned.

Warnings from the cleaning company echoed in her head. *Blood and other bodily fluids. Infectious materials. Bloodborne pathogens.*

Jamie grabbed her purse. No need to worry. Her desk was located away from where the shooting had occurred. She'd dash in, grab what she needed, and get out.

Twenty minutes later, Jamie arrived at the front of the Canfield building. She pressed the remote button to open the iron gate spanning the entrance to the small private parking lot. Just as Sam had reported, the yellow caution tape had been removed. She tucked her purse under the front seat, taking only her car keys and the electronic key card.

It'll be fine. No one is there. You're safe.

She'd made a promise, and Dana was counting on her.

With a quick flick of her wrist, Jamie swiped the reader and opened the door. Before she could take the first step, a rush of death and decay slapped her in the face. The stench surrounded her, shooting down her throat to her stomach. Her eyes watered. She reeled backward, cupping one hand over her mouth, gagging from the vile scent.

The door slipped from her hand, slamming shut as she stumbled to the side of the building. Back pressed against the sun-heated surface, she gulped in fresh clean air. The foul odor clung to lining of her nose, and bile rose in her throat. Even after several deep breaths, the quivering in her stomach continued.

Bracing one hand against the wall, Jamie made her way to the corner of the building. The lingering scent of decay wafted past her. Holding her breath, she stumbled to the side of her car.

Tears welled in her eyes, then started rolling down her cheeks. She couldn't—just couldn't—go into the building.

And that meant failing in her promise to Dana.

Rhys turned the corner onto Federal. Plenty of time to pick up lunch from Carson's and get back to Dana's by the time she finished running whatever errands she had on her to-do list. Along the way, he'd make a quick stop at the Canfield building to check the doors. Not that he didn't trust Sam and his deputies, but that didn't preclude any other intruders—curious or otherwise—from exploring.

The sight of the open gates to the parking lot proved his instincts were on point.

He flipped on the turn signal and pulled into the lot. Jamie was slumped against the side of her car. Blood raced from his head, leaving him a bit dizzy. Biting back the curse boiling in his throat, he whipped the Navigator into the spot next to where she stood.

He raced to her side and cupped her shoulders. "What happened?"

She spun around, her face drained of all color except for ocean-blue eyes wide with shock. A sob burst free, and she fell into his arms.

His heart bumped, his breath stalled. Her long lean body meshed perfectly with his. Better than he'd imagined. Pushing those wayward thoughts aside, he ushered her into the passenger side of his SUV, then dashed to the driver's side. Flipping open the center console, he grabbed a handful of paper napkins and held them out to her.

"I tried to go inside," Jamie said, her voice quivering as she dabbed the dampness from her face. "Go ahead. Tell me I'm stupid."

Rhys shifted sideways in the seat, and with a gentle touch, turned her face toward him. "It's not safe for you to be in there."

"I know, but I promised Dana I'd have the mock-ups for the new Main Street website for her review this afternoon. I'd left my notes at the office. I thought I could run in, grab them and get out, but I couldn't make it past the doorway. The smell was…" She shoved the napkins against her nose and mouth.

The odor had been bad enough when the scene was fresh. Since the building had been closed for over a day, he couldn't imagine how much worse it had become.

"Dana would've understood, and nothing is worth risking your health." He tipped a knuckle under her chin, tilting her head to face him. "Got it?"

A smile trembled across her lips. "Got it."

"Don't worry about the mock-ups. We have other things to discuss this afternoon."

"Something happened at your meeting this morning?"

Her eyes widened, and for a moment, he lost his train of thoughts in their hypnotic hold.

"More than I expected, especially after Dana left. I'll catch both of you up at her house." He turned on the ignition. "We need to hustle. Dana called in a lunch order at Carson's. I'll drive you back for your car after we finish."

"Wait!" She fumbled for the door handle. "I need my purse."

He was out of the vehicle before she could move. He grabbed the purse, locked her car, then jumped back in his own.

He slid a sidelong glance in her direction. His heart raced, blood roaring in his ears. Time to put himself on the line. "I have another bone to pick with you."

Her brow puckered. "Which is?"

"Your comment this morning to Sam. About not being my girlfriend."

"What about it?"

He grinned. "Would you like to be?"

"I'd love to be your girlfriend." The words shot out of Jamie's mouth without warning. She clamped a hand over her lips as a burning heat swept across her face. "I—"

"No take-backs." Rhys's retort rode the crest of a good-natured chuckle.

All the reasons she should have said no ran through her mind as Rhys shifted into drive and backed out of the parking space. They worked together. His mother was her employer. His best friend since childhood was her roommate. Their lives were intertwined already. If things didn't work out between them, she'd be the one to lose everything. Her job, her home, her friend.

Her heart.

All those risks raced through her thoughts while she studied the man beside her. His strong hands held the steering wheel with an easy competence. He radiated an outward confidence, but she'd seen the blows his armor had taken with the revelation of Dana's identity and his father's betrayal.

She closed her eyes and took a deep breath. The faint musky scent of his aftershave wafted to her nose, banishing any lingering odors from the crime scene.

Someone who didn't know Rhys McCall's past might assume from his open and friendly demeanor that he'd had the perfect childhood, a golden adolescence, and a bright future. During their brief acquaintance, she'd seen the respect shown to him. Not because of position or power, but due to his forthright nature and kindness.

And you think you deserve someone as good as him?

Maybe, maybe not, but she deserved the chance to find out. "Agreed. No take-backs."

"Next question. Have dinner with me tonight?"

"I'd like that." She nodded to Carson's Pizza and Sandwich Shop ahead on the right. "I'll run in and pick up lunch."

"Fair enough." He eased the SUV into an open space designated for carryout. "We can eat while I fill you and Mom in on what happened after she left. It concerns our new project and... well, other changes."

"What changes?" Door open, one foot on the pavement, Jamie halted, staring across the vehicle at him. Based on the slight uptick at the corners of his mouth, he seemed to be hinting at a surprise. "Never mind. I'll be right back."

She pushed the door shut and dashed into Carson's.

Wait till Paige hears that Rhys asked me out!

Paige Carson lifted a hand in a short wave as her roommate Jamie Danvers entered the restaurant. "Restaurant" being an exaggeration for the current state of the place. When funds ran out before the dining room could be completed, Paige had closed the beautiful pocket doors Rhys had installed until her finances improved. In the meantime, business was takeout and—fingers crossed—soon-to-be deliveries in the downtown core.

For now, the front area was decorated with several framed prints and a pair of cane-back benches in a glossy oak finish for customers waiting on orders.

Paige turned her attention back to her waiting customer. Early thirties, she guessed. Tall, and blond. And hot. Really, really hot. *GQ* swagger with a biker's gleam in his dark blue eyes. Definitely the sort of man who should have stuck in her mind. She'd seen him before, she knew it—she just couldn't remember when and where.

"Sorry for the delay. How about a bottle of water or a soft drink? On the house." She nodded toward a refrigerated case stocked with bottled beverages.

"Don't mind if I do." He flashed a quick, crooked smile. "Unless it'll get you in trouble with the boss."

"I *am* the boss." Paige laughed and held out one hand. "Paige Carson."

His grip was warm and firm. "Ben Hampshire. Pleased to meet you. Instead of water, can I get a coffee to go?"

"Sure." She filled a cup from the coffee dispenser located behind the counter and handed it to him. "I'll check on your order." With a glance at Jamie, she said, "Checking on yours too. Be right back."

Paige bumped open the door to the kitchen with one hip. Dana's order was packed and ready, but Ben's was still in progress. She grabbed the large to-go bag and carried it out to the front counter. "Another couple minutes, Ben."

Standing by the beverage case, he lifted one hand in response as he sipped from the cup.

"Here you go. Salads for you and Dana. Steak sandwich for Rhys. Anything missing? Oh, and Dana paid when she called in the order."

"Rhys asked me out!" The words exploded out of Jamie's mouth in an exuberant rush.

Paige grinned. "About time."

Jamie bit her lip. "Do you think I'm doing the right thing?"

"For pity's sake, Jamie!" Paige tossed her head. "I had a feeling about you two from the beginning. Go for it!"

"But Dana's my employer…."

"And he's Dana's son. It couldn't be more perfect. Now, go." She pushed the bag in front of Jamie. "I want details tomorrow!"

"Maybe not all the details." With a laugh, Jamie snatched up the bag and raced out of the building.

The door to the kitchen swung open, and Paige grabbed the bag Karen held out to her. "Ben, your order's ready."

Ben turned and walked back to the counter.

"Thanks for your patience. A copy of our menu is in your bag. You can save time by calling or ordering online."

"As good as the coffee is, I certainly will be back." Ben gave her a quick salute with the hand holding the cup as he walked to the exit.

Her gaze dropped to check the fit of his jeans. Yep, hot from the rear too. She frowned as the door closed behind the man.

Where have I seen you before?

Nick Warden strode through the doors of the Richmond International Airport. He located a position out of the rush of midday travelers and settled against one of the stone columns. Leaning back, he pressed one foot against the wall behind him. All he had to do now was watch for Megan's descent on the escalator.

According to biology and the eye of the law, Megan was his stepdaughter. In his heart, she'd been his daughter from the moment he'd set eyes on the seven-month-old cherub. That angelic state hadn't lasted much past the time she'd stood and put one foot in front of the other. When his ex-wife Callie married Megan's biological father last year, they moved to Denver, Callie proudly announcing that they were finally "the family they always were meant to be."

Not that he cared where his ex-wife chose to live. But taking his daughter almost two thousand miles away? Talk about a knife to the heart.

Despite the distance separating them, the bond between Nick and Megan remained unbreakable. Until the past month, when their communication had dwindled to complete silence. His confusion had turned to anger, then worry. Whatever happened yesterday in Denver had to be dire for Megan to leave so abruptly. Still, Nick intended to put the fear of God—and Dad—into her for refusing to answer any of his calls or texts.

His foot tapped a feverish tattoo against the concrete floor as he considered possible punishments.

Put her to work at the garage.
Enroll her in summer school.
Ground her for life.

His breath caught as a brown-haired young woman sprinted toward him, ponytail bouncing with each step. Her joyful smile melted into a sob, and tears flowed from her eyes. Nick straightened, barely having time to throw out his arms before she dropped both of her packs and fell into his embrace.

"I'm home, Daddy." She buried her face in his chest. Tears dampened his shirt as her words shot straight to his heart.

Hold her and never let her go.

Nick held off the inquisition until they were settled in his vehicle and headed south on I-64. He sent a quick glance in Megan's direction. "Start talking."

Megan squirmed in her seat, head bowed. Hair tie removed, her face was hidden behind a thick curtain of honey-brown hair. "I'm sorry I worried you."

A deep sigh made its way from his lungs to his lips. "Sweetie, I'm not happy about you taking off the way you did. First word I had from your mother was that you'd run away. Next, I receive a call—not from you—but from your friend asking me to pick you up here in Richmond. Whatever the problems were, you went about this entirely the wrong way."

Her head shot up, revealing red-rimmed eyes brimming with tears. Words burst rapid-fire through her lips. "I couldn't take it any longer! Nothing was ever good enough. Mom constantly took money from my bank account. She and Gary have this bizarre love/hate relationship. I'm tired of the nonstop fighting." Her shoulders slumped, and her fierce tone subsided into a faint echo of itself. "I couldn't stay any longer. I had a chance to leave, and I took it."

All the slights and irritation Nick had fed on over the past weeks disintegrated into dust. He knew firsthand how Callie manipulated situations, playing the victim and dealing out blame.

He eased one hand briefly from the steering wheel to squeeze Megan's wrist. "Why didn't you call me? When you moved to Denver with your mom and Gary, I told you I'd always fight for you."

"I couldn't. Mom...."

The hair on the back of his neck bristled. "Mom what?"

Megan turned her face toward the window. "She threatened to take out a restraining order if you kept contacting me. And

Gary... he said your interest was more than fatherly."

A flame raced through Nick's gut. "Son of a—" He bit back the remainder of the curse.

Emotional blackmail. Another Callie classic. It didn't work on him anymore except when it came to Megan. His ex-wife always knew how to use that weak spot. As for Gary's claim, the vicious lie was one more way the loser was attempting to cover his own failures as a father.

Neither Callie nor Gary were fit to be parents, but they refused to let Megan remain with the one person who'd been her constant. Not for love, but for the financial gain Nick's monthly child-support check provided. Some people might call him a fool for continuing to pay support for a child who wasn't his by blood. But he'd have been less of a man for refusing to acknowledge the daughter who was everything to him.

"I told Mom I wanted to stay with you. She kept harping on this being my last year before college. How I was the only one keeping her from having her happiness at last. It was all about what *she* wanted. I thought if I gave in this last time, then I could leave after graduation with a clear conscience. I wasn't going to let her hurt you or ruin your reputation because of my stupid decision." Megan straightened in her seat, stretching her legs. "I should have stayed with you."

"I always wanted to adopt you."

The admission was nothing new. Megan knew he'd tried repeatedly. She'd begged for it so many times over the years. He'd pushed the issue with Callie, but she "couldn't bear to deny Gary his rights."

Once again, Callie had played the odds. Keeping Gary on the hook for a child he'd never wanted and Nick in reserve as the father Megan needed.

"I know, Dad. I never blamed you."

But he did. The failure to make Megan his daughter in the eyes of the law stung deep in his soul. He'd done the best he could with the restrictions of being "just" a stepfather. But it wasn't what he'd wanted for Megan. Or himself.

He cast a quick glance in Megan's direction, and his chest swelled. His little girl always could turn his heart to mush.

"Hey." He nudged his elbow against her arm. "Happy Birthday."

Her lips curved in a slight smile. "You're happy I'm here?"

That whisper of insecurity in her voice ripped another piece of his heart. He gave her hand a second squeeze. "Don't ever doubt it. I'm going to call your mother, and let her know you're safe."

"Dad—"

"Unless you want to call."

Megan pantomimed zipping her lips. She folded her arms and slid down in the seat. He tapped a button on the steering column to initiate the call. Callie answered on the third ring.

"You find her yet?"

Hello to you too. "Megan's safe. She's with me."

Callie's voice shrieked through the speaker. *"She needs to get herself home! You tell her—"*

Nick tapped the volume control, wishing he could hit the Off button instead. He was immune to Callie's temper tantrums when they were directed at himself. Attacks on Megan were a different matter. "Megan's eighteen and can make her own decisions."

"A decision made after some persuasion from you?" Callie's voice dripped with insinuations. *"What did you promise her, Nick?"*

His breath hissed through clenched teeth. "Don't even consider making any accusations against my reputation. I know way too much about you and Gary, and what I don't know, Megan can fill in. If it comes to a fight, you will not win."

Nick jabbed the Off button with his thumb.

"You really did mean you'd fight for me, didn't you?"

He glanced to the side, seeing the hopeful glow shining on her face. With a nod, he returned his focus to the road. "You bet, and you're going to learn to fight for yourself. Right, Scout?"

"You bet. So, Dad, you hungry?"

He choked back a chuckle at the unexpected change to food. Definitely his daughter. "I could eat. Burger and fries?"

Megan boogied in her seat. "And chocolate pie."

The sound of her laughter made his day complete. Nick flipped the turn signal for the upcoming exit. *Diner food, here we come.* He'd text Dana from the restaurant. He couldn't wait for his two favorite girls to meet.

"Don't expect much." Nick led the way up the steps to the apartment over his garage. He opened the door, entered, then stepped back to see Megan's reaction.

Surprise, a touch of disappointment, then interest. Not bad, considering the place was something more befitting a college kid than a forty-six-year-old divorced man. It consisted of one large room, with a bathroom he'd created by throwing up two walls and a door.

Hands shoved in the back pockets of her jeans, Megan strolled around the area. "Not bad, Dad. You got a cool leather couch, big-screen TV, retro kitchen. Lots of light, good view of the ocean. I wouldn't mind having a place like this."

Nick chuckled and dropped onto the "cool couch." A welcome sigh crossed his lips as he stretched out the kinks from the long drive to Richmond and back. He patted the cushion beside him. "In that case, welcome home."

Megan plopped down beside him, mirroring his position. "I'm fine with this, Dad. Really. I'll just need some space in the bathroom and a dresser. I guess I get the couch...."

He rubbed a hand over his face. What had she dealt with over the past nine months to be so accepting of a dinky joint like this? Not that his current living space was workable long-term for the two of them. "Before we start renovating, what's the plan? College in the fall? Back east, I hope."

"I'm taking a gap year." The flat statement held both a question and a dare.

Karma came back to bite him as he recalled telling Callie he supported Megan's ability to make her own decisions. Which didn't mean he couldn't probe for her reasons. "Why the delay?"

One hand clenched into a white-knuckled fist. "I want time here to make up for all the months we've lost."

Nick chewed on that pronouncement as he studied his daughter. He'd raised her since before her first birthday and had an expert sense of when she was attempting to play him. This wasn't one of those times.

His silence must have weakened her already shaky confidence. She shrank into herself, shoulders bowing. "That's okay, isn't it?"

The insecurity threading through her quiet tone fueled the anger he'd tamped down since talking with Callie. "You know it is. But I get the feeling there's something more going on." He shifted, settling one arm along the back of the couch. "We've always been able to talk about things. Tell me—"

"I want a home! A real one."

Nick stiffened at the outburst. Had he done such a miserable job when they'd lived together?

"I didn't mean…" Megan buried her face in her palms. "I'm sorry."

He cupped the nape of her neck. "We've always been honest with each other. Look up here and talk to me."

"I didn't mean it the way it sounded." She sat up, knuckling the tears from her eyes. "With Mom, it was constant chaos. On and off boyfriends or husbands. BFFs and frenemies. Moving just because somewhere else was quaint or darling or 'the place to be.' I never felt like I had a home, just a place to sleep for the moment."

Nick nodded, but didn't reply. Megan needed to talk. He needed to listen.

"I felt safe whenever I stayed with you, but it never lasted. Knowing I'd have to leave hung over my head the entire time." Her brown eyes clouded. "That's what I meant when I said I want a real home. I don't want to go away to college just yet. I want to stay here and know I won't have to leave because of someone else's whim."

Not like his heart hadn't broken every one of those times as well.

"Those days are over. And while I'm happy you want to stay, that's not to say that you're going to sit around doing nothing."

She popped up onto her knees facing him, the impish smile he'd missed for nearly a year breaking free. "I'll get a job, Dad. I promise. I'll take online classes in the fall. I'll cook and clean. You won't have to do a thing."

He jerked his head toward the far corner of the apartment. "Grab my laptop from the table. Let's see if we can find any listings."

Her brow puckered in a frown. "Listings?"

"House. Apartment. We're going to need something bigger than this place for the two of us."

"You are the absolute best dad ever!" Megan hopped up, racing around the couch to the small two-seater table in the corner. Her sudden squeal sent his head reeling. "You got me a present? When did you have time to get this?"

She raced back to the couch. A purple gift bag swooshed by

his ear as she delivered a huge hug around his neck. He glanced back at the table where the laptop had been forgotten.

"Yes, I am the best," he said with a smirk. "But I didn't buy this." There was only one person who had access to his apartment and would have thought to deliver a present for his daughter. He took a deep breath. "I think my friend Dana left this for you."

The "Warden Brow of Inquisition"—a milder, more feminine version—winged in his direction. "And who is Dana?"

"Dana Canfield is a lady I've been seeing—"

A huff exploded past Megan's lips. "Oh, great! I escape one parent drama and get thrown right back into another."

The accusation burned the air, then sizzled off into the silence. Understanding the reason for her temper didn't mean he had to excuse the tantrum. Nick waited, allowing the quiet to continue until Megan squirmed in her seat.

Perfect.

"Scout...."

"What?" A note of apprehension squeaked its way through her defiance.

"When has it ever been acceptable to speak to me in that tone of voice?"

Megan scooted on the cushion, tucking one leg under the other. Face clean of makeup, tendrils of hair fluttering around cheeks still rounded in youth, she barely looked sixteen, let alone eighteen. Her rebellion fizzled into a conciliatory attempt at humor. "Umm... that would be... never?"

His snort of laughter escaped, mixed with Megan's soft giggle.

"I'm sorry, Dad. That was a really bratty thing to say."

Nick rolled his eyes. "Being the princess you are."

She swayed back in a pretend swoon. "Not a princess!"

His smile faded as he squeezed her hand. "Dana is important to me. I'm asking you to keep an open mind."

"I will, Dad. I just...." Her voice trailed off, replaced by a one-shoulder shrug.

"I know."

And he did. But Megan needed to understand that his life hadn't remained in stasis over the past year.

He picked up the gift bag, twirling it by the handles. Purple, good choice. Not too girly, not too juvenile. Thin streaks of silver running through the paper added a touch of sophistication that an eighteen-year old girl could appreciate.

She accepted it with a crafty smile. "So, Dad, I guess things must be serious if this Dana woman has a key to your apartment."

Busted.

There was more to the story than Dad was telling. A break-in at Dana's house. Safe place to stay. Blah blah blah. Megan would get to the bottom of that later. Right now there was a gift bag on her lap begging for attention. The birthday check from Dad had been awesome and perfectly timed, but it was weird that the only *wrapped* gift she'd received was from a total stranger. Knowing that Dad was eager to see her reaction, she made him wait by opening the card first.

Okay, cool card. Abstract watercolor of a beach, generic birthday wish, but inside....

Hi Megan. Welcome to PI. I'm looking forward to meeting you. Hope you have a wonderful birthday! Dana

She sounded... nice. Unless Dad had some major bucks other than her college fund stashed away, this woman probably wasn't after his money. Must be his body. She shot a quick glance under her lashes in his direction. All her friends at school agreed she had the best-looking dad. Most of the moms too, especially Kaylee's mom, who'd once felt the need to share one of her alcohol-fueled fantasies about Dad.

Megan dropped the card onto her lap, then pulled a tissue-wrapped object from the bag. A white cotton tank embellished with a screen-print of a morning sunrise lay atop a short-sleeve cardigan in hot pink. She knew Dad was waiting for a reaction, a comment—something—but she couldn't speak.

"Like it?"

"The sunrise on the tank almost matches the one on the card." She winced as soon as those words came out of her mouth, then shook her head. Lame. "I mean, yes. They're really pretty. But why would she do this? She doesn't even know me."

"Because she knows how important you are to me and how much I was looking forward to having you here." His knuckle gently lifted her chin, putting them eye to eye. "Give her a chance, Scout."

Megan nodded as she gently refolded the clothes. "I'll be sure to thank her, Dad. It was a really nice thing to do."

She won a Dad-grin from him, a flash of white teeth and crinkles around his eyes that proclaimed his pride in her.

"Get online and see what you can find while I check the voice mail for the garage." He pulled his cellphone from his pocket. "Later we'll take a drive to show you around and grab dinner."

Megan rose to retrieve the laptop. She cast a final considering glance at the tank and sweater. They'd go with both her jeans and her khaki shorts. It was a nice gesture, but she had a lot more checking to do before Ms. Canfield received the Megan McCallister seal of approval.

Chapter Four

Dana stood by the front window in the living room. It was silly to be watching for Rhys or Jamie to return. She should be spending her time working or unpacking a box or two. Anything to keep her mind off the call with Toddy.

He had every right to be upset with her. With all the bad and the good that had occurred over the past twenty-four hours, calling him hadn't even been a blip on her radar. He'd been her champion during those dark months after James's death, and he deserved better than that. More than a champion, he'd been a lifeline. Until her reliance on Toddy had become habitual, and she'd begun losing her self-confidence.

Starting over in a new location had been the best decision for her sanity and self-worth. She'd pulled herself free and started a new life on PI. It wasn't as if Toddy didn't have a multitude of friends and acquaintances to fill the void if he chose. To hear him brag, he had a plethora of enemies as well.

Toddy had been good to her throughout her marriage to James and an adoring grandfather figure to Joshua. Till Joshua took off without a word to her. Till James died from a senseless shooting. Till it was just Toddy and her left to grieve together.

Grief that now seemed two-pronged. She'd loved James, but a part of her now hated him. His lies and deception had stolen the life she should have had with Rhys. But having that life meant she never would have known Joshua.

As much as she craved answers, she dreaded what tomorrow could bring. The day she'd learn the extent of Toddy's knowledge of her past.

She could do it. After all, she'd had no problem facing Rhys's father. Erik McCall was a rat bastard even at the best of times. Chalk up that relationship to a slick-talking guy on the make and a naïve college freshman.

When Detective Kyle Lansing had revealed himself to be James's killer and had tried to force her at gunpoint to leave her office building, she hadn't let fear control her. She'd fought back, disarming Lansing with two blows from a tabletop metal sculpture and taking his gun. When he'd dared her to stop him from reclaiming that very same gun, she'd known she had the courage to shoot him. But someone else had beaten her to it.

Her breath caught, and she pressed a fist to her breastbone. Nick and Rhys would be appalled at her thoughts. As much as Rhys had deemed her a "badass mother" after hearing of her efforts, Dana was certain he'd meant it as a one-time vote of approval and not a license to go rogue.

Rhys's Navigator pulled into the circular driveway in front of the house. Jamie stepped out of the passenger side, then retrieved a restaurant carryout bag from the back seat. Rhys meanwhile opened the back of the vehicle and hefted a cardboard box from the cargo area. He shifted the box to one arm and lowered the lid.

A gentle warmth filled Dana when the two of them—young, beautiful, and vital with life—stood face-to-face, smiling as unheard words passed between them.

The tension between them this morning was gone, replaced with a new awareness, and Dana heartily approved. With a slight smile, she walked to the foyer to open the front door.

"Did you have a problem with your car?"

Jamie wrinkled her nose. "Long story, and I don't come out well in it. I'll take this to the kitchen. Before we eat, Rhys has something to show you."

"Hey! No hints," Rhys called. He stood for a moment, watching until Jamie passed from his sight.

Adorable. Dana hid another smile, then addressed her son with a mock scowl. "What made you think this house needed another box to unpack?"

He dropped a quick kiss onto her cheek as he headed toward

the living room. "You'll like this one, I promise."

I have a surprise for you!

A child's voice echoed through her memory. How many times had Rhys scurried to her side, eager to show off a picture he'd drawn or a treasure he'd discovered on the playground at their apartment complex? She sank down on the couch, watching the corners of his mouth twitch as he struggled to contain a grin.

"Wait for me!" Jamie rushed into the room and dropped to her knees on the floor, palms resting on her lap.

"You two have me totally intrigued." Dana scooted forward on the cushion. "I'm warning you. I'm expecting something big."

Rhys flipped the top off the cardboard box, then lifted out a large accordion folder. "You will not be disappointed."

Dana cast a quick look at Jamie for a clue of some sort. Jamie's gaze, however, was locked on Rhys. More than mere awareness, a connection of some sort had been born between the two of them.

His nimble fingers made quick work of untying the ribbon wrapped around the folder. The musty, sweet scent of aged paper wafted to her nose as Rhys pulled a sheet from the folder. "Last night I looked through another box from our old apartment. Since one of them contained the photographs that proved you're my mother, I thought I might find something else."

If the Fates had been cruel enough to separate her from her son all these years, they'd also been kind enough to leave clues to reunite them. Erik McCall's attempts to erase all traces of Rhys's mother hadn't succeeded entirely. Thanks to the insistence of Thomas Carson, Paige's father, belongings from the apartment where she and Rhys had lived still survived. Stored at first at the Carson home, then later moved to Rhys's place.

Her hand trembled as she took the paper. Breath stilled in her lungs as she viewed Rhys's birth certificate.

Her gaze ran hungrily over the details, such as date and weight and length. Facts suppressed by years of manipulation, but instinctively remembered in her heart. The inked imprint of two tiny feet was her undoing.

Kissing ten little toes. Playing piggy. Listening to his giggles.

"Mom?"

The laughter of the child she remembered faded into the voice of the man her son had become. She looked up and saw the concern on his face. "I'm okay. It's just..." She held up the certificate. "Seeing your little feet...."

"Oh, geez." A light blush ran up his neck.

Jamie pushed from the floor and scooted onto the couch. "How precious!" Her eyes widened. "Rhys Christopher McCall."

He cleared his throat in a deliberate move to shift their attention. "If we can move on, there's something else you should take notice of."

Dana glanced back at the document, reading further.

Father Erik McCall. Mother Catherine Dennison.

Catherine.

Katie D.

Kate.

A wave of dizziness washed over her. She didn't hear the snarl that Erik gave to her name. Instead, she heard loving voices, long forgotten, whispering in her mind.

"My family called me Katie D."

A slow smile crossed Rhys's lips as he withdrew another paper. "Well, Katie D, here's another piece of the puzzle."

Her birth certificate. The true one.

Catherine Avery Dennison.

Father Christopher Dennison. Mother Carolyn Avery.

"Says you were born in Connecticut. Never thought I had New England roots."

Memories swirled at the edge of her consciousness. So close. So elusive.

"Your middle name was after my father." She rocked, forward and back, arms wrapped around her stomach as snippets filtered through. "We visited during a winter break. They spoiled you that entire visit. They gave you a tricycle for Christmas. It was too big, but you loved sitting on it. It had a handle on the back so I could push you."

She dropped her head into her hands, fingers clutching her hair. How many other memories were locked behind this brick wall in her brain? "Where were they when all this happened? Why didn't they come to you?"

Why can't I remember?

"I don't know, Mom." He rubbed her back as she had done when he was child, his words soft and soothing. "We have names. We have a place. We have a starting point."

She sat up, wiping away a tear with one hand, squeezing his with the other. "You're right. We know more than we did."

He squeezed her hand in return. Their gazes met, excitement mixed with the uncertainty of the still unknown. "We'll find your past, Mom."

"All in good time." Reluctantly, she handed the papers back to Rhys, watching as he returned them to the folder. "Right now, let's eat lunch while we discuss this new project."

The meal started around the table in the nook, then moved to the kitchen island, where Rhys spread out several architectural drawings. Dana and Jamie, plates in hand, joined him.

"This is the front elevation. I drove by the building on the way here so Jamie could see it compared to this proposed view."

Jamie leaned over the counter, murmuring as she studied the sketch. "Luxury condos. Perfect for the upscale commuter who wants to get away and live in a quiet community."

"Our marketing guru is on the job already." Rhys nudged Jamie's arm. "However, there's one change I need to make."

He pulled a pen from his pocket and wrote two words on the sketch.

The Dennison.

Dana fought back tears. Seeing the name that had once been hers, one that was part of a legacy Rhys could now claim, gave her hope. "Oh, honey…."

"I couldn't call it anything else, Mom." A quick grin erupted. "Although we could name it the *Katie D*, if you prefer."

"Let's stick with Dennison." Her arms went around him for a brief hug. "Thank you. I was already excited about this project, but this makes it all the more special."

"For me as well." He gestured toward the table. "Let's sit down while I fill you in on my discussion with Kevin."

Once reseated, Rhys continued. "Overall, Kevin accepted the news of my return without an argument. I think he was relieved, especially since he hasn't been there long enough to settle into his own job, let alone know how to run the entire company. Although he wasn't as pleased when I told him I would be acting as CEO. On the plus side, you two have a good handle on Main Street, and I can keep a closer eye on the construction side."

"Do you know who owns the building?" Dana asked. "And

is the owner even willing to sell?"

"That's my next piece of news. The owner is John Marcum, and he was very interested when I contacted him. He and my granddad were old buddies, which worked in my favor when I asked for a first refusal."

"Is anyone else interested in the property?" Jamie asked. "You mentioned it's been vacant for a long time."

"Not before today, and that first-refusal agreement worked in my favor." He looked at Dana. "Turns out Kevin overheard us talking. He wants a buy-in. He also claims to have deep pockets." At their curious looks, Rhys added, "Trust fund."

Dana gave him a considering glance. "What's your gut feeling about that?"

"I'd like to hear your opinion first."

She rose and began clearing the remains from their lunch. When Jamie moved to assist, she motioned for her to remain seated. Restoring order helped her process her thoughts.

"We need the funding, and this is a quick way to get it. However, a partnership gives Kevin voting rights on what we want to do. Unless he intends to be a silent investor, which I doubt. I say we estimate the job, see what we can finance on our own, and then decide. Another option though would be to look for other investors."

Jamie frowned. "What's to prevent Kevin from trying to purchase the building before you arrange financing?"

"Kevin hinted during our discussion that *someone else* could buy the building. I informed him about the first refusal. John and I signed an agreement, so we're protected from Kevin swooping in with his trust fund." He gestured toward the papers on the island. "I want to look inside the building. I have the blueprints from city hall, but it's not the same thing."

Dana whirled around from the sink. "I would love to go with you!"

"I'd like that too, Mom, but not until I check it out and make sure it's safe."

She pushed back her disappointment. "I bow to your expertise on that matter." With a quick look around the kitchen, she nodded in satisfaction. "Why don't we go back to the living room?"

"What about parking?" Jamie asked as she stood. "Would that be leased or an add-on to the condo purchase?"

"There's one building at the end of the block that's separate from the Dennison," Rhys said. "If we can purchase that as well, it would be perfect for parking."

Dana lingered behind as the two discussed the parking issue. Standing at the island, she ran her palms over the paper, smoothing the surface. Onsite parking could be a deal breaker for some buyers. She looked up from the drawing. "Go on. I'll bring in the drawings in a moment. There's something I want to check."

After a curious look, Rhys departed, and she returned to the island to study the sketch again.

The building covered the entire block with one exception. The outstanding lot that sat on the corner of Ocean and Concord across the side street from the fitness center.

No...

She rotated the paper, tracing her finger along the street. She knew that building. She'd slept there last night.

Nick's garage.

Chapter Five

Ben Hampshire closed the door to his suite at Porter's Bed and Breakfast. Right now, he was the only tenant, and that suited his purposes. No disruptions. No nosy strangers. Even Maisie Porter was not what he'd expected. She made him feel welcome without inquiring overmuch into his business.

Her delight in renting the third-floor suite was unmistakable. He figured the elderly lady, having converted her Victorian home into a B&B, needed the extra income. He paid two months in advance, explaining occasional business trips might interrupt his stay. He wanted to secure a ready place whenever he returned to PI.

Ben crossed the sitting area into the bedroom. A glance out the window revealed Mrs. P strolling along the length of the back fencing, checking on her rose bushes.

He pulled the cell phone from his pocket and tapped the number to call his employer. He dropped onto the bed as two rings sounded before the line was answered.

"Hello, Benjamin."

"Mr. Stoddard."

"You have news for me?"

"Surprisingly, not much gossip about the shooting. A few stories are going around, but the official theory is that Lansing was responsible for the shooting of Mrs. Canfield's husband, as well as involved in other crimes. One of his partners decided he was a loose cannon and took him out."

Ben flexed his gun hand, reliving those seconds when he'd popped three bullets into the traitor cop. The look on that sap's face when he'd realized what going rogue had cost him had been a pure delight.

Stoddard's hearty chuckle filled the silence. *"He met a well-deserved end. What about Mrs. Canfield? Any suspicion cast her way?"*

"None that I heard. Mostly shock and sympathy. The lady's gained a good reputation in her short time here."

"Excellent."

"There's more." Ben paused. Mr. Stoddard was not going to be pleased.

"Continue."

"Mrs. Canfield knows Rhys McCall is her son."

"How?"

Ben winced at the volume of anger ripping through that one word. "I haven't discovered that yet, but she definitely knows. I overheard Mrs. Canfield's assistant mention it to another woman."

Her name was Paige.

Paige with the beautiful brown eyes and cinnamon brown hair. Paige who made the best cup of coffee he'd ever tasted.

"This changes our focus. I'll cancel the search for Joshua. Rhys McCall is our new target. Fortunately, we know exactly where to find him." The joy in Mr. Stoddard's voice was unmistakable.

"Shall I proceed since I'm here?" Who else could Stoddard trust to do the job?

"I'll send someone else to take care of Mr. McCall."

What? Hot denial shot through his body, and Ben rolled to his feet. He didn't need someone messing in his business. "I can handle this."

A brief silence, conveying a subtle warning, filled the line. Stoddard cleared his throat before resuming. *"You've established a presence on Providence. I don't want any attention drawn to you when the target meets his demise. If there's any problem prior to the job being completed, advise me immediately."*

Ben paced to the window. Mrs. Porter had completed her circuit of the garden and was making her way back to the house. A slow, steady pace. A game old gal. He had to admire how she never gave in to whatever aches and pains plagued her.

"Understood."

"I knew you would, Benjamin. That's why I count on you." A single click ended the call.

Ben returned the phone to his pocket. Mrs. P returning to the house was a sure sign dinner would be ready soon. Meals other than breakfast hadn't been included in the original agreement. However, Mrs. P claimed that she loved to cook and might as well do so for both of them. A deal he couldn't turn down, especially after the first meal. The woman cooked like a dream and was more than happy to fill him in on all the happenings in PI. Little old ladies collected gossip, true and false, in way that could make the CIA cry with envy.

He walked to the front of the suite and opened the door. He sank against the frame as heavenly scents rose from the kitchen area. Nothing beat a home-cooked meal. All in all, this was a sweet setup. Not the most exciting gig, but a pleasant break from routine. He said a quick prayer that nothing jinxed his stay or forced him to clean up possible loose ends.

Anyone who cooked like Mrs. P deserved to live.

Tuesday was a slow night at the Lighthouse Cantina, something Dana appreciated as she gazed around the area. Less than a dozen tables were occupied, and a small crowd of singles lingered around the bar at the far end of the pavilion. Music played over the speakers loud enough to feel festive but still allow conversation to be conducted at a normal tone.

With Jamie and Rhys on their first official date and Nick spending the evening with his daughter, Dana had decided to treat herself to a girl's night out. She took a sip of her margarita, then set the glass to one side.

Looking across the table, she noted the faint frown decorating April Davis's patrician features. Their friendship had begun when April had acted as the realtor during Dana's search for a house on PI. Another layer was added to the relationship when April's son Kevin assumed a position at McCall Construction on the heels of Rhys's abrupt dismissal. What April still didn't know was the connection between Dana and Rhys.

Rhys was insistent about publicly acknowledging her as his mother. Something Dana craved as well, but when, in all the craziness, would be the right time? She couldn't let her hostilities with Erik ruin whatever fragile link remained between Rhys and his father.

Until Erik recovered, any revelations would have to wait. For now, she was grateful to have someone with whom she could spend some girl-time.

"Thanks for joining me for dinner. Especially on short notice."

April's frown dissolved as she looked up from the menu. "I'm glad you called. I wanted to get together sooner, but I know you've been busy settling in." The frown returned. "I heard about the shooting at your office...."

Dana heaved a sigh. No escape from the subject, but to be fair, April's comment radiated concern, not rabid curiosity. She hesitated before going with an abbreviated version. "The man who was killed apparently was involved in my late husband's murder. As for who shot him, I never saw the person."

April's blue eyes darkened with alarm. "Does the sheriff have any leads on who this other person is?'

"Nothing as of this morning when I spoke with him. They're checking security tapes from the ferry, both on PI and Sutton."

"Does he think the person is still in the area?"

Dana shrugged. "It's possible. Sheriff Wallace seemed to think the shooter didn't mean any harm to me."

Her throat closed, choking her words. Past insecurities, laid to rest after a year spent climbing out of a cocoon of grief and the unknown, pushed against her reserves. She drew a deep breath and pushed those dark threads aside. "I'm letting Sheriff Wallace handle the investigation and putting my energy into my new life here."

"Good for you."

Conversation halted, and they leaned back in their seats as their dinners arrived. After the obligatory "the plates are hot" warning, the server inquired about drink refills, then left with a flirtatious wink. He was barely out of earshot before they burst out laughing.

"He has to be younger than Kevin," April said. "And probably your son as well. How old is he?"

Fork halfway to her mouth, Dana froze. *She means Joshua. Not Rhys.* She hated continuing the deception. Revealing the truth—and how—was something she and Rhys needed to decide before much more time elapsed.

"Joshua is twenty-five."

"Same age. Let me switch over to realtor mode for a moment. Everything okay at the house. No problems?"

Relieved by the change in subject, Dana settled back in her chair. "Nothing so far. The patio doors have been replaced and a security system installed. The windows are next in line. I'm still unpacking boxes."

Well, she had every intention of unpacking those boxes. Someday.

April shook her head. "You are much too busy. All that, plus those renovations on Main Street. I have an idea. The yacht club has an incredible salon and spa. I'll request a guest pass for you, and we'll make a day of it."

Dana hesitated. She couldn't imagine spending an entire day, losing all that time, at a spa. Then again, why not? She didn't *have* to work every moment of the day. If it took longer to finish unpacking boxes, then obviously, those weren't things she needed at the moment. "Sure, it sounds great. By the way, I have some other news. I met someone—"

"Nick Warden!"

Dana's mouth dropped open. "How did you know?"

"Know what?"

"That I'm seeing Nick."

"I didn't. You are?"

She felt as if she'd been dropped into an impromptu comedy routine. "I am, but why did you say his name?"

April nodded toward the entrance leading to the inside seating area of the cantina. "His picture's on the wall."

The picture Dana had taken. The one Paige had submitted for the Man-of-the-Month contest. The one that had caused such a chain reaction, Nick had had to close his business for the day while the sheriff's department had cleared the onslaught of traffic. All female drivers, stopping by the garage to see him in person.

She twisted in her chair and saw the poster, encased behind a glass-fronted frame, for the first time. The photograph, still saved on her digital camera, fell far short of the six-foot version.

A love affair sizzled between the dark blue T-shirt and denim jeans and his hard workman's body. Sweat glistened on his face and arms, and his hair stood slightly spiked, as if a woman had just run her fingers through the dark strands. The stance, the body, the attitude all proclaimed this was a man who got the job done.

And did it well.

A smidge of jealousy coursed through her veins as women lined up to have their picture taken in front of the poster. She shook those feelings away. After all, she was the one with firsthand knowledge of what lay beneath that T-shirt and jeans.

All mine.

April waved one hand to gain Dana's attention. "Back up a moment. You've been here less than a month, and you've already met someone? You *have* been busy."

From anyone else, the comment would have sounded demeaning. Even though April did have society connections, she'd never shown the least sign of a "mean girls" mentality.

"We met my first day here. What can I say? We hit it off."

"I can see why. He's a handsome man." April glanced at the poster again. "Nice too. He stopped to help when my car had a flat tire."

"He mentioned that." Dana took another sip from her glass. "What about you? Anyone interesting in your life?"

A shadow darkened April's blue eyes. She set the glass on the table with careful precision. "Not exactly. Possibly." A short laugh spilled out. "Sorry. I didn't mean to sound so vague. There is someone. A man I knew many years ago before I married Kevin's father. I thought he was the one, but… well, circumstances."

"He's here on PI?"

April nodded.

"A second chance might be on the horizon?"

"I hope so. It's superstition on my part, but I don't want to say anything until I'm more certain of how this is going to progress." Her mouth opened as if to say more, then clamped shut. "It's complicated."

A feeling Dana lived with every day.

"I'll keep good thoughts for you." She would do exactly that. April deserved the same type of happiness she'd found with Nick.

"Thanks. And if it does work out, the four of us will have to double date one evening."

"You, me, and our two guys. Sounds like a perfect night."

Rhys parked in the driveway next to Paige's house. Before Jamie had moved in with Paige, he would have rounded the house and entered through the backdoor. No knocking or ringing a bell. Just a shout-out and another scolding reminder that doors were meant to be locked.

Today, he climbed the front steps and pressed the doorbell. He spared a moment to glance down at his clothing. Dark gray slacks, blue shirt. Black shoes polished to a shine. As a concession to the still-warm evening, he'd left his sports jacket in the SUV until they arrived at the restaurant. He hadn't dressed up for a date in an embarrassingly long time, and a first date with Jamie called for extra effort.

He switched the bouquet of gerbera daisies from one hand to the other. Daisies seemed like a safe choice for a first date. Nothing over the top.

No, damn it. He should have bought roses. He glared down at the bouquet. The happy yellow faces smiled up at him, saying *Nah, you're good. Trust us.*

Jamie opened the door, and his heart bumped into a crazy beat as he took in every detail. The deep purple of her summer dress turned her eyes an incredible blue, the skirt fluttering around her well-toned calves. Blonde hair flowed loosely around her shoulders. Around her neck, a dragonfly charm swung from a delicate gold chain.

His fist tightened around the stems of the flowers. Energy zapped through his veins, and in this moment, he knew his life was changing. Jamie was the calm in the storm that surrounded him, glowing with a light that drew him into a warm embrace.

"Hi. You're right on time. Come in. I just need to get my wrap." The words rushed out as she backed away from the entrance.

Rhys stepped over the threshold, closing the door behind him. He cleared his throat and held out the bouquet. "These are for you."

She stared for a moment at the daisies, then reached for them with both hands. "Thank you. They're beautiful."

"So are you. You look amazing."

"You look very handsome." She smiled. "But you always do."

They stood for a moment, grinning at one another out of simple joy. He finally stirred. "I guess we'd better get going. We have a reservation for seven."

"Let me tell Paige—"

"I'm right here." Paige appeared behind Jamie. "Both of you. Up against the door. Picture time."

Rhys groaned. "What is this? Prom night?"

Paige flapped one hand, edging them in reverse until their backs were against the door. "First date. You'll thank me later. Rhys, arm around her. Jamie, snuggle in."

They obeyed. Not because Paige said so. Because they wanted to. A sultry fragrance shot through his senses as Jamie moved into his embrace, wedge sandals putting her mere inches short of his own six-one height. Her fingers warmed the cool cotton of his shirt against his back, and instinctively, he cupped his palm around the curve of her hip. Jamie's eyes widened at the too-familiar embrace. Before he could remove his hand, she shifted closer, her smile warm and reassuring.

Somewhere in the haze that surrounded him, he heard the click of the camera as he stared into Jamie's upturned face. He'd barely have to lower his head to touch his lips to hers.

"Ahem." Paige's voice broke through the spell that bound the two of them. The smirk on her face matched the one in her voice. "If you can look my way for a moment?"

Rhys straightened as Jamie lifted the bouquet in front of her. Paige snapped several more shots before he called a halt. "We need to leave if we're going to make our reservation," he said, not wanting to but needing to end the embrace.

He waited patiently while Jamie and Paige exchanged a girly hug and a few whispered comments, then traded the bouquet for Jamie's wrap and purse. Seconds later, they walked down the front steps to the silver SUV.

As he drove to the restaurant, Rhys searched for a topic that wouldn't include work or his family drama. When Jamie settled back in the leather seat with a sigh and extended her legs, he nodded toward the floor in front of her.

"Nice, isn't it? Having enough room to stretch out your legs."

A giggle escaped through her lips. "I've ridden in cars with my knees almost up to my chin."

He nodded. "Been there too. Paige thinks it's hilarious. By

the way, whatever she said about me while we were growing up, take it with a grain of salt."

Jamie shifted slightly in the seat to face him. "Actually, we don't spend much time discussing you." Her teasing smile suggested the opposite.

"Hmm. Just in case, let me know if there's anything I need to deny or explain."

"You're lucky having a friend like Paige." Her voice dropped. "I'm lucky too. When we first met, I couldn't believe she would offer a total stranger a place in her home."

"Paige has a good heart, but she's no fool. She sensed she could trust you, and she was right." He flipped on the turn signal as they reached the Crossroads intersection. "Traffic's light tonight. We shouldn't have any problem making our reservations."

"Tell me about Embers. What's it like?"

His cell phone rang, signaling through the media system in the console. He bit back a curse before tapping a button on the steering wheel. "Hello. This is Rhys McCall."

"Mr. McCall, this is Nurse Donovan at Rollison Memorial Hospital. I'm calling because your father has regained consciousness. He's asking for you."

A slow rush of air passed through his lips. "Tell him I'll be there as soon as I can."

"I'll let him know. Thank you."

With a short goodbye, Rhys ended the call.

Why now? Why tonight? Shame immediately rushed through him. Despite their recent hostilities, he couldn't enjoy a night out to dinner while leaving Dad waiting alone in a hospital room.

"Jamie, I'm—"

"Don't apologize."

He smacked the heel of his hand against the steering wheel. "I didn't mean it that way. Dad's awake, able to speak. It's amazing, especially after the injuries he received. I just…."

"Needed a break."

She rested her palm on his leg, a brief gesture of comfort. Before she could withdraw it, he laid his hand upon hers, intertwining their fingers.

"Exactly. But, it is what it is. I'll double back and drop you off, then head over to the hospital."

"Absolutely not! I'm going with you."

"Not the best idea. I don't know what I'm walking into. My dad is irritable under the best of circumstances. He could be throwing bedpans by the time we get there."

"Then we'll duck. If he gets too bad, I'm sure the nurses will either restrain him or sedate him."

Rhys chuckled, releasing the tension that had begun to rise again in his chest.

"I'll check if we can get a later reservation for dinner. If not, we'll find something else." She squeezed his hand. "You don't have to do this alone."

His breath stumbled at those words. If they'd ever been directed at him in the past, he couldn't remember. When he braked at the next intersection, Rhys lifted her hand to his lips for a quick kiss. "Thank you."

Both hands back on the steering wheel, he returned his attention to the road. A slight smile played on his lips. Date night wasn't turning out to be what they'd planned, but he was still spending the evening with Jamie.

Holding Jamie's hand while they walked into the hospital seemed the most natural thing in the world. Some women would have unloaded an earful about having their evening disrupted. Others would have accepted it along with delivering a subtle dose of guilt trip. Jamie didn't do either of those things.

Rhys could tell she was disappointed. He was too. But she accepted the change with good grace and offered ways to make his situation easier. She remained in the lobby working to reschedule their dinner reservation while giving him time with his dad.

By now, Dad had been moved into the step down ward. Private room, of course. A glance through the glass door revealed Erik McCall lying motionless, eyes closed. An IV line ran from one arm, the other one supported in a sling.

Rhys slid the door open. He tapped on the frame, then crossed to the bed. "Hey, Dad."

Erik stirred, blinking several times, his gray eyes clouded. "Son."

"How are you feeling?"

"Ten rounds... with a wrecking ball." The words came out staccato, broken by a laborious attempt to breathe. "Better than... first woke up. Couldn't move."

A chill ran through Rhys's veins. Dad had always been active and an avid outdoorsman. Camping. Fishing. Construction work. He'd never cope with having a life less than that.

"Did you get a look at the person who attacked you?"

"Punk ambushed me... crowbar."

Rhys winced.

Erik closed his eyes, took several deep breaths, then opened them. "Careful." Another deep breath. "Kate..."

"Let the sheriff sort this out." The last thing Dad needed at this point was to send his blood pressure skyrocketing with a rant about Dana.

"Need you... work..."

He rested a hand on his father's shoulder. "Starting back there tomorrow."

Erik's eyes widened, then he tilted his head in a slight nod. "Good."

Rhys glanced up as the door opened and a nurse entered. "Looks like my time's up. Don't worry about work. Can I get you anything before I leave?"

"Shot of whiskey?" Something between a smile and a grimace washed across his father's face.

"No need for whiskey, Mr. McCall," the nurse said. "I'm here with your pain meds."

"Dad, I'll check in with you tomorrow. Get some rest."

A brief tilt of his chin was all Erik managed before sinking back into his pillow.

The nurse nodded as she readied the injection for the IV. "We'll call if there's any change."

After a final glance at the bed, Rhys walked out of the room. He paused in the hallway, watching as the nurse administered the medication. Erik McCall had made enemies of his own throughout the years. Though none Rhys could think of who would attack him in that manner. The assault lacked the full-on confrontation of Keg Lansing or the finesse of the person who'd shot the detective.

What had happened to Erik McCall seemed personal. Very personal.

Jamie stood by the front windows of the hospital. Twilight was setting in, but the flow of cars and visitors continued much like the evening tide of the ocean. She wrapped her arms around her middle, remembering the warmth of Rhys's embrace.

He kissed me!

An impulse. A quick touch of his lips to the back of her hand. The sincerity of the gesture though was unmistakable. The awareness that had sparked between them from the moment they'd first met had grown from a flicker to a flame. When they'd posed for that first-date photo, something inside her had clicked into place. She'd wanted to turn fully into his arms, and when she'd lifted her gaze to meet his, she'd seen the same yearning in his.

Her phone chimed, and she checked to find a text from Paige.

How's it going? How's the food? Here's a pic of u & R.

A small gasp escaped Jamie's lips as she viewed the attachment. The stained glass insert in the door made the perfect backdrop. Despite Rhys's quip about prom pictures, the pose struck her more as an engagement photo.

Wow. Talk about getting ahead of herself. She stroked a fingertip across the dragonfly charm on her necklace. Why not hope for that very thing? Why not believe that a relationship with Rhys was one more good thing she could have in her life?

A thud of heels drew her attention. She turned to see Rhys walking across the waiting room. He looked tired. And sad. His lips moved into a smile, but she could see the effort behind it.

"Ready?" he asked.

"Embers didn't have any later reservations available."

The hostess at Embers had been sympathetic to the situation, but unable to help. Which meant coming up with a Plan B. The plan wasn't what she'd been promised, and certainly not what Rhys had intended. But it included the two most important parts of the date—food and being together.

He raked his fingers through his hair. "Let me think."

"I have it covered." Jamie tucked her arm through his. "The cafeteria is open for another half hour."

Rhys ground to a halt. "No way. I'll find something—"

"We're both hungry. You're tired."

He dipped his head, then looked up with a grin. "With an unspoken 'and cranky'?"

She returned the smile. "Perhaps."

The salad bar was closed. So was the grill. They scored the last ham and cheese sandwiches and an iced tea each, then settled at a small two-seater near the front of the cafeteria. Toward the back, chairs rested on top of tables, and a custodian mopped the floor.

"Before I forget...." Jamie pulled a small plastic bag from her purse. "I checked out the gift shop while I was waiting." She set two candy bars on the table. "Dessert." Next a small candle. "Ambiance." With a flick of a disposal lighter, the final purchase in her bag, she lit the candle.

Rhys turned the label to face him. "Hyacinth?"

"The other options were Fresh Grass and Bubble Gum."

"Good choice." He looked down at his sandwich. "Bon appétit."

They'd each taken their first bite when the custodian passed by. "Fifteen minutes till we close. And no lit flames. Safety hazard."

Rhys hastily swallowed, then picked up the candle. "Make a wish."

His eyes glowed as he watched her, a flicker from the candle, a flame from his soul. Jamie pursed her lips and blew out the candle. Rhys's gaze held hers as he leaned forward.

His lips met hers, the kiss short but sweet. Unexpected for where it occurred. Precious because first kisses always are.

A dimple flashed in one cheek as he sank back in his chair. "My wish came true."

She reached across the table, taking his hand in hers. "So did mine."

Chapter Six

Dana stared across the vast expanse of the Atlantic Ocean at the approaching Virginia coastline. Less than a month ago, she'd made her final move to PI, never expecting events to unfold as they had. The life she'd lived for over twenty years had been a sham. Her husband had been a liar, and the son she loved had been borne by another woman.

Beside her stood the son who'd lived in the shadows of her memory for that same length of time. Reunited by the most extreme coincidence imaginable. A chance remark sparking a faint memory and an unexpected miracle. Her life could have continued, knowing Rhys McCall only as a business partner, perhaps as a friend as well. But any chance of regaining that infinite connection of mother and son would have been lost.

She dabbed a fingertip to the corner of one eye, hoping the oversized sunglasses hid her distress. Obviously not. Rhys wrapped an arm around her shoulders in a brief hug. She pushed the glasses on top of her head and looked at him. Tall and handsome, with unmistakable glimpses of the child she'd had for such a brief time.

"Thank you for coming with me."

Rhys shook his head. "I didn't really give you a choice."

"No, you didn't." She squeezed his hand. "I'm glad. I need you to be there when I confront Toddy."

His gaze shifted toward the mainland ferry terminal coming

into view, then back to her. "What's your gut feeling? Could he have lied to you all these years?"

"James did, and I believed him." Dana planted her back against the railing. "I was so stupid!"

"You had no reason not to believe him."

"Nothing was real to me. Nothing was right. How could the only memories I had be false when they were so vivid in my mind? I should have asked more questions. Should have pushed harder for answers."

"And put yourself at risk. Something happened—intentional or accidental—to the real Dana Canfield. You could have ended up dead with another woman replacing you."

She pushed away from the railing, looking around frantically. "Now I'm putting you at risk. I can't—"

He caught her by the shoulders. "It's going to come out anyway once you confront Toddy."

Dana wrapped her hands around his forearms. "You *do* think he's involved, don't you?"

"I'm not discounting it. One thing's certain, I will keep you safe."

Another long-ago memory burst into being. She stepped back and rested one arm along the wooden railing. "You made that same promise to me once before."

He faced her, mirroring that same pose. "Yeah?"

"You'd learned how to unlock the door of our apartment, but there was a second latch higher than you could reach. One day while I was in the kitchen, you climbed up on a chair and unhooked that latch."

Recognition flashed across Rhys's face.

The door was open. Terror gripped her heart, squeezed the breath from her lungs. A gray haze washed across her vision, seeping into her body and stealing strength from her arms and legs.

"Rhys!" All her waning energy blasted into that one fervent scream.

He wouldn't… couldn't… Dear God, he had. A rush of adrenaline cast away the debilitating haze, and she bolted into the hallway. The doors to the three other apartments on their floor were closed. The other residents had classes at this time. If one of them had been home, they would have marched him back to her apartment.

The stairs. She raced to the stairs. Without a doubt, the front door had been left open by some of the guys in the building who were too damn lazy to close it behind them.

Don't you dare have gone outside!

She rounded the stairs at the final landing, twisting her ankle. Biting back the pain, she grabbed the railing and forced her way down the remaining steps. Staggering across the entryway, she stumbled onto the stone porch, stopping, sagging in relief as she saw her son.

He sat on edge of the porch, toes tapping against the top of the next step as he watched a soccer game in progress across the courtyard. She limped across the porch, easing down beside him. He jumped to his feet, excitement lighting his face as he pointed across the street.

"Mommy, look. Soccer! Can we play soccer at the park today?"

"No park today, sweetie." She took his hand in hers, needing that touch to assure her he was there and safe.

His lower lip puckered, stopping short of a pout. "Why? You said we would go to the park today."

She drew him between her knees. "Because you disobeyed. You unlocked the door and went outside without permission. I had no idea where you'd gone."

He stabbed a finger toward the top step. "I was right here."

She cupped his chin, holding his gaze. "But I didn't know that."

A shadow darkened his moss green eyes. He gazed up at the second-floor windows of their apartment, then back to her. A small hand stretched out, wiping away a tear she'd missed before sitting down. "I scared you. I'm sorry."

She drew him to her; he fell against her. Arms around one another, they sat for a silent moment.

"The rules are for a reason, Rhys. To keep you safe."

He drew back, his face solemn as he nodded. He cupped her face in both tiny hands. "When I get bigger, it'll be my turn to keep you safe."

Rhys spoke, breaking into her thoughts. "For the longest time, I felt responsible for you being gone." She started to protest, but he held up one hand to stop her. "As time went on, I realized there was nothing I could have done. This time, I'll keep that promise. I *will* keep you safe."

So much rode on the upcoming meeting with Toddy. She needed answers, but she feared what those answers would be. She wasn't the only one invested in the meeting. Rhys's life had been impacted as well.

A blast from the boat's horn sent a jolt through both of them. They walked to Rhys's vehicle in preparation for disembarkation.

Dana watched as her son maneuvered the SUV off the ferry and through the terminal parking lot. Strong and sure. Confident and in control.

He wasn't a man to give his word lightly. Fate had kept him from fulfilling that promise he'd made as a child. From this point on, he'd risk his own life to ensure she remained safe.

And that scared her more than anything else.

"Mrs. Canfield, your host has already arrived. If you and your guest will follow me, please."

Rhys's step slowed as they followed the maître d' past the main dining room, his architect's eye taking in the heart-pine wood floors and antique stamped-tin ceiling. Stone walls gave way to a small private alcove enclosed in a circular half-wall of glossy wood and etched glass. Soft music played from unseen speakers, muffling any passing sounds of footsteps or conversation.

The man seated at the table rose in greeting, arms outstretched toward Dana. "There's my girl."

He stood a few inches taller than Dana, overall fit but with a few extra pounds around his waist. Hair more silver than gray was combed back from a tanned and weathered face. Watery blue eyes sat over a hawk-like nose.

Rhys stayed where he was as the two exchanged greetings. After a brief kiss on Dana's cheek, Toddy stepped back, hands cupping her upper arms. "You look tired. You're not sleeping again, are you?" He shook his head. "No wonder, with that Lansing business."

Exasperation flickered across Dana's delicate features. "Toddy—"

He dropped both hands, cutting off her protest as he turned to Rhys.

"So you're the plus-one today, young man."

Rhys extended his hand. "Rhys McCall, sir."

A faint frown creased Toddy's brow, then cleared. "The business partner. Good enough." A clap on the shoulder followed the hand clasp. "None of that 'sir' stuff. Call me Toddy. We're all friends here. Have a seat, everyone. I ordered appetizers. Little something to get us started."

Steamrolled. No other word for the hit-and-run introduction.

Dana's warnings on top of the conversation he'd overheard at her house still hadn't prepared him for the man in the flesh.

The waiter moved around the table, filling each glass with chilled champagne. Toddy lifted his glass. "To old times."

"And new beginnings." Dana lifted her glass.

Toddy placed several appetizers on his plate. "Sweetheart, catch me up on your little shopping mall project."

Rhys bristled, but a covert hand gesture from Dana cooled his jets.

"You know very well the project is not a shopping mall. We discussed it too many times before I left." She threw a teasing look in his direction. "You're not forgetting things, are you, dear?"

Toddy's hand stilled over his plate, a gesture so brief Rhys would have missed it if he hadn't been focused on the man's every move and reaction.

A second later, Toddy chuckled. "Touché." His smile faded. "What's your plan when this project is completed? Certainly there's not enough work on the island to keep you occupied full-time."

"I've had a few inquiries so far. And Rhys and I are working on developing a new project." She looked down at her plate. "But that's not why I'm here. I have another reason for wanting to see you in person."

Interesting. By all appearances, Toddy would be a likely candidate to approach for a financial interest in the Dennison. However, Dana totally avoided the topic.

Nerves? More than just that. The stiff posture, the hand resting on her lap in a fist, the tight pull of muscles at the corners of her eyes and mouth told him the true story.

She's scared.

Scared to hear the answers Toddy would give. Scared to know her world could shatter once again. And there was nothing he could do to prevent that blow.

"And here I thought you missed my good looks and charming personality." Toddy winked, then gestured to Rhys. "Try the crab cakes. Marvelous." He looked back to Dana. "Remember that little place we stopped at along the way back from Joshua's baseball finals in his senior year? Not much on ambiance, but the food was outstanding."

"I remember, but—"

"Did you play sports in school, Reid?"

"Rhys. I played basketball."

Toddy nodded. "Got the height for it. Joshua did too. Basketball, baseball, soccer, track. Well, everything but football." He pointed his fork in Dana's direction. "Mom here wouldn't agree. Too violent. Every year I'd take him Christmas shopping for his parents. He knew exactly what he wanted for his father. Mom gifts, oh, they took *hours*. Had to be just right. Nothing less than perfect for his mother." His gaze softened as he stared into the distance. "What good times we had."

Rhys shifted in his chair, concentrating on the loneliness in the old man's voice, the yearning for a time that was forever gone. Why wouldn't Toddy cling to memories of happier times and the one person he could still call family? If his stories were drenched in sentimentality, perhaps that was due only to the man's over-the-top personality.

And not the stirrings of jealousy Rhys was fighting to suppress.

"Toddy, I need you to listen to me," Dana said, a firm note in her voice.

He dabbed the corner of his napkin to his mouth. "Of course, dear. What is it?"

"Do you remember when we first met?"

A quizzical look crossed his face. "That's a bit bizarre. Sweetheart, are—"

She held up one hand. "Answer the question."

Toddy sat back in his chair with a barely heard sigh. His gaze dropped to his plate, and when he looked up, a small smile teased his lips. "The first time I saw you, you were lying on the sofa in the sunroom. Frail little thing. Barely a bump beneath the blanket. Joshua was sitting on the floor, head against the seat cushion, holding your hand. When he saw me, he put a finger to his lip and said, 'Quiet. Mommy's sleeping.' Such a tiny little solider protecting his mother." He blinked away a sheen of moisture and cleared his throat. "To answer your question, we didn't meet officially until the following day."

Protecting his mother. The image seared a path through Rhys's brain. His fingers closed into fists. He drew in a deep breath, struggling to keep his composure as color rose in Dana's cheeks, her voice lifting in frustration.

"You didn't come to our wedding? Never saw a photograph?"

"I knew you only by name. I was living overseas at that time, remember? I received an invitation to the wedding but wasn't able to make the trip." Worry lines deepened around the corners of his eyes. "Why are you bringing this up now?"

"Detective Lansing was one of the responding officers when I had that car accident."

His frown deepened as he continued to eat. "Quite an odd coincidence."

"I don't think so. Especially since my identity was switched with the woman who died in that wreck. The woman who died was James's real wife. I'm not Dana Canfield."

Toddy's face grayed, and he lifted a trembling hand to rub the side of his neck. "That can't be. Honey, you—"

"Don't you dare suggest that I'm having delusions! It explains all those memories everyone told me had never happened. Why Joshua was so confused. What it doesn't explain is why James lied. Why he perpetuated a fraud that kept me from my own family for over twenty years."

"Is this based on something that Lansing fellow said? Hardly a reliable source."

It was Dana's show, but Rhys couldn't remain silent any longer. "It's more than a matter of switched identities. It's about a woman who lost the life she should have had with her own son."

"Her... son?" Toddy looked from Rhys to Dana and back again. His shoulders sagged, and the creases in his face deepened, aging him years in mere seconds.

Rhys extracted several photographs from his inner jacket pocket. "We have proof, if you'd like to see."

"Yes, I would." Toddy's hand shook as he took the photos. His eyes widened, and a soft gasp expelled past his lips. He looked up, tears pooling in his eyes, his voice hoarse with grief. "Who *are* you?"

"Catherine Dennison McCall." She extended her hand toward Rhys, and he took it without hesitation. "And Rhys is my son."

Toddy's gaze flew back to the images, then to Rhys. "I don't know what to say, what to think. All these years, then by mere chance the two of you find each other." His head bowed. "To believe this means believing a man I called my godson, a man I loved and respected like a son...." His voice broke into a single sob. "How could he have committed such a heinous act?"

Toddy's fist clenched around the photos.

Rhys rounded the table, rescuing the precious photographs before they were crumpled. He tucked them back into his pocket, then returned to the opposite side of the table. Standing behind Dana's chair, he rested his hands on her shoulders. "That man you loved and respected cost me my mother. I grew up thinking she was dead."

"I had no idea…" Toddy's haunted eyes stared across the table at Dana, his words barely more than a whisper. "You thought I knew."

Dana lifted her chin, taking a guilt-ridden blow she didn't deserve. "I hoped not. I prayed you didn't. But I had to ask these questions. I had to see your face and hear your voice when you answered them."

Rhys gripped the back of the chair where Dana sat. Was the old man a good enough liar that he could fake that level of anguish? Or was he just selfish enough to care more about his own hurt feelings than for all that Dana had suffered?

Rhys gave Dana's shoulders a gentle squeeze, then returned to his chair. "What happened to the other woman?" he asked.

Toddy frowned at the sudden question. "Her family"—he looked at Dana—"*your* family would have dealt with those details, I suppose."

"I never knew where my mother was buried," Rhys said.

"I'm sorry to hear that," Toddy said with a slight bow of his head before turning his attention back to Dana. "By the time I arrived, you were recuperating at home. As far as I knew, the other woman was responsible for the wreck."

"She was responsible," Dana said softly. "The driver of the blue car was cited as causing the wreck. According to the official records, Catherine McCall was the driver. But I'm Catherine, and I was driving a red car. That means the real Dana was at fault. So I come back to what did James know and when? If the switch was a mistake, why didn't he correct it?"

"I don't know." Toddy's helplessness faded, replaced by a surge of defiance directed in Rhys's direction. "The only one who possibly could explain what happened at the hospital that day is your father."

"He hasn't been cooperative with any details."

"How unfortunate." Toddy's dry tone indicated his own lack of sympathy for Rhys's situation. The anger in his face cleared as he turned to Dana. "Knowing what you do now...?" His voice broke, stalling his question.

"We're still family, Toddy. I can't erase those years like they never happened."

"And Joshua?"

Dana cast an apologetic look in Rhys's direction before she replied. "Joshua will always be my son." She stirred restlessly. "Under the circumstances, I think we should cancel the rest of our luncheon."

Silence filled an awkward pause before Toddy responded. "I suppose that might be best."

Dana touched her fingertips to the back of Rhys's hand. "I'm going to freshen up. I'll meet you outside."

Rhys stood as Dana pushed back her chair and walked away.

I don't blame you.

How could he blame her for loving the child she thought was her own? The mother he remembered could have done nothing less than that. And throughout all she'd endured, all the lies she'd been told, he took comfort knowing that a part of her had never forgotten him.

He stared at the empty doorway, holding back the urge to follow. Dana would want to regroup and compose herself in private, the same way he would.

In the meantime, he'd make the most of these final minutes.

Toddy rose and walked to where Rhys stood, his gaze resting on the now-vacant doorway. "I owe you an apology."

Not what he'd been expecting. Rhys shifted into Toddy's line of sight. "For what happened to my mother?"

A hint of anger flickered in Toddy's blue eyes, then washed away. "No, for today. It must have been uncomfortable for you to hear me reminisce about Joshua and the close relationship he had with his mother... with Dana."

"I was four years old when this happened. I have some memories of her. Others we've recalled together. I know firsthand what a wonderful mother she is. I lost years with her because of the selfish motives of a coward." He ignored Toddy's wince and plowed on. "I can't fault Joshua because he lived the life I should have had. What I don't understand is why he walked away.

Whatever issue he had with his father, Dana didn't deserve to be abandoned. Joshua hurt her deeply."

"We're all hurting." Toddy lifted his face toward the ceiling.

Rhys struggled to reconcile the jovial if somewhat sarcastic first impression he'd had of Toddy with the grief-stricken man beside him. He studied the man's upturned profile. His jaw was set, but his mouth quivered.

"That girl captured my heart from the first time we met. Lost, but so determined. She pushed herself through physical therapy so she could be the mother Joshua deserved and made a miraculous recovery. She kept saying 'My son needs me.' She was the light of the family. But that light went out after Joshua left. Things were never the same between her and James after that. When James died, that was just one more blow for her."

Toddy squared his shoulders, hands shoved in his blazer pockets. "The light went out of my life as well when she fell into a deep depression. Rumors swirled about James's murder, about their marriage. Cruel, hurtful gossip. I protected her through all that. It broke my heart when Dana decided to move... but it was what she needed to do. A fresh start." He shook his head. "And look what's come of that."

"The truth. That's what came of it. Tell me, do you call it supporting Dana when you imply she's off her meds? Medication she probably never needed to take in the first place?"

Any hint of cordiality faded from the older man's manner. "Obviously you were eavesdropping on our recent conversation." His glance shifted to the doorway where the maître d' waited. "David, our plans have changed. Can you have Mr. McCall's car brought around?"

"Certainly, I'll have your bill prepared and be back in a moment." He turned to Rhys. "Mr. McCall, if you'll accompany me, I'll escort you to the valet station." Looking at Toddy, he asked, "As for your car, sir?"

"Calling my driver now." He waved his cell phone. "Oh, and Mr. McCall?"

Rhys halted at the doorway, turning.

"Over the years, Dana struggled with bouts of depression. I found making a quip helped spark her temper. Put a bit of fight back in her. I don't expect you to understand. After all, you haven't known Dana as long as I have." He dropped his gaze back to the phone. "Have a good day."

The dismissal was as smooth and cutting as Rhys had ever seen. If it wasn't for Dana waiting for him, he'd finish the conversation in a way Toddy wouldn't like.

He glanced around the vestibule. Finding no sign of Dana, he walked outside. Still no sign of his mother. Enough time had passed that she should have exited as well. Toddy hadn't emerged either. A dark suspicion rose from his gut. He was starting to go back inside when the door behind him opened.

Dana emerged as Rhys's SUV arrived at the foot of the steps. She paused, half-turning toward the entrance. "Wait. I didn't tell Toddy good-bye."

Oh hell, no.

Whatever regard Dana held for the man—good, bad, mixed—Rhys wasn't about to let her suffer any further distress. He nodded toward the waiting vehicle. "He'll have to understand."

Dana hesitated, then nodded. Her mouth eased into a soft smile as she tucked her hand into the crook of his arm.

Their conversation halted as Rhys maneuvered the Navigator through the afternoon traffic. Once on the main road, he sent a glance in Dana's direction. She sat with both hands in her lap, staring out the window. He expected sadness, anger, even suspicion. Not this bizarre stillness so at odds with her natural vivacity.

"What do you think?" he asked. "Do you believe him?"

Dana sighed. "I don't know. If James could lie to me, why not to Toddy as well? The three of us were all the family Toddy had. First, Joshua left, then James died, and I moved away. The look on his face when he realized I thought he was in collusion with James..." She rubbed her hands over her arms as a shiver overtook her. "He looked so heartbroken."

"He seemed sincere." *Seemed.*

"What did the two of you talk about after I left?"

"He apologized for boasting about how wonderful Joshua was since he didn't know about our relationship, and how hard it must have been for me to hear those stories." A snort followed. "Then he proceeded to say how you pushed yourself to recover after the accident because—quote—your son needed you."

Dana shifted halfway in her seat. "Oh, he makes me furious! One minute gracious, the next moment popping off cruel remarks."

"Like those off-your-med remarks he makes to you."

"You asked him about that?"

"Sure did. He said it was his way of jump-starting you out of your ongoing bouts of depression."

"Bouts of depression, my ass. He's a pompous old coot who gets his kicks pushing people's buttons." She sank back in her seat and shook her head. "I'm not being fair. Yes, I was depressed after Joshua disappeared and then James was murdered. My God, who wouldn't have been? Toddy stood up to all the gossips who tried to destroy my reputation. The ones who claimed I was having affairs, that James and I were on the brink of divorce. He defended me because we're family, and he cares. I can't forget that."

"You're being more than fair. All I heard the entire time was how this affected him."

"Nothing new there." She tapped the back of her hand against his shoulder. "Do you feel better after telling your mom on him?"

With one remark, Dana eased the darkness that had lingered over their day. "As a matter of fact, I do. Thanks, Mom."

"I love hearing that word."

"I love saying it."

"There's one thing Toddy said that we need to consider. Erik may be the only other person who can provide additional information about that day."

Rhys flipped on the turn signal as they approached the entry to the ferry terminal. "Right now, Dad's not able to give us any information, even if he were inclined to do so. But as soon as he's better, I will get answers from him."

Chapter Seven

Main Street Village sat comfortably between yesterday and way back when. A few indications of the modern day—stoplights and crosswalks—had crept in, but otherwise the shopping area clung to its traditional roots with cobblestone streets and brick sidewalks. A one-time Victorian wedding-cake residence at the corner of Main and Canal was now a bed and breakfast. On the opposite corner, a former five-and-dime had been converted to a 1950s-style restaurant. Framework houses had become clever little shops. Junk competed with antiques, T-shirt and souvenir stores with coffee and tea shops. Tradition mixed with trendy, from an upscale boutique and original art, to estate jewelry and vintage clothing

The overall effect was charming, but there was considerable work to be done. Sidewalks had buckled from the roots of trees planted along the block. Benches were needed for visitors to rest or sit while enjoying an ice cream cone or soft drink. Sign posts were missing or faded. Streetlights were various styles, rarely matching.

Strolling along the sidewalk, Jamie marveled at Rhys's vision for the revitalization. Winning a go-ahead from both the council and the merchants was a testament to his reputation and powers of persuasion.

Following Dana's instructions, she stopped in at the Take Me Home gift store and introduced herself to Sally Van Kirk, vice president of the Merchant's Association, and explained the reason for her visit.

Short and rotund, the woman bristled with energy. "I'm all for this renovation. What lady doesn't need a makeover every now and then? And these old buildings along this street can sure use one." She paused in the middle of refolding a stack of T-shirts. "This is a good thing for the village. Bart Caine knows it too, even though he'll gripe to anyone who'll listen."

"I plan on speaking to Mr. Caine next about some ideas to promote Main Street and help increase your sales. Since you're the vice president—"

Sally held up one palm. "Sweetie, I don't know a thing about marketing. Anything you do will beat the nothing being done now. I've met Mrs. Canfield, and I trust her. If you work for her, that's good enough for me. Goes double since Rhys was the one who brought her here. That boy wouldn't be going through all this if it wasn't to make things better."

Jamie held one of the T-shirts—purple with white daisies—against her shoulders. Maybe next paycheck. She looked back to Sally, unable to contain a smile. "You knew Rhys when he was growing up?"

"I've known him since he was four years old and watched him grow up. The Carsons lived three doors down from us. They practically raised him. When the boy wasn't working for his daddy or Tom Carson, he did odd jobs around the neighborhood. Did all our yard work. I found out Harold was only paying him five dollars and made him up it to fifteen. Harold decided that gave him the go-ahead to supervise the job. I'd always slip Rhys an extra five along with a handful of cookies for having to put up with the old coot."

Sally's face softened, a smile crossing her lips as she gazed out the window. "I'll never forget the day I was sitting on my front porch, and this big red pickup stops in front of the house. Rhys came bounding out of that truck and up my front steps, saying, 'Mrs. V, I'm here to take you out for ice cream.' I was the second one to ride in that truck."

"Let me guess. Paige got the first ride." Jamie refolded the shirt and returned it to the stack. She pictured a teenage Rhys, his face beaming with pride over a truck he'd earned through his own efforts.

"Paige got the first ride. But I got the first *date*." Sally chuckled as she reached under the counter and pulled out a pink bag with a black store logo. She tucked the T-shirt into the bag and extended it to Jamie.

"Oh, I can't, Sally."

"Honey, I may not know about marketing, but I know a bit about word-of-mouth advertising. You're going to be walking up and down this street, and everyone you pass is going to see that bright pink shopping bag with my store's name on it." She jiggled the bag. "Welcome to PI."

Jamie accepted the gift, touched by the gesture. "Thank you, Sally."

A gentle pat fell on her arm as they walked to the exit. "Don't you fret about Bart. He may bark… and bite… but he's a good enough businessman to listen when it comes to making money."

Her mood lighter after talking with Sally, Jamie walked down the block toward Caine Jewelers. The sun washed the area in a hazy golden glow. Just ahead of her, an older couple strolled hand in hand. Walking in her direction, a young couple laughed as they pushed a baby stroller. Gurgles erupted from within the carriage as it bumped along the uneven pavement. Across the street, another young couple indulged in a PDA just short of inappropriate.

Her eyes misted behind her sunglasses. As sweet as Sally's story had been, it twisted something inside her. Every story she'd heard about Rhys detailed his work ethic, his generosity in helping others. Losing his mother at such a young age had to have damaged his sense of security. Especially if his father had been a transitory figure. Paige's family might have filled a gap in his life, but they couldn't have closed the wound in his soul.

Rhys gave and gave, but did anyone give back? Did anyone notice? Or care?

I care.

And one way she could prove that was to help make this project a success. She charged ahead with a decisive step, ready to confront the dragon named Bart Caine.

A soft chime sounded as she opened the door to Caine Jewelers. Walking into the shop was like stepping into a mixture of the past and present. Original wood showcases polished to a gleam had been updated with modern glass. Classical music played from hidden speakers. In the far corner of the shop, an elderly gentleman sat behind one of the cases. His head was bowed, glasses perched low on his nose.

"One moment, please."

Gentle voice, kindly manners. He didn't look like a dragon. Didn't sound like one either. Still, surface impressions could be deceiving. Jamie pressed a hand to the pit of her stomach. How much influence did Mr. Caine have? Enough to sway those who were on the fence, even to turn the opinions of those who agreed with Sally?

The renovations would continue either way, but the fallout from disgruntled merchants could be devastating to Rhys's reputation. She had to convince the jeweler that the inconveniences would be worthwhile in the long run and get him to approve the promotional plan.

But how? *Think, Jamie, think.* What would persuade him best? Sally's words echoed back to her: *...listen when it comes to making money.*

She strolled around the shop, noting the merchandise he carried in addition to jewelry. Ceramic boxes. Gold keychains. Wedding and baby gifts. Tokens for graduations and engagements. She stopped to examine a display of wooden boxes, opening and closing the lids. Comparing the sizes and considering uses as ideas clicked in her mind.

"How may I help you, young lady?" Hands clasped in front of him, Bart Caine delivered a slight bow.

She pulled a business card—one of Dana's with her own contact information noted on the back—from the side pocket of her purse and extended it to him. "I'm Jamie Danvers with Canfield Designs."

"Hmm." The pleasant demeanor dissolved, replaced with hints of what she'd been warned about. "Here to wreak more havoc on the area? The streets are a mess." His expression hardened, his bushy brows drawing together. "Between the noise and the dirt, I'll have to close *my* store when the work reaches this block. Why *my* corner was selected for that clock...."

"I'm sorry about that, but I have some ideas—"

Mr. Caine held up one hand. "Ideas are what created this mess. I don't want to hear any more."

"Mr. Caine, if you would give me a chance—"

"Miss Danvers, you have forced me to ask you to leave my store." He nodded toward the door. "Good day, and don't come back."

Mr. Caine turned and walked to the work area behind the counter.

Tears sprang to Jamie's eyes, and her mouth trembled. Head bowed, she exited the shop. Her vision clouded, she tripped on a raised bit of sidewalk and grabbed on to the tree causing the problem. The bark bit into the palm of her hand, and she pulled in a shaky breath. All she needed was to fall on her face to top off the day.

She hurried down the block, sniffing back the tears that threatened to fall. How could she visit the other merchants in her current state? Even armed with Dana's drafts, why would the shop owners who had expressed interest in updating their shops listen to her? She'd only embarrass herself and ruin any goodwill Dana had built.

Why did I think I could run a marketing campaign? Even if it was for a group of merchants on a small island, that didn't mean it wasn't important. Tourist traffic was vital for those shop owners, especially during the winter months, when the number of visitors dropped to nothing. She was fooling herself thinking her ideas were anything but fluff.

She stopped at the corner, rummaging in the side of her bag for a tissue. Her fingers grazed the business card she'd attempted to give to Bart Caine. She slid the card from the pocket, running one finger across the embossed design, then turned it over where her own contact information had been written.

The tightness in her chest relaxed. She took a deep breath as Dana's voice whispered a reminder to her.

"You've more than earned it."

A fire ignited in her. The only way she could mess up was to walk away. She needed to find a way to connect with Mr. Caine's concerns. They had to be about more than money.

My store. *My* corner.

But what else?

Jamie crossed the street, then walked back in the direction of the jewelry store. She stepped to the edge of the sidewalk, studying the front of the building. The structure was old, but well-maintained, with script on the window stating *Established 1847.*

Pride. Ownership. Belonging.

She pulled her tablet from her bag, then swiped and tapped until she found the image she needed. Shoulders squared, Jamie marched back into the shop.

Mr. Caine looked up from his work area and scowled. "Miss Danvers—"

"I neglected to answer your question before I left. I'd like to do that now."

Mr. Caine walked around the glass case. Before he could argue further, Jamie pushed her sunglasses on top of her head and met him halfway.

"You asked why your corner was selected for the clock." She turned the tablet to face him. "Mrs. Canfield found a photograph of Caine Jewelers with the original street clock."

The old man studied the image, slowly nodding. "Installed in 1897. Caine's fiftieth anniversary. It was taken down during World War II and the metal donated for the war effort."

Jamie gestured toward the front windows. The pounding of her heart subsided, her breathing slowed. "Which is why your corner is the perfect place for the new clock. Twelve feet tall, black and gold. Everyone who sees it will immediately notice your shop." She took a deep breath. "Especially with a few minor updates to the exterior."

Seeing the protest forming on his lips, she raced on, recalling the suggestions Dana had recommended. "The only updating needed is black trim for the door and window frames. Gold paint for your signage. You have so many beautiful items here. They just need to be showcased. Updating Main Street is Rhys and Dana's part of the project. Mine is working with the merchants to communicate those changes toward helping to improve sales."

A crafty gleam entered the old man's eyes. "I noticed you looking at those wooden keepsake boxes. I agreed to stock them for one of the local craftsmen, but they're not selling. People say they have no use for them. What do you suggest?"

Energy surged inside her, unfazed by the challenge.

"They do have a use. People don't realize it yet." She tapped a finger on one of the smaller boxes. "iPod player, charger and earbuds." She tapped the next size larger box. "Recipe cards." An oblong box. "Crayons and markers." A larger one still. "This one could hold silk scarves, keys, any number of things. You can set up a display with different combinations to show shoppers why they need one. Your sign says you do engraving which makes one of these boxes a perfect gift for a birthday or Christmas." Her eyes widened. "If we can find miniature clocks similar to the one being installed, those would be perfect souvenirs. Beautiful and practical."

Mr. Caine rocked back on his heels, arms crossed over his chest. "All that right off the top of your head."

"I'm just getting started, Mr. Caine." She pointed to one of the walls. "I noticed you have photos of the shop from over the years. Those would make wonderful postcards." Her eyes widened. "And for the website!"

"Website." He shook his head. "I'll have to sit down for this one, Miss Danvers. Let's move behind the counter. No promises other than I'll listen."

A broad grin broke across Jamie's lips as she followed him to his work area.

During the next hour, Jamie saw both the gruff and the gentle sides of the man. At times, he seemed to argue for the sake of it, leading her to wonder if he wasn't extending the conversation merely to have the company. Bit by bit, he conceded, usually to her pleas of "Let's try it. We can always change it, and you can say 'I told you so.'"

Not having finished mock-ups actually worked to her advantage. The basic shell encouraged Mr. Caine to contribute his own ideas. Some good, others she persuaded him to compromise on. She ended the meeting with detailed notes and a promise to check back in two days with a draft version.

After lunch at the Garden Tea Shoppe, Jamie paid visits to the other merchants. Armed with Dana's drafts and her own knowledge of merchandising, she soared through the conversations with ever-growing confidence.

Leaving her final stop, Old Time Toys, Jamie was assailed by the sound of construction equipment. Bart Caine had labeled the noise intrusive, but to her it was the sweet sound of success. She walked to the temporary parking area. Tossing her purse and shopping bag onto the passenger seat, she settled behind the wheel.

What a perfect day. Sally is behind us one hundred percent, and the merchants like Dana's designs. Best of all, Mr. Caine is coming around. I know I can convince him to give my ideas a chance.

Baby steps, she warned herself. She had to make sure she had answers prepared for any questions or roadblocks Mr. Caine might present. Enough patting herself on the back. There was plenty of work waiting at Dana's house. If she pulled this off, maybe she would consider treating herself to those earrings that had caught her attention on the way out of Caine Jewelers. Layaway, of course. Her first check was allocated to paying Paige for rent, along with other monthly expenses.

She turned the key in the ignition, and the engine responded with a whine. The next attempt was more pathetic than the first one. "Just what I don't need."

Thought you knew it all, didn't you? Got a big head. Just goes to show...

She pushed away the vicious flow of her mother's voice in her head and reached for her cell phone. *It's just a setback.* "I can handle it."

She could, and she would.

His wallet a little lighter, his heart a lot fuller, Nick made his way down the east alley behind Main Street to the parking area. Plans were falling into place, and he couldn't wait to spring his surprise on Dana. Couldn't wait to see the blush on her pretty face and the sparkle in her dark eyes when he asked the most important question a man could ever ask.

How lucky could a guy get? A woman both gorgeous and smart by his side. His daughter back home where she belonged. Very soon, he'd have the family *he'd* been meant to have.

Yes, sir. I am one lucky guy.

Not that there weren't some bumps in the road. His promise to look at rentals this evening had weighed on him all morning. His apartment wasn't suitable long-term for a father and daughter, but putting life with Dana on hold until Megan went off to college didn't sit well either. The kid had dealt with more than her share of drama over the years due to Callie's life choices. Was it fair to expect her to accept a ready-made family because he'd fallen in love?

Damn straight it was. He'd been her champion through thick and thin, and he expected no less from her.

Which doesn't mean dropping a bomb her. Give her a chance to meet Dana. Once Megan met Dana, she'd love her as much he did.

Problem solved.

Good mood restored, he crossed the lot to his truck. Officially, the garage was closed for a second day, but he had a backlog of work to complete. He shifted directions when he saw Jamie Danvers standing by the side of her car, cell phone in hand.

"Afternoon, Jamie."

Her head shot up, the frown on her face easing into a relieved smile. "I was just looking up your number to call you."

"What seems to be the problem?"

"It won't start." She bit her lip, then asked, "Would you mind trying to jump it?

"Give it another try." He listened as she turned the key in the ignition, then shook his head.

"Could it be the battery?"

"More likely the alternator. I won't know for sure until I get it to the garage. I'll drop you off wherever you need to be, then head back to the garage for the tow truck. I'll need your keys." He paused. "Unless you want to have someone else check it?"

"No, that's why I was trying to call you." Jamie dropped the car keys into his open hand.

Nick waited while she retrieved her purse and a shopping bag, then led the way to his truck. He opened the door for her, then crossed around to the other side.

"About the repairs… I just started my job with Dana…"

The blush creeping up Jamie's cheeks told him more than the words she'd yet to say. "Let me check the car over and work up an estimate. We can figure out payments if need be. Besides, I owe you for helping set up that dinner at Dana's house."

"You don't owe me anything. I was happy to help."

"Seeing as it took most of your Saturday, I certainly do owe you. At least as much as those three weeks of lunch I gave up in exchange for Paige's help." He shook his head. "I must have been crazy doing that. The garage is still getting slammed over that poster."

Jamie chuckled. "So business picked up?"

Nick snorted. "Don't share that with Paige. She'll take credit for it." He maneuvered the Expedition off the lot and followed the detour out of the construction area. "Where can I take you?"

"Dana's house."

"How long until you can get back in the office?"

"The sheriff's department released the site today. The cleaners will start tomorrow. They estimated at least two days to finish."

Nick grunted. "Don't envy them that job." When Jamie didn't answer, he changed the subject. "Do you know what time she and Rhys are due back?"

Jamie glanced at the clock on the console. "Probably not for another hour."

Another hour at least to find out if the trip had been worth the stress it put on Dana. He doubted it. Guilty or bystander, this Toddy fellow didn't sound like someone who would roll over and tell the truth. "I'd like to have been there to see that guy's face when she confronted him about Canfield's lies."

"I don't like him."

The flat pronouncement took him by surprise. "You talked with him?"

"Dana had the call on speaker when she talked with him yesterday." An exasperated sigh fell from her lips. "He seemed concerned about her, but the next moment he was so demeaning. Suggesting she was 'off her meds' and shouldn't drive in her condition."

Nick snorted. "Did she rip him a new one?"

Jamie laughed. "Not entirely. She was holding back until she could see him in person."

"I wish I could've been there with her." Nick heaved a deep sigh. "But too many people might have put the guy on guard."

"You had a lot going on as well," Jamie said. "How's Megan?"

"Settling in. We had a couple good talks. What's helped her the most is knowing she never has live under the same roof as her mother again."

He cast a glance in Jamie's direction, expecting to see a shocked expression instead of guarded curiosity.

"Do you think they'll ever resolve their issues?"

His "dad senses" suggested something similar might be going on with Jamie. "Not all things can be fixed. Some people aren't satisfied being happy, and they resent anyone who is. They play the victim and lay guilt trips on others that have no basis.

Best thing to do is walk away and save yourself the grief."

"It's not always that easy."

"No, not always. I would have washed my hands of my ex-wife years ago if it hadn't been for Megan." A quick glance showed the tight look had eased somewhat on Jamie's face. Finances might play a part, but something else was eating away at the girl. For now, all he could offer was one more piece of advice.

"Don't waste energy trying to change things with someone who doesn't have your best interests at heart."

"Like breaking a bad habit."

Nick chuckled. "Good analogy."

"Thank you. For the pep talk and coming to my rescue. I was so relieved when you walked up to my car." A faint frown creased her brow. "Did you have another call in that area?"

"Ah… no. I had an errand on Main Street."

Nick could sense Jamie's mind running over the list of merchants. A sudden gasp confirmed she'd made the very connection he'd wanted to avoid.

"Were you at Caine Jewelers?" She twisted in her seat, a brilliant smile erupting. "Are you… Did you…?"

He couldn't hold back his own grin. "That just might be a yes."

Downtown PI was not the most promising area for a job-hunting eighteen-year-old with limited experience, but Megan wasn't discouraged. It was cool to walk around and check out the town. A day at the beach would have been better, but not by herself. There had to be kids her age here. If school wasn't out yet, maybe she could scoop the competition for a summer job.

Lots to do later today. Dad was even closing early so they could look at houses. A finger of guilt nudged her, wondering if her arrival was throwing a wrench into his—whatever—with Mrs. Canfield.

Dad dating a widow. With a murdered husband.

Weird.

Spying the two-story Canfield Designs building, Megan crossed the street. She paused in front of the window, then cupped her hands to peer inside.

"Help you, miss?"

Megan jumped, whirling around to face a tan shirt covering a broad chest. A silver star pinned to the shirt winked with reflected sunlight. She craned her neck upward. "No, just curious."

She started to step away, but the lawman blocked her retreat. "I haven't seen you around here."

"And I don't talk to strangers."

With a grunt, he tapped the star on his shirt. "Sheriff Wallace."

Megan's mind raced to the recital of friends Dad had shared the previous evening. She broke into a wide smile, holding out a hand. "Oh, sure. You must be Sam. I'm Megan. My dad is Nick Warden."

If the lifting of his eyebrows meant anything, she'd caught him off guard. He shook her hand. "Here for a visit?"

"Nope, I'm here to stay. I've been living with my mother in Colorado. Now that school's out, I'm here with Dad." She swept a quick glance across the street. "On foot patrol today?"

His eyes narrowed, raking her over with *the look*. The one adults gave when trying to discern an honest question from a lightly sarcastic remark. He ignored the inquiry, jerking his head toward the building she'd been peering into. "Were you looking for Mrs. Canfield?"

"Actually I'm job hunting." With a step back and then to the side, Megan maneuvered herself around the man's solid frame.

The doofus took the hint. He stepped out of her way, giving a nod. "Tell your dad hello for me."

"Sure thing, Sam. See you around." With a wave, she strolled away, keeping to an easy glide.

She continued down the street, stopping in front of a red brick building with a green-and-white striped awning. Carson's Pizza and Sandwich Shop.

Cute place and even better, a *Help Wanted* sign in the window.

She opened the door and walked inside. Several people were lined up at the front counter. She waited until the line cleared before approaching. Despite the recent rush, the woman behind the counter greeted her with a perky smile and upbeat demeanor.

"Welcome to Carson's. What I can I get for you today?"

"An application." Megan gestured toward the window. "I saw your sign that you're hiring."

Relief swept over the woman's face. "Oh, thank God." She grabbed a sheet of paper from under the counter, then handed it and a pen to her. "You can have a seat at the table in the back to fill out the application. By the way, I'm Paige Carson."

"Megan McCallister."

Application in hand, Megan walked to the four-top table. She glanced around before sitting down. As this was the only table in the area, her chances didn't bode well for a waitressing position. Unless a dining room existed behind the set of closed sliding doors.

Still, a job was a job, and she'd made a promise to Dad. Within minutes, she'd completed the form and walked back to the front counter.

"All done? Great, let's talk." Paige motioned toward the table, pausing to bump open the door to the kitchen. "Karen, I need you to watch the front for a few minutes."

Megan resumed her former seat while Paige took the chair opposite.

"Paige, I don't see any other tables. Is the job for the kitchen?" Megan tilted her head toward the closed doors. "Or is there a dining room?"

Paige cast a sour look in that same direction. "There is, but I don't have the funds yet to finish it. When I opened, it was strictly carryout. I'm expanding to delivery. The job opening is for delivery plus kitchen prep. Hours would be ten a.m. to two p.m., with deliveries between eleven and one. Tell me about your restaurant experience."

Megan gestured toward her application. "Two years at a place called Frankie's. It's a family restaurant. I waited tables, did prep work. Sometimes I worked the take-out counter along with the register."

Paige frowned. "Where is Frankie's? Is that in Sutton?"

"Oh, sorry. That's a small chain in the suburbs outside of Denver. I just moved here."

"Denver?" Paige looked at the application, then back to Megan. "You're Nick Warden's daughter."

Was that a good thing or not? From Paige's tone, Megan wasn't quite sure. "I guess you know my dad."

"He gets his lunch here often." Paige smiled and held out a hand. "You're hired."

"Just like that?" Megan narrowed her eyes. "No background check? No drug test?"

Paige lowered her hand. "Background checks and drug tests cost money. The job is part time, minimum wage. The sheriff's office is across the street. If you rip me off, I know where your dad works."

Megan sat back in her chair, grinning. Her new boss was no pushover. She held out her hand. "Works for me. I accept."

After a handshake, Paige stood. "I'll get the rest of your paperwork."

Megan pulled her cell phone from her pocket. Dad to the rescue again. The extra phone he had wasn't the most up-to-date, but it was good enough for now. At least she could text her friends back in Denver.

Speaking of texts... Her fingers dashed across the screen.

Dad! I got a job!!!!!!!

Chapter Eight

Rhys's plans for an early return to PI were aborted when Dana spied Tina's, a small walk-up food stand, opposite the ferry terminal and insisted on stopping. What could he do other than indulge her request? Besides, they'd both missed lunch and deserved a treat. It wasn't champagne and crab cakes at Callavicci's, but hot dogs and an ice cream cone hit the spot on a warm spring day.

Ice cream cones... something about.... Time raced backward, and he recalled a scene much like the one around him.

A small wooden building with two walk-up windows. He couldn't see over the counter, so Mommy lifted him to let him trade his dollar for a chocolate cone.

"You took me for ice cream when I was little."

Dana's lips curved into a soft smile. "There was a place just off campus. Much like this one. Every Saturday we walked to the park so you could play, then we stopped for ice cream."

He sat on the bench, legs swinging, cone clutched between both hands. Mommy sat beside him, holding napkins. Just in case.

Always napkins. Never a cone.

"You did without." He met her startled gaze. "All those times we went for ice cream, you never bought one for yourself. You went without so I could have it."

"You obviously haven't dealt with a toddler eating an ice

cream cone. Every time it started to melt, you'd yell for me to help. Believe me, I got my share of ice cream."

She hadn't denied his observation, but the explanation she offered eased his conscience. Slightly. "I'm starting to realize how much you had to sacrifice by having a kid while trying to get through college."

"Because it wasn't a sacrifice. It was a joy. Nothing meant more to me than you."

He'd opened the door to their past. Might as well ask another question, one that had plagued him throughout the years. "Did Dad ever not want...?"

Dana set her palm on top of his hand, not allowing him to finish those words. "Not want me to have you? Never. I'll give him credit for that. Not that he was happy about the pregnancy, but that was aimed at me." Sunlight filtered through the leaves of the trees next to where they sat, haloing her. The gentlest of smiles bloomed across her face. "When I found out I was expecting a baby, I was scared, but ecstatic. I wanted you from the very first moment I knew you were a reality."

"I remember Dad coming to see me on and off. Did he give you any financial support?"

"It fluctuated, depending on his work. Sometimes not much. Other times, more." Her gaze winged over his shoulder, faint lines fanning around her eyes. "He was furious that I didn't move to PI and make things easier for him." Her gaze shifted back to him. "You know what the commute is now from PI to the mainland. Can you imagine what it was like twenty-some years ago? There's no way I could have continued to attend school. Living on PI meant taking a low-paying job just to cover the bills. I wanted more for you, and I wanted more for me."

He couldn't blame her for that. "That day we confronted Dad in his office, he mentioned you'd intended to transfer out of state."

"I don't remember, but it seems likely. Probably to Connecticut where my family lived." She gathered the trash on the table, stuffing it into her now-empty drink cup. "Things would have been so different for both of us if I had."

Rhys took the cup from Dana's hand and set it into his own. "When I think back on our times together, I remember being happy. If we lacked anything, I didn't know it because you made life an adventure."

She wiped a stray tear from the corner of one eye. "I needed to hear that. To know that you felt secure and loved."

As they walked back to the SUV, he thought what his life could have been after his mother's "death" if not for his dad, Mom and Pop Carson, and his best friend Paige.

And what would life would have been for Joshua Canfield after his mother died, if not for Dana?

"Company," Dana said as Rhys turned the SUV into her driveway.

Nick and Jamie stood beside Nick's vehicle. Jamie's car was nowhere to be seen. A smile broke across Nick's face, and he walked in a slow, long-legged stride to meet Dana as she opened the door and stepped out. His arm slipped around her, and she leaned into that strong embrace.

"You okay?"

"No." It hadn't even occurred to her to soften her response. Lies had played too much a part of her life, and she needed every bit of comforting Nick could offer. She gazed up into his face, those strong, solid features reassuring her. "Having you here makes it better."

A low chuckle tickled her ear.

Her hand stayed clasped in his as they walked around the vehicle. Rhys's gaze dropped momentarily to their linked hands, then rose back up along with a quick nod of acceptance.

Jamie rushed to her other side. "Are you all right?"

"I'm more confused than ever. Would you mind if we call it a day? I don't think I can concentrate. Let's start out fresh in the morning." She looked around, connecting Nick's presence with Jamie's missing vehicle. "Is there a problem with your car?"

"It wouldn't start when I was leaving Main Street. Fortunately, Nick was there and drove me back here. I didn't think you would be back this soon."

"Since we're calling it a day," Rhys said to Jamie, "I'll give you a ride home."

Nick held up one hand. "Jamie, I'm going to get caught up with Dana, then head back to the garage to get the tow truck. I'll have an estimate for you some time tomorrow."

"Thank you both," Jamie said. "Dana, I'll see you in the morning."

After final good-byes to Rhys and Jamie, Nick and Dana entered the house. They walked into the living room and sat down on the couch. Dana kicked off her pumps and stretched out her legs. Nick mirrored her position, but left on his shoes. He caught her hand in his, resting them on his thigh.

"How bad?"

"We didn't even stay for lunch." She blinked, swallowed, ordered herself not break down.

And failed.

Tears rolled down her cheeks, and she fought back a sob.

"Come here." Nick pulled her to his chest.

Strong arms anchored her, allowing her to ride out the storm until she could speak. "It was horrible! Toddy didn't believe me until Rhys showed him the photos of us when he was a child. When he realized that I suspected he'd been involved, he looked so heartbroken."

"You believe him?"

She leaned back to view his expression. "I have no reason not to believe him. Other than I'm scared. I believed James over all the inner warnings I had, and it cost me years with my son. What if I trust the wrong person again? Rhys had to sit there while Toddy went on and on about what a great mother I was to Joshua. How accomplished Joshua was and what wonderful times we had together. If it wasn't that he blathered on about it before I confronted him, I would have suspected him of taunting Rhys."

"Maybe he did know and was doing exactly that."

"But if he's innocent, I hurt him for no reason."

"There was a reason. To learn the truth and protect yourself. If he is innocent and cares for you as he claims, he'll get over it." He dropped a gentle kiss on her brow. "Will you be all right here tonight?"

She summoned that core of resolution, the one that carried her through the deepest, darkest of times. Nick had his own concerns, and she wasn't about to steal time away from his daughter this soon after her arrival.

She sat up, brushing his mouth with a kiss. "I'll be fine. You need to be with your daughter. Is she settling in?"

"Clothes, shoes, and makeup all over my apartment. So, yes, she's settling in. I can't blame her completely. The place isn't set up to accommodate a teenage girl."

She had plenty of room. Three extra bedrooms' worth. "Nick—"

"I'd like the two of you to meet. How about dinner tomorrow night? The three of us."

Had he guessed the question she was about to ask? She fought back another wave of disappointment. It wasn't as if they had to wait forever. But even the slightest delay seemed a heavy burden. She wanted—needed—normality.

"Tomorrow's fine. Here? You can try out the grill. Six o'clock work for you?"

"Sounds good. I'll pick up some steaks. You take care of the sides?"

"Deal." She scooted away, placing a cushion's width between them. "There's something else we need to discuss."

Nick raised one eyebrow in judgment of her retreat. "Lay it on me."

"It's about a new project on Towne Square. The vacant building next to your garage."

His expression cleared. "What about it?"

She explained the gist of the project. "The question came up about parking."

His quick mind immediately filled in the blanks. "And you want my property for that." He narrowed his eyes. "Did McCall suggest you try to influence my answer?"

The question would have triggered her temper if it hadn't been for the wide grin on his face.

"If I wanted to influence your answer…" She rolled to her knees, eliminating the distance between them. Her slim skirt rode high on her thighs as she straddled his lap. "…I'd do it like this."

Her palms glided up the hard muscular chest to rest on his broad shoulders. A flutter of lashes, pouting lower lip, whispery tones. "Please, Nicky baby? Say yes. For me?"

His entire body shook with laughter. "Do not… ever… call me Nicky."

She twirled a forefinger through his dark hair. "Whatever you say, baby."

His hands settled on her hips as she started to retreat. "Glenn Thornton wants me to buy him out."

She dropped the act, leaving Nick looking half disappointed, half relieved. "Who is Glenn Thornton?"

"Owns Crossroads Body Shop."

"And...?"

"He's looking to retire. A while back, he asked if I'd be interested in buying his business. I wasn't eager to take on more debt, but told him I'd think about it." His gaze heated. "But since you asked me so nicely...."

She pressed her hands against his chest. "Don't do this for me."

"I won't." His palms stroked a lazy path down her thighs. "But I will consider it for you." He lifted his hands from her hips. "Right now, I need to get back to work."

Fingers intertwined, they walked to the front door. Nick paused, placing a hand on the nape of her neck. "Things are crazy right now, but we'll get through them." He dropped a quick kiss on her cheek. "I love you."

"I love you too." She cupped his face before he could move away and planted a solid, steamy kiss on his mouth.

He grinned and tapped his forefinger to the tip of her nose, then dashed down the front steps.

Dana stood in the open doorway until Nick exited the driveway, then she walked back to the living room. She played over the conversation with Toddy and the subsequent one with Rhys. Toddy was right about one thing. Erik might have information he didn't even realize.

One thing was for certain: she wasn't waiting around for Rhys to question his father. She had questions of her own to ask the rat bastard, and he was in a place where he couldn't walk away.

Dana rested one hand on the metal bed railing, gazing down at Erik's sleeping form. He still snored in his sleep. The things she remembered that should have stayed forgotten.

We shared a life for a short time. Shared a bed. Saw the worst of each other. We created a beautiful child.

Resentment pushed its way into those memories. A child who missed having a mother in his life because of this man's selfishness.

He didn't know.

Rhys believed that, and Dana needed to accept that possibility as well. Though it didn't relieve Erik of having walked away based on the word of a stranger.

You owe me answers.

Erik's face twitched, and he stirred restlessly. A low moan slipped between his lips, and his eyes snapped open. Dana moved into his view.

"Oh, God. You?" A louder groan followed as his hand groped at the side of the bed. "Where's that damn call cord?"

"Do you need the nurse?" Dana glanced down, spying a cord dangling from the side of the bed.

If his glare had any power, it would have scorched her. "No, security. To bounce your ass out of here."

She shrugged. "While you look for it, you can answer some questions."

"Nothing to discuss." His burst of energy expelled, he sank back into the bed. His lips tightened in a face that was far too pale.

"You have details about the day I was in that wreck. Information that might explain what's happening now." She leaned over the railing. "I... need... to know."

Stormy gray eyes narrowed into hard slate. "I... don't... care." He turned his face away from her.

"Not even if Rhys is danger?"

His head swiveled, and he groaned from the swift movement. "Something happened to him?"

"No, but it might." Her grip tightened around the metal bar. "Don't you understand everything that's happened to us points back to the day of the accident? Something you don't even realize you know is making you a target."

"So this *is* your fault." He fumbled one-handed for his cell phone from the lap table.

"No, you idiot. Now, will you please answer my questions?"

"Sorry. Can't remember a thing." Head bowed, he tapped on the device. "Anything else?"

Dana snatched up her purse. "Try harder to remember. It

might save your life."

His grunt this time was tinged with exasperation. He looked up, jutting his chin toward the counter behind her. "Hand me the charger on your way out."

Dana picked up the free end of the cord. "This one?"

Erik rolled his eyes. "Yes, that one."

She jerked the cord from the socket and sniffed at his outstretched hand as she walked to the doorway. "Work on your memory." She dropped the cord into the wastebasket and walked away.

Dana stormed down the hall. Erik was the same selfish jerk he'd always been. He'd rather leave himself open to danger than help her. That was fine if he wanted to take that risk. But she wasn't willing to chance the danger spreading further in Rhys's direction.

I can't allow that to happen… I won't allow it.

Her heart raced, her hands shook. She couldn't drive in this condition. A cup of tea and a few quiet moments. Exactly what she needed before getting behind the wheel of the car.

Dana walked to the cafeteria. The impromptu hot dog and ice cream cone seemed like hours ago. A bowl of soup, a small salad, and a cup of tea restored her balance and reaffirmed her resolve.

I'm not taking no for an answer, Erik.

Her heels clicked on the tile floor as she walked back to Erik's room. The glass door was shut, the drapes drawn partially. Dana stepped to the edge of the window to glance in.

A woman stood next to the bed. The smile on Erik's face seemed out of place on his pale, drawn features as he looked up at her. She swept a palm across his brow, brushing back strands of his gray hair, then leaned over the bed to exchange a tender kiss.

Dana shuddered. What woman in her right mind…?

The woman straightened, looking directly at her.

…a man I knew many years ago… he was the one…

April.

Dana stumbled back from the window. The meal she'd just eaten rolled in her stomach. She caught her breath, then rushed down the hallway. She heard her name, but ignored the call. By the time she reached the lobby, the footsteps echoing behind her caught up.

"Dana, stop!"

Dana halted, then turned to face the woman who might not remain her friend for much longer. At any moment, the stunned gaze locked on her would morph into knowledge.

It came in waves, and Dana felt each blow. The soft gasp. The dropping of the patrician jaw. The widening of the pansy-blue eyes.

"You're Rhys's mother."

Dana nodded, struggling to speak. "When you mentioned the man in your past... I didn't know...." Her throat closed, and she stood in silence, waiting as April considered that answer.

"We need to talk somewhere more private. I'll meet you at your house." April walked away before Dana could protest or agree.

Another layer to the secrets and lies that had changed her life. What part had April played in all this? Or was she another innocent bystander who was now paying a price?

Dana had met April Davis for the first time at this very house. Of course, it hadn't been hers at the time, but once she'd seen the house, she'd known it was the one. Something about the traditional structure called to her. A four-bedroom house was a ridiculous purchase for a woman living alone. Back then, she'd never dreamed of meeting a man like Nick Warden, let alone that their initial attraction would explode into love and possibly lead to marriage along with a stepdaughter.

And she'd never expected a business transaction with her realtor to bloom into friendship. One that now seemed destined to end.

They didn't speak until after entering the house and settling on the couch in the living room.

"There's so much to my story I haven't shared with you," Dana said.

"You told me your husband had been killed before you moved here. A couple days ago you told me you were dating Nick Warden. Now I find out you're Erik's ex-wife." April shook her head. "I'm confused over all these men in your life and why you kept these secrets."

Secrets. They'd engulfed her life, drowning her in layers of deceit. How could she make April understand all the bizarre events that she herself was struggling to accept?

"I was in a car accident when Rhys was four years old. I had a head injury and was in a coma for several weeks. The other driver was killed. When I regained consciousness, I couldn't remember anything prior to that time. I was told my name was Dana Canfield. My husband was James, and I had a son, Joshua. Several months ago, I found the job posting for the Main Street renovations. After I moved here, by chance I mentioned the date of that accident to Rhys. The same date his mother died in a car accident. The coincidence struck him as strange, so he searched until he found photographs. Pictures of the two us when he was a child."

April crossed her arms over her chest and frowned. "That's when your memory returned?"

"Bits and pieces. So many things I'd never forgotten, but I'd been told never happened. I thought for so long they were false memories. Brain damage, or so I was led to believe." Dana tapped two fingers to her temple. "I was told I never had a little boy who loved to draw and play soccer. The little boy I had liked cars and baseball."

"Your husband had to have known."

"Exactly." Her lips trembled. "James knew and let the lie continue."

"This doesn't make sense. Erik would have known the other woman wasn't you."

"Someone at the hospital told him I was the one who died. Erik never confirmed my so-called death and left me with strangers. He took Rhys and returned to PI." Tears rolled down her cheeks, and her voice quivered. "Rhys grew up never knowing where his mother was buried or being able to visit her grave. However Erik felt about me, he owed Rhys that comfort."

She expected April to protest. To defend Erik's actions. But she remained silent.

"There was no love lost between us." Dana wiped a hand across her cheek. "Erik had bad boy written all over him when we met, and I wanted nothing to do with him. But he was charming and persuasive, and I was seventeen. When I told him about the baby, he accused me of getting myself pregnant." Her mouth curved in a half-smile. "I corrected him on several aspects of human biology."

"He wasn't like that when I knew him." April's eyes darkened with tears of her own. "I thought we had the beginnings of something special. When I didn't hear from him, I concluded he wasn't interested. I returned to college and married a man everyone said was suitable. Mitch Davis wore the right clothes. Belonged to the best fraternity. Knew all the right people. His family was in our social set. Later, I found out that was all surface, and *he* was the true bad boy."

"If Erik was interested, and it seems he must have been, why didn't he follow you?"

April's mouth thinned into a tight line. "Mitch and some of his friends beat Erik up and put him in the hospital. By the time he was released, it was too late."

And that was when a bitter, lovesick fool met a naïve college freshman.

So many "what ifs." So many tangled threads and lives, with each step back revealing another player who contributed to the chain of events. Erik and April's history explained the quick hiring of Kevin Davis.

Was that why Erik pushed Rhys out of the company? To replace him with April's son, even if Mitch Davis was Kevin's father? If April did have that much influence, she might be the key to getting Erik to talk.

"I went to see Erik today to discuss what happened the day of my accident. He might have seen or heard something that could help us find out who's behind this." Dana took a deep breath, praying for the answer she needed. "Erik won't talk to me, but he might talk to you. Will you help me?"

April bowed her head, her chest rising and falling as if in rhythm to her thoughts. When she looked up, her eyes were rimmed in red. "Right from the beginning, you and I hit it off. We had so much in common. Single, same age, grown sons. You were so open and lively and funny. I knew we could be friends." Her voice trembled, and she paused briefly. "At the hospital today, right before I saw you, Erik had just told me that Rhys's mother was alive and here on PI. When I looked up and you were standing outside his room, I knew you were that woman."

Dana caught her lip between her teeth. Tears welled again, and she blinked them back.

"I didn't hear all the details from Erik. I'm sure there's more to the story than you've told so far." April lifted her slim shoulders in a slow shrug. "The truth is somewhere in between. That's the way it usually is, isn't it?"

Dana pressed her fist against her breastbone. Hot flames flickered through her at the thought of losing April's friendship.

"I'm sorry if I've made you angry," April said. "I don't excuse Erik's decision, but I don't know the reason behind it. I want a life with Erik, but I don't want to lose our friendship either." She paused, then nodded. Firmly. Decisively. "I'll ask Erik to talk to you about that day. He'll do it for me."

A portion of the heaviness in Dana's heart lifted. "Thank you. For listening. For offering to talk to Erik."

April rose and held out her arms for a hug. They embraced, then Dana walked with April to the door.

"We'll work this out. By the time this is over, we'll have that double date I suggested." April waved as she walked across the porch. "You'll see."

Dana waved in response and closed the door. The news about Erik's aborted courtship of April tugged on her heartstrings. Slightly. It still didn't excuse his actions at the hospital. As for their disastrous relationship? They both owned equal responsibility for that. Though from the few words April said about her ex-husband, Erik might have been the better choice for her than Mitch Davis.

Wonder where Mr. Davis is these days and if any of his buddies are still on PI? She'd have to pass that information on to Sam.

Her gaze landed on the thick folder Rhys had left on the floor beside the couch. She had nothing else planned for tonight. She could check for any other names or dates.

Dana laid the birth certificates on the coffee table. Seated cross-legged on the floor, she sorted through her own folder of personal documents that she'd stored in the home safe. Finally she located the birth certificate she'd previously known as her own.

Dana Denise Colby. Father Robert Colby. Mother Anna Avery.
Dee Dee Colby.

Somewhere in the dark corners of her memory, she knew that name. Dee Dee. A name she'd heard but never called herself.

The paper slipped from her fingers, her arms falling limp at her sides. She struggled to draw a deep breath as a rush of acid raced from her stomach to her mouth. Forcing herself to sit up, she reached with a trembling hand for the other certificate.

Catherine Avery Dennison. Father Christopher Dennison. Mother Carolyn Avery.

Anna Avery.

Carolyn Avery.

Both papers fell to the floor, and she buried her face in both hands.

What did you do, James? What did you do?

Chapter Nine

"A new guest checked in today," Maisie Porter said.

Ben set his glass of iced tea on the table between them. He should have been bored by the slow pace he was being forced to live. But somehow, the hot lazy days on PI suited him. Not forever, but for now.

Lounging in a rocking chair on the back porch while his landlady sat in the porch swing filled him with a serenity he'd rarely known. He rocked, keeping time as her knotted fingers somehow made swift work of peeling and snapping something called pole beans.

He looked closer and saw the tight set of her mouth. "Guess you see all kinds of people, don't you?"

"That I do."

Ben waited, knowing that Mrs. P would fill the silence. He might not know the name of the new guest, but he'd bet money on why the person had arrived at this particular time.

"Down here from Richmond, so she says. Doctor's orders. Stress-related anxiety." Mrs. P sniffed. "Won't help her any. She might have left the city behind, but she brought herself with her."

Ben burst out laughing. "That's one of the keenest observations I've ever heard."

Pink crept across the old woman's cheeks. "Getting a bit too comfy with you. Here I am gossiping about one of my guests."

"What happens on the back porch, stays on the back porch."

He picked up the glass, took a sip. "Guess I'll meet her at dinner."

"She informed me she'd find better food elsewhere." A shrug suggested Mrs. P didn't care, but the slight tremble in her voice suggested otherwise.

Ben forced a smile. "Well, good. Just the two of us."

"Suits me fine. Now, if you don't mind giving this old gal a hand getting up, I'll start on dinner."

"Don't mind at all."

He carried the pan of beans in one hand and opened the back screen door with the other. Tailoring his step to accommodate Mrs. P's slower pace, he followed her into the kitchen.

"Ham on the menu tonight," she said. "Along with parsley potatoes, beans, and hot rolls." She peered up at him through the glasses perched on her nose. "How's that sound to you?"

"Sounds like I'll have to run an extra mile or two to work off the second helping I plan on eating."

A schoolgirl blush raced across her cheeks. "Ben Hampshire, you are a charmer."

Ben tipped a forefinger to his brow in salute as he left the kitchen.

He climbed the steps to the second floor and located the room with the locked door. It took him less than ten seconds to jimmy the lock. He eased inside the room and slid the deadbolt.

The cloying scent of perfume was his first clue, and the only one he needed to know who Mr. Stoddard had sent to eliminate Rhys McCall.

Idiot.

The sun was setting, the shades were drawn. A lamp by the bedside provided sufficient light to see as he made his way across the room. For someone who'd checked in only a few hours ago, the woman had made a hell of mess. She'd apparently dropped her clothes as she'd walked to the bed. He kicked a stiletto pump aside, walked across a silk dress that likely cost a cool grand, and stood by the bed. Clad in the briefest of lingerie, the woman lay with one arm crossed over her face, bent knees turned to the side, red hair splayed across the pillow.

The calculated pose looked ridiculous, but he didn't expect anything less from an egocentric loose cannon like Vicky Towers.

"Wondered how long it would take you to come calling," she said, lowering her arm. She rolled to her feet to stand mere inches away from him. "And here you are."

"To warn you not to screw up. What are you even doing here? All you have to do is eliminate McCall."

Vicky walked to the bureau, running a finger across several bottles. "I saw him. I stopped him on the street and asked for directions. He's very handsome. If I can find a secluded place, I might keep him hidden for a while." She met his gaze in the mirror, all cold blue eyes and hot red lips. "I like to play with my prey."

"You're playing a dangerous game. Mr. Stoddard doesn't allow mistakes."

Vicky turned, resting the heels of both hands on the bureau top. "*Nathan* told me to use my judgment."

She gave a long stretch, a pathetic attempt to showcase a body he had no interest in, followed by a giant yawn. "You're boring me, Benjamin. This girl needs her beauty sleep."

"Sleep on this."

In a flash, he pinned her against the wall. He read the lurid anticipation in her eyes, the smirk teasing her lips in her expected conquest over him. She learned how wrong she was when he shoved the barrel of his gun beneath her jaw.

"You do anything to hurt that old lady downstairs, I'll kill you." He jabbed the gun, tilting her head upward. "Understood?"

The fire still blazed in her eyes, this time with hate. "Got it. Now get your hands off me."

"My pleasure." He returned the gun to his pocket, then walked to the door. He paused, hand on the deadbolt. "This is your only warning."

A quick check of the hallway revealed it was safe to exit the room. He closed the door before Vicky's curses could follow him. The faint crash of glass sounded as he walked away.

If that was one of Mrs. P's antiques, he might have to end Vicky's visit to PI sooner than she'd intended.

Chapter Ten

Dust clung to the walls. The windows were filthy, and the floors were warped in places. The air was musty. But overall, the old Marcum building was in better shape than Rhys had expected. Partially due to John Marcum's sense of responsibility in having regular inspections to maintain the integrity of the property. Sentimentality, no doubt, played a part in that decision as well.

Rhys ran his hand over the railing of the staircase leading to the second floor. Solid as the day it had been installed.

By a McCall.

I want this.

More than he'd wanted the Main Street renovations. This project would mean working with Dana from the beginning. What could they have accomplished if they'd had all those lost years together? Would they have gone their separate ways or forged a collaboration of their talents?

Dana might have remarried, giving him half brothers or half sisters. He would have grown up knowing his maternal grandparents. Cousin, uncles, and aunts. He might even have been an uncle by this time. On the other hand...

He would never have known Paige.

He might never have met Jamie.

Rhys sank down on the steps as the might-haves and might-nots swarmed over him. The mixed emotions Dana battled over their own lost years versus having never known Joshua became clear to him. Loving one person didn't take away from the love for another.

He shook his head. No time to waste on things he couldn't change. He'd accomplished what he'd intended on today's walk-through. His memory was refreshed, his sketches updated with notes and plenty of pictures to share with Dana and Jamie.

Exiting the building, he walked next door to Nick Warden's garage and entered through one of the open bay doors. Jamie's blue Ford was parked in the left bay. Nick stood at the front counter, tapping on a computer screen.

Their initial interactions had been less than positive. A situation that had changed when Nick realized Rhys was Dana's son, and not a romantic rival. Racing together to save her from the man who'd killed James Canfield had further solidified a measure of respect between them.

"Morning. Just getting started on Jamie's car, if that's why you're here." Nick walked around the side of the counter, resting one elbow on the surface. "Or would this be about the building next door and my property?"

Considering Warden's tone didn't sound antagonistic, Rhys plunged ahead with that very topic. "Dana mentioned you'd think about it. In case you decided no, I wanted to check if renting a portion of your back lot would be feasible."

Nick shook his head. "Not a good idea, given the volume of traffic I have in and out of the lot most days." He straightened, sparing a quick glance around the area. "I have a niche business here. I have customers who work downtown or pass by this way. I live in a small apartment upstairs. With the emergency on-calls I handle through the sheriff's department, I could have my loan paid off in a couple more years."

It made perfect sense. It wasn't the answer he'd wanted, but it was the one he had to accept. "I understand."

Rhys followed as Nick walked to the front of the garage. They stood just shy of the sidewalk. When a driver passing by waved at him, Nick lifted a hand in response. He paused as a motorcycle roared past, louder and faster than the legal limit. "Haven't seen that one before now. Some kid must have gotten a graduation present."

"Sam'll put a stop to that quick enough."

"No doubt," Nick said. Scuffing a foot along the sidewalk, he returned to their discussion. "Glenn Thornton's looking to retire. He's asked a couple times if I was interested in buying his body shop. Did Dana mention that to you?"

"No, she didn't."

Nick glanced away, his mouth crooking in a half-smile. Rhys had a feeling he really didn't want to know what had generated that reaction.

"I've thought about it on and off. More so after talking to Dana yesterday." Feet planted, Nick shoved his hands into his back pockets. "I called Thornton this morning, told him I was interested. I've looked over the building and equipment previously with Glenn. I'm meeting with his realtor later today to look at the property itself. As I recall, the customer parking is limited. Might need to reconfigure that area." He shook his head. "Not your problem though, and I'm getting way ahead of myself."

If Nick was already thinking about the new property, odds were good he was ready to make the move. The issue now, as always, was money. Meeting Nick's asking price along with the other funds they needed. As much as he hated to admit it, accepting Kevin's offer might be the only option that would permit them to meet the deadline set with John Marcum.

"I appreciate your considering the request."

"I need to make changes in living arrangements now that Megan's staying with me. Might be time for other changes. Lots to work out still."

Their handclasp didn't seal the deal, but it warmed the growing relationship between them.

Rhys paused outside Nick's garage to check his emails. He tapped out several quick responses, then tucked the phone away. Next stop was McCall's.

Behind him, the drone of a motorcycle grew louder. He glanced over one shoulder. The driver had jumped the sidewalk at the corner and was speeding directly for him. His heart thumped. No time to retreat to the garage. He wouldn't make it to the corner. Couldn't dodge into the street.

He jumped onto the concrete ledge framing the windows of the Dennison, then leaped for the fire escape. Momentum carried him to the second rung. He hefted his body, curling his legs upward.

The motorcycle sped below him, skidding to a halt at the corner. Fury radiated from the tense set of the driver's body. Head covered by a full helmet, the driver gave a single nod, a warning of future retribution, then raced away.

Rhys dropped to the ground. He wobbled, falling back against the grimy window as Nick reached his side.

"Did you get the plates?"

Rhys shook his head, his chest heaving in deep gasps. "Call the sheriff."

"I already did."

Jamie waved as she entered Carson's front door. Standing behind the counter, Paige returned the salute and gestured toward the lone table in the back.

"Have a seat. I'll be right there."

Jamie walked to the four-top table now known as "the front office." Seconds later, Paige arrived, carrying two bottles of water. She set a bottle in front of Jamie, then dropped into one of the chairs facing the front of the restaurant.

"Whew! I think the noon rush is over." Paige grinned. "So, Operation Date Night."

"Thanks for helping. And letting me borrow your Jeep too." A frown crossed Jamie's brow. "Are you sure you have a ride home after work?"

A wave of one hand dismissed Jamie's concerns. "Not a problem. Molly Kincaid said she'd be glad to drive me home." Paige leaned forward. "I think Tom Hunter has a crush on her."

"Hmm. The deputy and the dispatcher?" She nodded. "Could work."

"As for my part in Date Night, I'll be ready at the appointed time. Fingers crossed it goes better than your first date." Paige held up two hands, demonstrating.

"Do *not* jinx me!"

"Just saying." She opened the water bottle and took a deep drink. "Have you met Megan yet?"

"Not yet." Jamie looked around. "Is she here?"

Paige pushed halfway out of her chair, stretching to look out the window. "I'm expecting her back soon. She called a while ago to check if there were any more orders. I need to rethink this delivery process. As word spreads, it's going to be difficult for her to carry everything and make multiple trips." A crafty smile crossed her lips. "Say, you're good with ideas."

"Let me give it some thought." Jamie bit her lip. "Paige, do you think…?"

Paige glared across the table. "Think the date is good idea? Yes. Think Rhys likes you? A thousand times, yes. Good grief, Jamie. He asked you out, didn't he? Asked you to be his girlfriend even, which is so stinking cute, it's almost sickening. I wish some guy would look at me the way Rhys looks at you."

"Sam does."

Paige snorted. "Not that he's done anything about it."

Jamie smiled. "Maybe *you* should."

The bell over the door jingled as a brown-haired girl entered the restaurant, calling out a greeting to Paige. She dropped her collection bag into the locked drobox under the counter, then grabbed a bottle of water out of the case.

"Hi. You must be Megan. I'm Jamie Danvers, Paige's roommate," Jamie said as the girl dropped into the seat beside her. "I also work for Dana Canfield. Your dad may have mentioned her."

"He has. We're having dinner at her house tonight," Megan said. She pushed a dollar bill across the table to Paige. "For the water. Sorry I took so long. I was down the street helping out at the dog cart."

Paige tucked the bill into her pocket. "What dog cart?"

"The hot dog cart." Megan took a long drink from the bottle, then recapped it. "Man, is it ever hot out there."

"You're on the clock for me, and you're helping—" Paige jumped to her feet. "Where is he?"

"Gone by now. Anyway, I was still working for you. So, here's how it went down."

Paige dropped back into the chair. "This better be good," she muttered.

"It's the best. I see the cart. The guy is cute, so I decide to stop. We chat while people buy their lunches. He fixes the hot dogs, and I pack them into bags… along with a flyer for Carson's. By the way, I gave out all of them."

"He didn't catch on?" Jamie fought back a smile. No need to

tick off Paige any more than she already was.

Megan shrugged. "If so, he didn't stop me. When anyone asked for a certain type of drink he didn't have, I suggested they check out Carson's and mentioned that we deliver."

Paige looked slightly mollified. "I'll let it go this time, but this guy—"

"Cole." Megan wiggled her eyebrows. "Wavy brown hair. Great arms. Cute butt."

"Never heard of him." Paige looked at Jamie. "Do you know him?"

"No, but I haven't been here that long either."

"I didn't see him yesterday, but Dad and I didn't get to town until midafternoon. I figured it was a usual thing when I saw him today. You know, summer food? Turns out he's a psychology major working on some theory about why people make certain food choices. I didn't listen to all of it."

"Do you plan to stay the entire summer with your dad?" Jamie asked.

"Probably longer. I'm taking a break before starting college."

"Will you be going back to Denver for college?"

"No way. As long as the DNA-donors live there, I'll stay on this side of the country."

Jamie frowned. "DNA?"

"Sperm and egg donors."

Paige coughed, then slammed a napkin to her mouth to catch spewing liquid. She recapped her bottle and set it to one side. "Didn't expect that."

"The... donors..." Jamie said. "That's your biological parents?"

"Callie is. I have my doubts about Gary. She says he is, but I think it's wishful thinking on her part. As far as I'm concerned, Nick Warden is my dad and has been as long as I can remember. Even after Callie remarried, twice after she and Dad divorced. During which time, Gary popped in and out whenever the whim hit him."

"Wow." The soft whisper slipped out of Paige's mouth.

Megan nodded. "Not to mention the guys she dated in between her marriages. One time was a faker named Liam who couldn't keep his accent straight between Irish and Australian. I stayed with Dad while they took a two-week trip to the Bahamas. Six more weeks passed before she remembered to tell

Dad they were back in town."

Jamie gasped. "She *forgot* you?"

"Forgot. Buzzed. Didn't care. My birthday happened during that time. Dad took me to a dude ranch. We camped, rode horses, hiked, fished. Best present was two months with Dad without Psycho-Mom. Plus she totally forgot my birthday, and I escaped the humiliation of a 'pretty princess' theme party."

They sat in stunned silence, Jamie finally responding. "I'm glad you're living with Nick now. He's a great guy."

"He's the best." Megan pushed back her chair and stood. "If there's nothing else, boss, I need to head home and clean up."

"Sure. Go on. I'll see you tomorrow."

Once the door closed behind Megan, Paige shook her head. "Wow. I thought Rhys's dad was a poor example of a parent. He doesn't sound so bad compared to Megan's mother. Can you imagine having a mom like that?"

Jamie turned in her chair. She stared out the front window, her eyes landing on Megan waiting to cross the street.

She could imagine that situation with no problem at all.

Chapter Eleven

Mentally, Nick had already replaced the sign above the building with one that read *Warden's Auto and Body Shop*. Between Glenn Thornton's yen to retire and April Davis's eye on a sale, he couldn't come up with a single question they couldn't answer.

April's suggestion for the limited customer parking was one he hadn't expected. Next door to the body shop was a large lot where a silver bullet diner and drive-in, originally owned by Thomas Carson, once operated. After he'd passed away, Paige had continued to run the restaurant until opening her own business downtown.

Nick walked the length of the vacant lot, mulling over his options. He could continue what he was doing. Getting along. Paying off his current loan. Putting a little money aside as he could. While he was playing it safe, someone else could buy Thornton's business and do exactly what he was considering. Combo body and engine repair shop. If that happened, he could be left scrambling for customers.

Running a garage with time off for fishing. That had been the plan when he'd come to PI. It had taken only one look at a curly-haired brunette to change his life completely. Mysteries, guns, and murder. A daughter, a stepson-to-be, and an almost fiancée whose best friend—he glanced across the lot to where April stood—was dating said fiancée's ex-husband.

Thankfully Dana had sent a text stating *April's dating Erik. More later.* Which explained the curious look Ms. Davis had given him when he'd arrived. As for buying the old Carson location, it was anybody's guess how Paige would react to his offer. Didn't take much for either of them to spark the other's temper.

He reached the end of the lot, taking one more look around. *I'm going to do it!* It felt right. Right enough to push aside the queasy discomfort of the additional debt. He quickly covered the distance back to the shop where April Davis waited.

"Find out how much for Carson's. I know how much Thornton wants for the building and equipment. I'll figure up a counteroffer. I want inspections on both too."

"I can do that. Give me a day or two to pull the information together."

His decision wiped out any lingering sense of discomfort. He escorted April to her car, a sleek white Mercedes, then walked back to his own vehicle.

Megan looked up from her phone as he slid behind the wheel. "Does this mean we're going to live in a silver tin can?"

Nick chuckled. "That's an idea. However, I was thinking that could be the office. If it's in good condition, I'd like to keep it."

"If it helps you make a decision, I counted cars along this road. Lots of traffic could mean lots of customers. Convenient location, easy access."

"You were listening?"

She twirled the cord of her earbuds around one finger. "Camouflage."

"I'll keep that in mind." Nick settled back in the seat. By this time of day, the flow of traffic was headed south, leaving the direction back to town open.

Megan toyed with the hem of her sweater. "Dad, how young is Mrs. Canfield?"

Interesting question. Not 'how old' but 'how young.' "She's my age."

"My age in man-speak?"

"I have no idea what that means."

"When Kaylee's parents got divorced, her dad told her mom that his girlfriend was his age, thereabouts."

"Thereabouts means…?"

"Somewhere between his age and Kaylee's." Megan shot a quick glance into the side mirror as they pulled out of Thornton's.

"Mrs. Davis looks like a trophy wife. You know tall, blonde, thin, classy."

As he waited out the pause, it occurred to him that April and Callie shared a number of physical similarities. Classy being the exception.

"What does Mrs. Canfield look like?"

"She's mid-height." Just tall enough to tuck her head under his chin. "Slender, nice figure." With a world-class... everything. "Brown eyes." So deep and dark, he could get lost in their depths.

A quick glance at Megan's face confirmed none of those wayward thoughts had passed his lips.

"I bet she thinks you're hot."

"Hope so."

Megan giggled. "All the girls at school agree I have the best-looking dad."

"Me or Gary?"

"You, of course! I told them Gary was my stepfather."

"And they believe it?"

"Sure. I look nothing like either of those two. My middle name is Nikole. Why wouldn't they believe you're my bio-dad? Besides, I have this theory."

Nick paused at the intersection of Colonial and Magnolia. After a glance in either direction, he turned right onto Magnolia. "Go ahead."

"I think you and Callie had a drunken one-night stand. She wanted to get pregnant to force Gary to marry her. When he did one of his see-you-later exits, she manipulated a meeting to get back with you."

"Why didn't I recognize her?"

"Because of the drunken ONS."

His laugh came out in a derisive snort. "Have you ever known me to get blackout drunk?"

"Maybe she drugged you. I don't know. It's a theory in progress."

Nick let her chew on that theory the rest of the drive. Megan needed time to adjust. Just as he'd had to do when making all the changes in his life. He could tell her a thousand times that hearts trumped blood, but believing was something she had to do on her own.

He eased the truck into the driveway in front of Dana's

house and shifted to face Megan. If it took a thousand and one times, he'd say it again.

"You're my daughter in every way that counts. No DNA will ever change that." He tapped his chest. "It's from the heart, and you captured mine from the moment I set eyes on you. Got it?"

"Got it." Her smile told him she accepted that answer, but a painful longing lingered in her eyes.

"Believe it. Now, let's go. I'm starving."

Which will it be? Insta-mom? Besties? Possessive girlfriend?

Megan didn't know what to expect. She held her breath as the door opened, expelling it as Dana Canfield appeared.

She wasn't a femme fatale, but she wasn't a trophy wife either. Dad's description hit the high points, but it fell short of the woman herself. Her hair was a cloud of dark curls. No gray that Megan could see, but the color might not be natural. High cheekbones, full lips, at least one dimple on display. No obvious work done on her face.

She cast a quick glance at Dana's outfit. Cute cropped pants in hot pink and a white cotton sweater flattered the "nice figure" Dad mentioned.

She looks like a mom. Not quite a stay-at-home mom, but not a soccer mom either. Or one with the misguided notion that forty-five was the new twenty-five. She looked nice and normal.

Maybe.

"Hi," Dana said, stepping back to allow them inside. "Come in!"

Prompted by the gentle touch of Dad's hand on her back, Megan stepped over the threshold. He followed, pushing the door closed behind him.

"Hey, sweetheart."

"Hey, you."

Megan watched as they exchanged a brief kiss. At least it wasn't a tango of tongues such as she'd had the misfortune of witnessing on a regular basis between the DNA-donors. Still, the night was young. When Mrs. Canfield turned to her, she steeled herself.

"I'm happy to meet you, Megan."

She's nervous. A reaction Megan hadn't expected.

"I'm glad to meet you too, Mrs. Canfield."

"Please call me Dana."

"Oh, and thank you for the sweater and tank." She plucked at the hem of the cardigan. "I should have thanked you sooner, but…"

"I understand. You've been busy." Dana looked around. "Dinner's almost ready. Why don't we head to the kitchen?"

A glance to the left revealed a stuffy dining room. To the right, a living room that didn't look like it was straight off a showroom floor. Color here and there. Comfy sofa. Nothing as cool as Dad's black leather one though.

The kitchen was primo. Built-in appliances, double oven, huge island, porcelain tile floor. If she gave a hoot about cooking, a kitchen like Dana's would be the kind to have.

"Megan, I hope you like salmon." Dana shot a glare at Nick. "We were going to have steak…"

Nick held up both hands, palms outward. "Sorry. Crazy day. At least I called to let you know we wouldn't have time to grill."

"Which meant lucky me got to do the shopping."

Megan frowned. Dana seemed to be angry, but there was no heat in her tone. Both of them seemed attuned to one another. A look. A touch. A smile. Seeing Dad so happy made her happy, but it also brought a pain to her chest.

"Scout?"

She looked up, seeing a questioning look on Dad's face.

"Sorry. Yes, that sounds great. Dana, is there somewhere I can wash up?"

"Right down the hallway on the right. Feel free to look around."

Well, heck. Permission took all the fun out of snooping. Still, she took advantage of the offer to peek into rooms and check closets. She circled to the living room, which provided a clear view of where Dad and Dana stood at the island.

They worked together in an easy harmony. Dana chopped and assembled salads. Dad swiped an olive, and when Dana caught him, he slipped one into her mouth. At one point, they turned from opposite directions, nearly running into one another. They laughed and sidestepped around each other, Dana continuing to carry plates to the table. Dad halted, turned to watch. Not with a leer as Gary would have done, but with a joy she hadn't seen in him before.

Dad loves Dana.

The realization hit her like a punch to the gut. How selfish could she be? Thinking that Dad had been living in a bubble since she'd left. Or that he'd put his life on hold because she was…

Home.

Words from her first day on PI echoed back to her. *I want a home.* That's what Dad wanted too. What they both needed. The rattle of dishes, the opening and closing of the refrigerator, the mingled laughter and gentle teasing. Sounds that meant nothing by themselves, but together, they signified a home.

You're right, Dad. As usual.

She returned to the kitchen. "Sorry to take so long. I took you up on your offer to look around. I didn't go upstairs."

"That would have been fine if you had."

"What can I do to help?"

Dad set out pitchers of water and lemonade, Megan finished setting the table, and Dana plated the food. With three sets of hands, dinner was ready within minutes.

Megan responded when conversation was directed to her, but otherwise she preferred to monitor the discussion. Understanding the dynamics between Dad and Dana couldn't be left to chance. She half listened as Dad related their trip to look at the property he was thinking of purchasing.

"Do you need the extra lot?" Dana asked.

"Thornton's parking lot isn't that big. The additional lot would allow space for drop-offs the evening prior to an appointment if needed. I'm thinking about moving the office into the old restaurant."

"Is there a problem with the existing office?"

"The breakroom and restrooms need to be updated and enlarged. It'll also be cleaner and quieter for the office staff to move to the other building. I'm going to ask Rhys for an estimate on what the changes will cost."

The corners of Dana's lips tugged at a smile. "Are you now?"

"Uh-huh. Which I'll add to the asking price for my lot."

Megan's head shot up. "Wicked move, Dad."

"I thought so." He looked across the table. "Dana?"

She brushed her hands. "I'll leave that discussion up to the two of you. I don't envy you moving the couch out of the apartment."

"Good point. I might add Rhys helping me move that beast to my list."

Megan shot a glance in Dad's direction. Surely he wasn't clueless enough to discuss looking for a house? He was smarter than the average guy, but he was a guy. Geez, they were crazy for each other. So far, she hadn't found a thing she didn't like about Dana, and she trusted her instincts. She couldn't have survived all those years with Callie if it hadn't been for a BS detector that had grown more refined over the years. The last time she'd ignored those instincts, she'd ended up in Denver. A mistake she didn't intend to make again.

No way was Dad putting his life with Dana on hold because of her. Someone had to put these two on track, and it was up to her.

"Dana, the pesto on the salmon is delicious. Can you teach me how to make it?"

A pleased glow lit Dana's features. "I'd love to."

"Great. I love this house, and it's going to be so much fun with all three of us cooking dinner. Or we can alternate. That would be fun too. After all, it's silly for us to look for a place to live when we'll be moving in here soon. You have set a date, haven't you?"

The "dad glare" winged in her direction, turning the giggle bubbling in her throat to a gulp.

Dad shook his head. "Way to step on my agenda, Scout."

Megan's eyes widened at her blunder. She tapped her napkin to her lips and pushed back her chair. "In that case, I'll excuse myself so the two of you can discuss that in private."

Silence followed her out of the room.

"My daughter's a brat." Nick pushed the door to the dishwasher closed and flipped the latch.

"She's adorable." Dana dropped the dishtowel onto the island and whirled around. "Oh, Nick. I love her already. She's full of life and sass and totally adores you."

After the disastrous meeting with Toddy followed by April's

revelation, tonight's dinner—especially the exchange between Megan and Nick about the future—lifted her spirits more than she'd hoped. A sudden panic filled her. "What if Megan was teasing about living here? What if she—"

"Don't borrow trouble. Megan says what she thinks. Sometimes she's blunt and uncensored, but honest."

"Like her dad?"

A half-shrug admitted the resemblance as he trailed a fingertip along her arm. "From the moment you and I met, it's been zero to sixty."

Dana smiled. The description perfectly matched their whirlwind courtship. "I wouldn't have it any other way."

His gaze shifted to something serious, and Dana caught her breath. Was he going to ask her? Here and now?

The chug of the dishwasher and the lingering hint of seafood took the place of sweet violins and roses. Pendant lights suspended over the kitchen island fell short of the ambiance that candlelight would have provided. But the situation couldn't have been more romantic. Couldn't have been more real.

Nick caught her hand and held it to his chest. The beat of his heart and the warmth of his body forged a commitment of its own. His tobacco-brown gaze held her captive.

"Marry me?"

Blunt and unvarnished. No artifice or pretense. After all the lies and hidden truths that had plagued her past, she savored the simple words, straight from his heart. His name passed her lips in a gentle sigh as she cupped his face. That strong, handsome, honest face.

"You give good proposal, Mr. Warden." She lifted on tiptoe and pressed a kiss to his mouth. "And that's a definite yes."

The seductive murmur drew a chuckle from Nick, a wicked gleam in his gaze. "I aim to please, Ms. Canfield."

"In that case…" Deep breath. *Go for it, Dana.* "Move in with me? You and Megan?"

One corner of his mouth lifted. "No place else I'd rather be."

He said yes! The only question left to ask was…

"When?"

He shifted into a hip-shot stance, reminding her of the first time she'd seen him. Standing outside his garage, leaning against the building, coffee cup in one hand. The other hand had gone to his chest, playing out a heartbeat. At the time, she'd thought the gesture was aimed at her BMW convertible. But it hadn't been.

His heart had been beating for her even before they'd met.

"How about late summer, early fall? With your projects and relocating the garage, the next couple months are going to be busy."

"That could work for the wedding." She paced from the island to the stove and back. "For the move, why wait? Pack the essentials, you could move in tomorrow. Then—"

"Whoa, honey. We have some planning to do there too."

Her spirits dropped and immediately she scolded herself. Talk about being a brat. She was the one who wanted everything. Now. And that wasn't fair to Nick.

"You're right. You'd have to drive across town to work. Megan wouldn't be able to walk to Carson's. There's no need—"

He stopped her midstep, wrapping an arm around her waist. "There's every need. But we need to tell Megan and Rhys first." He tapped the tip of her nose. "Knowing you, you'll need a project plan outlining everything to be done and in what order."

"Excuse me for being organized."

"Keeps things neat, but I do love it when you show that impetuous side."

Dana bumped her fist against his chest. "I'll show you the depths of my impetuosity once you move in."

"Looking forward to it. In the meantime. I have a surprise for Megan in my truck. Graduation gift. I'd like to give it to her now, if you don't mind."

"Of course I don't."

He kissed her. Hard, deep, and with a passion that left no doubt of his devotion. "I love you."

"I love you too." The power of his kiss had ignited a wild pounding in her heart while her mind clicked off a to-do list. Nick could tease all he wanted about her attention to details. But the sooner those details were put into order, the sooner the two of them could start sharing that big bed of hers upstairs.

Sooner was much better than later.

Regaining her composure, Dana walked to the living room, wondering about the upcoming surprise. Nick had once mentioned that he wanted Megan to have memories rather than possessions.

Still, graduation was a major milestone in his daughter's life.

Megan sat curled up on one end of the sofa, thumbs flying across the screen of her phone. She looked up, and to Dana's surprise, set the phone aside. "Hey, where's Dad?"

"He went to get something from his truck." She gestured toward the phone. "Am I interrupting?"

"No, I was texting with my friend Jillian. I didn't get to say goodbye to any of my friends except Amber before I left." She glanced toward the front window, then back to Dana. "Is this weird for you?"

"Oh, Megan. My entire life for the past month has been nothing but weird. But this—you, me, Nick—it feels right. I know it's too early for you to think that way."

Megan shrugged. "Not really. That's what's weird. I came here wanting to spend time with Dad before going off to college. I wasn't expecting him to have someone new in his life. Dad deserves to be happy, and I can see you make him happy." Her head dipped as she drew a deep breath. "I'm sorry for what I said at dinner. I didn't mean to embarrass you or put Dad on the spot."

"I'll give you a pass. And let's call it assertively honest."

Megan snickered. "I'll try that on Dad." Her smile faded, and a tremor entered her voice. "It wasn't only about Dad. It was about me too. It would be cool to have parents who love each other. To live in a home with dinners around the table and to celebrate holidays when they actually occur. To know how a real family can be."

Her mother's heart winged out to the lost child who lived within this teenage girl. "I don't presume I can take the place of your mother—"

"Callie didn't set the bar that high."

"I'd love to be your mom, and I'm thrilled that you want to give me that chance. One thing you never have to doubt is how much I love your father."

The click of the front door, followed by heavy footsteps across the foyer sent both of their heads turning. Large gift bag in hand, Nick walked to the sofa. He waved one hand at Megan.

"Scoot to the center."

"Is that for me? Dad, you already gave me a birthday present. I even have money left over from your check."

Nick took the vacated seat and set the bag on the floor in front of Megan. "That was your birthday present. This is for graduation."

She grinned. "Sweet." She pulled a layer of tissue paper from the bag. Her face wrinkled into a frown as she lifted a garish red cloth onto her lap. Further rummaging revealed a mortarboard cap. "It's my cap and gown. I brought it with me so you could see it."

Nick stretched out his legs, hands resting on his stomach. "That's what I figured when I found it on the floor next to the couch."

"Oh... sorry." She plopped the cap on her head.

The wink Nick shot over to Dana warned her the surprise was still to come.

"I talked to Sean McLain, the principal at PI High School. He's agreed to let you participate in the graduation ceremonies."

Megan's jaw dropped, and a blush raced across her pale skin. Shoulders shaking, she buried her face in the folds of the gown. The cap tumbled to the floor.

Nick rested one hand on his daughter's back. "You okay, Scout?"

Megan lifted her tearstained face and leaned against him. "It's what I wanted. For you to be at my graduation and see me walk the stage."

"Principal McLain gave me two tickets."

"Oh, my gosh, Dad, when is it?"

"Saturday, eleven o'clock. You'll need to be there by ten."

Megan wiped at her tears and bolted up, whirling toward Dana. "Can you come too?"

Dana blinked back her own tears. "I wouldn't miss it."

Megan beamed. "This is the best gift ever. This is the best day ever!" She hopped to her feet. "I have to call my friends."

To Dana's surprise, she received a hug from Megan. One with the same fervor as the one Megan delivered to Nick.

Grabbing her phone, Megan headed outside. "I'll be on the patio. Let me know when you're ready to leave, Dad." She paused at the exit, hand resting on the handle of the French door. "Dana, I think I want a room overlooking the garden, but I'm not sure since I haven't seen it yet. Can we talk about that? Also, would you go shopping with me for things for my room? I mean... whenever you two decide what you're doing."

"We'll talk about it."

Megan shot them a thumbs-up, then dashed outside.

Nick patted the cushion and shot a grin at Dana. She scooted next to him and settled into the crook of his shoulder. He wrapped one arm around her and his chin nudged the top of her head. "Congratulations. It's a girl."

"I'm looking forward to having a daughter."

He lifted her hand, rubbing a thumb over the indentation where she'd once worn her wedding band. "You're not going to argue about getting a ring, are you? 'Cause I already have it planned."

"Good heavens, no! I want a ring." Her head rocked with the silent laughter rumbling through his chest. "It doesn't have to be an extravagant one."

"You will love it and think of me every time you look at your hand."

Dana tilted her head, smiling up at him. "My hot, sexy guy is getting me a hot, sexy ring."

"For my hot, sexy woman." A knuckle under her chin lifted her lips to his.

A faint breeze swept across the room. Dana glanced over Nick's shoulder to see Megan standing in the entrance to the patio, holding her phone a few inches from her ear.

"Sorry to interrupt, but am I having a graduation party?"

"We were discussing that very thing," Nick said.

Megan rolled her eyes. "Dana?"

"Divide and conquer," Nick murmured in Dana's ear. "Starting already."

She elbowed him. "Nick and I'll discuss it."

"Perfect." Megan turned her attention back to her phone. "I'm back. Of course, they're having a party for me. I—" The door closed, cutting off the remainder of her conversation.

"Spoiled…." Nick shook his head in mock sorrow.

"Pooh. She's spoiled only enough to know she's loved. Now, about this party—"

"Leave the details up to me. It's under control."

"You have a plan? This fast?"

"You bet. Who planned that dinner party on your patio?"

Dana took her turn at rolling her eyes at Nick. "Paige and Jamie."

"Exactly." Nick stretched out his legs and yawned. "Megan won't expect much on short notice. She just wants to brag to her friends back in Denver that she had a party too."

"So, Mr. Warden, are you going to be this involved in planning our wedding?"

Humor faded from his face. "Much as I'm not in favor of a long engagement, there may be a hitch in our plans. We need to find out if you're still legally married to Erik McCall."

A fire having nothing to do with the hot, sexy man she was going to marry ignited inside her. Over twenty-five years later, and Erik McCall was still screwing up her life.

Chapter Twelve

Rhys rummaged through his briefcase, looking for the USB drive containing his notes on Towne Square. Working out of three locations—Mom's house, the Canfield building, and McCall HQ—wasn't going to work full-time. Four, if he counted his house.

Granted, Mom's house was short term until the cleaners cleared her office building. Which was due for completion today. He'd have to check with Jamie on that. Best solution would be to consolidate everything at McCall. Dana and Jamie could meet with him here. His preference though was for the Canfield building. Somehow Dana had known exactly the environment he'd needed when she'd decorated his office there. She'd captured the spirit of PI with straw-yellow walls and random accents of Carolina blue and winter white.

Why not both?

That could work. Mornings at one location. Afternoons at the other. In the meantime, he couldn't spend any longer looking for the flash drive. He had a good memory and could knock out a new set of notes in the morning.

No late night tonight. He had a date with Jamie, and this time she'd asked him out. First time for everything. Leave it to Jamie and her clever mind to surprise him.

"Lose something?" Stacy Andrews strolled into the room.

Then again, Stacy didn't stroll. She strutted, sashayed, swayed.

A knock-out body, red hair, blue eyes, and a Cupid's bow mouth. She had a keen wit, a sharp mind, and didn't hesitate to let Rhys know she was interested. Sometimes he wondered if her flirting was more of a game. Something to tweak his attention, probe for mutual interest, or irritate him out of boredom.

She slid onto the top of his desk and crossed her legs to reveal an expanse of shapely thigh.

"Get off my desk."

"I have something for you." She held up his missing USB drive. "You left it on my desk so I could copy your notes to the network files." Her scarlet nails tickled his palm as she dropped the device into his hand. "That reminds me. I need to reactivate your network permissions."

"Thank you." He dropped the USB into his briefcase. "Now get off my desk."

The hemline scooted closer to the finish line as she slid off the desk. With a wiggle and a tug, she pulled the skirt into place. "Have I told you how happy I am you're back?"

"Several times." He stood up, case in hand.

"I'm serious. You don't realize how good it is to have someone else here who knows what they're doing."

The switch from flirt to professional never failed to amaze him. Stacy was smart and no doubt knew more about certain facets of the business than he or Dad did.

Rhys circled around her and walked to the door. She fell into step with him. "Set up a meeting for us for early tomorrow afternoon," he said. "I want to go over all the active and pending projects."

"To celebrate your homecoming, how about we go out for drinks? We can talk over all those pesky details and get them out of the way."

"Tomorrow is fine, and I have plans for tonight. You have a good evening."

He walked to the stairwell as Stacy grumbled a "you too" at his back. Minutes later, he was in his car, heading home to get ready for his date. Jeans and a T-shirt, Jamie had ordered. Casual. Strictly casual.

When their first date had gone sideways, Jamie was the one who'd saved the evening with her ever-creative thinking. As for that kiss? It couldn't have happened anywhere less romantic, but the touch of her lips had ignited all those feelings he'd been suppressing since they'd first met. Jamie's cool beauty, clever mind, and gentle heart had captured him in a way that hot-as-hell Stacy could never do.

What did Jamie have planned?

The question plagued him the entire drive to Paige's house. Whatever Jamie had in mind, she'd joined forces with Paige, and he wouldn't put anything past his best friend. Surely Jamie wouldn't go too far with any shenanigans. Then again, Paige could be persuasive, evidenced by the text he'd received from her just before leaving work.

Go to my house. Use your key. Wait inside. Stay out of the fridge. xoxo

"Anybody home?" No response. No answering sounds. "Paige? Jamie?"

His voice echoed through the house. He waited, listening. Nothing. The hairs prickled at the back of his neck.

Had something happened to Paige and Jamie while they were waiting for him? The motorcycle incident might have been a malicious prank, except it seemed targeted deliberately at him. He'd downplayed the incident when he'd told them about it. No reason other than his own suspicious mind to think it was more than that.

After a shooting at Dana's office, then an attack on Dad? Good thinking, McCall.

The back door. Had Paige left it unlocked again? He took a single step toward the kitchen when the doorbell rang. His heart jumped, and he slowly turned. A glance through the living room window revealed Paige's Jeep parked at the curb, and he let out a breath. When he opened the front door, Jamie was the one standing there.

A blush-pink gypsy blouse sat low on her shoulders, highlighting the dragonfly necklace he'd noticed before. A short denim skirt showcased her long, tanned legs. Legs that ended in a pair of beaded strap sandals and nails polished a shimmering gold. His gaze traveled upward to her blonde hair, loose and tousled, landing finally on sparking blue eyes and a kissable set of lips.

Casual might have been the dress code for the evening, but the pounding of his heart was anything but.

"Uh... sorry. Come in." He stood back, allowing her to pass, then closed the door. "I was going to say you look great, but I couldn't get the words out of my mouth."

Her lips parted, and a faint flush blossomed across her cheeks. "Thank you." She held out a small package. "This is for you."

The daisies printed on the wrapping paper were a call back to the flowers he'd given her. He glanced around, didn't see them. Did she keep them by her bedside? He traced a finger over the smooth surface before edging his thumb along the taped fold. He pulled the paper away to reveal a framed photograph from their first date. Not the more formal one where they'd faced the camera. The one where they'd stood a little closer, looking deep into one another's eyes.

A perfect reminder of a perfect moment.

"It's not much," Jamie said. "Just a token..."

His gaze jolted upward, realizing his silence had inadvertently led Jamie to doubt his appreciation. "It's perfect." He swallowed back a sudden rush of emotion. "I can't remember the last time I received a gift for no reason."

And certainly not one with such significance.

"I'm glad you like it." Her beautiful smile bloomed again. "Are you ready for the rest of our date?"

"Am I ever!"

She took his hand, and they stepped outside. After Rhys locked the door, they walked to the Jeep. When Jamie headed for the driver's door, he halted.

"Wait. What are—"

"I'm driving," she said, cutting off his protest. "Remember? I'm taking you out tonight."

He stared at her for one long moment. Date Night was throwing off his game in more ways than one. He didn't know the rules or what to expect.

Palm resting on the door handle, Jamie waited, silent and smiling until he turned and walked to the other side to take the passenger seat. Resting his arm on the open windowsill, he asked, "So what's on tap for our date?"

Jamie threw a teasing smile in his direction. "You know, the usual. Drive-through. Movie."

Drive-through? There were no chain restaurants on PI, and

none of the hometown businesses offered that kind of service. Whatever Jamie had planned had him stumped. Which was more than okay. The mystery obviously was part of her plan, and he intended to sit back and enjoy every minute. Watching a woman behind the wheel on a date gave him an entirely new perspective.

Jamie navigated through the back streets of downtown PI before turning into an alley. She braked to a stop behind one of the brick buildings. A building he knew well, due to all the time he'd spent renovating it.

A crackling sound rippled through the cab of the truck.

"Welcome to Carson's. Can I take your order?"

Jamie reached under the seat, pulling out a blue walkie-talkie. He grinned, knowing that its red counterpart was inside the building. He and Paige had run around the neighborhood as kids, testing the distance on those devices.

"Picking up an order for Danvers."

"Be right out."

Less than a minute later, the back door opened, and Paige glided on a pair of inline skates to Jamie's open window. A laugh deep from his gut broke loose.

"Order for Danvers. Two date-night specials."

Jamie settled the drinks into the cup holders, then passed a fragrant bag to Rhys. He breathed deeply, sighing at the delicious aroma of beef and onions.

"Have a good evening." Paige tipped a finger to her brow in salute, then skated toward the back entrance.

"I'm impressed. You pulled off the drive-through."

"Best I could do under PI conditions." She braked at the mouth of the alley, glanced over at him. "Fry, please."

He pulled a hot French fry from the bag, lifting it to her lips as she leaned her head in his direction.

"Whoa, hot."

He ripped the wrapper off a straw and inserted it through the lid of one of the drinks, then held it out to her. She took the cup and drew a deep drink into her mouth. He jammed the other straw into his cup and swallowed a long, cold gulp of his own.

He dug out another fry, popping this one into his mouth. "Are we going to have the fries polished off before we get to the movies?"

"Maybe." She cast him another flirtatious smile, and he fell a little bit deeper.

They were heading back south on the same road they'd just traveled. By habit, Rhys glanced to his right as they neared the site where the original Carson's restaurant once operated. To his surprise, two vehicles were parked on the lot. Nick Warden and April Davis stood facing the building. The woman's hands were gesturing as she spoke. Warden stood with both arms crossed over his chest.

"Whoops. I thought we'd park there and eat." Jamie accelerated past the old restaurant site. She sent an apologetic smile his way. "Let me think."

"I know somewhere we can go." A quiet place with plenty of privacy. Perfect if the evening progressed the way he hoped. "My house."

She gave him a look that sent his senses tingling. "Tell me which way."

The area became more rural as they traveled south. A two-lane road, trees lining one side, simple one-story cottages sprinkled along the way. Rhys's home was the last one along the lane before it widened into a sandy beach.

Jamie braked short of turning into the carport connected to Rhys's house. "You live on the beach?"

"Not as glamourous as it sounds."

The one-story shotgun house wasn't what she'd expected. Clapboard siding, tin roof, concrete pad with a metal awning for parking.

"What's your pleasure? Inside or on the beach?"

"Beach, please." She parked the Jeep and hopped out before Rhys could circle around to assist her. When they met at the back of the vehicle, he had the two drink cups in his hands.

"Let me take those." The cups were slick with condensation, and no doubt, the ice half-melted. *Yuck.* The food was probably cold as well. "Let's just go inside."

"No, ma'am. You promised me a beach picnic." He nodded toward a trash can sitting by the edge of the driveway. "Dump these, then pop the back of the Jeep. There should be a couple blankets. I'll grab some bottles of water and give the food a quick nuke."

Jamie chuckled as Rhys took the food bag and dashed into the house. The man just couldn't help himself. He was a fixer, a caretaker.

She had the blanket rolled under one arm when he returned, the strap of an insulated bag slung over one shoulder, the necks of two water bottles tucked between his fingers. A short walk later, they were settled on a yellow and pink blanket, their sandals and sneakers set to one side, and dinner spread out on paper plates.

The sun hung low in the sky, still blazing and brilliant as it diffused into a subtle wash of peach and pink across the horizon while they ate. Above, seagulls squawked out last calls before retreating for the evening, leaving only the rhythmic sounds and hypnotic sway of the tide.

"I'm surprised no one else is on the beach. I guess everyone goes to the one on the north side." Jamie popped another fry into her mouth, one of the few they hadn't consumed on the drive south.

"That's the public beach. This area is private. Most of the residents are older and don't come down here very often. The sheriff's department patrols a couple times a night." He pointed to the shoreline behind her. "I own the next three lots after my house."

Her eyes widened as she viewed the expanse. "How did you…?"

Rhys chuckled. "Afford it? One I picked up for unpaid taxes. Cost me less than four hundred dollars. The house on the farthest lot had been vacant for a number of years. It was in bad shape, and the heir sold it for the cost of the lot. I bought the first lot here just after I graduated high school, mortgaged it, and bought another. I kept watch on properties for sale while I was in college and working upstate."

"What do you plan to do?"

She waited for his answer as he chewed and swallowed.

"I haven't figured that out yet. I've received several lucrative offers, but I don't want to see South Pointe turned into a summer playground for society mainlanders."

"Paige said a number of homes had been purchased as

summer or weekend getaways."

"Unfortunately, Dana got thrown into that category when she first arrived. The fact that she intended to put down roots helped negate that."

"Plus working with you on Main Street. And dating Nick Warden."

"He's a good guy." Rhys shrugged. "I'm getting used to the idea of the two of them dating."

Should she mention Nick's trip to Main Street? He'd all but confessed the reason for his visit had been to go to Caine Jewelers. Nope, better to leave the news to unfold on its own.

"I owe you a big thank you," Rhys said as he uncapped the water bottle. He took a long drink, then replaced the lid.

Jamie looked up from clearing away the remainder of their meal. "For what?"

He set the bottle to one side, then stretched out on the blanket, hands cupped under his neck. "For not being a datezilla."

Stretching out beside him on her stomach, she propped herself on her elbows, feet in the air. "Which is?"

"Going crazy because every detail of the date didn't work as you planned."

"You fixed it."

"So did you when we ended up at the hospital to check on Dad. If it had been left up to me, we would have driven around PI for who knows how long, looking for a place to eat." He rolled onto one elbow, facing her. "I don't know a thing about your family. Do they live near here?"

Her stomach dropped. Family wasn't a subject she wanted to delve into too deeply. *Keep to the basics. That's all he needs to know.*

"Upstate. My dad passed away over ten years ago. I have two sisters, both brilliant. One's a scientist for a pharmaceutical company. The other is a forensic accountant. My mother teaches physics."

"What did your dad do?"

"He was a freelance writer. He did voice-over announcements for ad agencies. Acted in local theater. Loved to read." *He loved me unconditionally.*

"Sounds like an interesting guy."

"The best." She smiled. For the memory. For Rhys tucking a lock of hair behind her ear. Both men had that same innate gentleness.

"Do you see your mother often?"

"My mother and I... we're not close."

Rhys's eyes widened at her curt tone, and she rushed to change the subject. "I met Sally Van Kirk this week. She mentioned knowing you growing up."

He grinned. "Used to cut her grass."

"With Harold's supervision." Rhys rolled his eyes, and she laughed. Sitting up, she stretched her legs, flexing her toes. "She told me about the red truck you bought."

"Lot of lawn work, bussing tables at Carson's, and construction work at McCall's went into buying that truck."

"That's where I got the idea for this date. I wanted to re-create a high-school date. Something simple and fun. I brought a DVD player to put on the dash in the Jeep so we could watch a movie while we ate."

"I'm fine without the movie. Besides, I prefer the view here." He sat up. "I have a suggestion. Where does your mother live? If it's not too far, we can take a weekend to go visit. I'd like to meet her."

A wave of dizziness washed over Jamie. Her arms fell limp in her lap, and she choked back the food threatening to rise from her stomach. She jumped to her feet.

"No! Absolutely not!"

He leaped up from the blanket. "I'm just saying—"

"Don't you understand? Aren't you *listening*? This isn't something for you to fix, and I don't need you to fix *me*."

She spun on one heel, fleeing down the sandy beach.

"Jamie!"

Go ahead. Run away.

She ground to a halt, fighting away the hateful echo. "What am I doing?"

Ruining things like you always do.

It was only ruined if she ran away. Just like with Bart Caine, she had to trust, to believe that all was not lost. Which meant no more running away. Not now. Not anymore.

Jamie turned. She had to face her actions and ask for more than forgiveness. She needed to ask for understanding.

Rhys slowed to a walk several feet away. As he closed the distance, she saw the anger banked beneath the grim set of his jaw and the fire in his dark green eyes. With each step he took, the tightness eased in his face, the softness returned to his gaze.

She met him halfway and took his hands in hers. "I'm sorry."

"I didn't mean to upset you. You said I didn't listen, but I didn't hear anything to warrant—"

"My over-the-top reaction?"

"A simple 'no, thank you' would have sufficed." A slight note of humor filtered into his voice.

She dropped his hands, shoved hers into her hair. "I'm not going to let her ruin.... No, *I'm* not going to ruin this."

"'Her' being your mother?"

She ducked her head, nodding.

"Hey, when it comes to parent issues, I'm standing right there in line with you." He took her hand and started walking back toward their picnic area.

Jamie scoffed at the unspoken challenge. Finding an example wasn't hard. "My dad and I had a special bond. He was the one who took me to ballet class and recitals. He encouraged me to try out for the school paper and school plays. I could talk to him about anything. My mother was furious that he encouraged what she considered 'worthless pursuits.' Though to her way of thinking, I might as well pursue those interests because I didn't have the brains for work that had any value."

She caught the side glance Rhys sent her way though he remained silent.

"She didn't want a third child. She had the two daughters she wanted, but if there had to be another one, it needed to be a boy. Instead, she got another girl. Not an intellectual, petite, dark-haired little girl like my sisters, but a gangly blonde with her head in the clouds. My dad loved all of us, but my mother couldn't stand that Dad and I shared a special connection. One day..."

She stopped, paralyzed by the power the memory still evoked. Strong arms surrounded her, pushing away the bubble of time past.

"You don't have do this."

The soft whisper lured her into safety. She wanted to stay there even if the illusion was temporary.

"Yes, I do." She pulled free so she could see his face. "When I was fourteen, I overheard my mother ask Dad why he seemed to favor me. He said how much I reminded him of his younger sister who died when she was fifteen. My mother's reply was…" She took a deep breath, steadying herself. "…'I should be that lucky.'"

Rhys's expression went stock-still. A soft breath hissed between his teeth. "Damn her to hell and back."

If he'd dropped the f-bomb, she couldn't have been more shocked.

"Jamie, if I'd known—"

"But you didn't." Jamie buried her face in both hands. "This is so embarrassing. I'm an adult, and I'm still letting things my mother said influence my life. When you mentioned going to visit, all I could think was how she'd denigrate my job and insist that I only got the position by dating the boss's son."

He wrapped his hands around her wrists, gently lowering her hands. "Look at all you've accomplished in just a few weeks. Promotions for Paige's restaurant, marketing plans for Main Street, winning over Bart Caine when Dana couldn't. You even faced down Sam with nothing more than a blueberry muffin."

An unexpected giggle bubbled in her throat. Logic and humor. With those two weapons, Rhys vanquished her demons for the moment. He saw a truth she couldn't view through her own eyes. All those things he'd mentioned had been driven by her natural instincts.

She rubbed the dragonfly between her fingers, drawing strength from the tiny charm.

"Does that have a special meaning?" Rhys asked, nodding toward the necklace. "I noticed you wear it a lot."

"It's my spirit totem. Like the hummingbird seems to be for Dana. Silly, huh?"

"Not at all. Dana bought that hummingbird statue for good luck, and it saved her life."

They stopped at the edge of the blanket.

"This necklace was the last Christmas gift I received from my father before he died." She took a deep breath, thinking back, then told Rhys what her father had said.

"It's more than a piece of jewelry, sweetheart. I picked the dragonfly especially for you."

"What does it mean?" She held the chain in front of her. The dragonfly danced as sparkling rubies—her birthstone—glistened down its back.

"It represents joy—and you are my joy. But it also represents transformation."

"What does that mean?"

"Change. Not letting yourself be held captive to someone else's vision. Allowing yourself to grow and be the person you are meant to be." He touched a fingertip to the charm, sending it dancing again. *"Believe in yourself."*

Believe.

She'd never forgotten those words. Throughout the years, she'd replayed them again and again in her mind, but in her heart, she'd never truly trusted them. She'd allowed the critical words of others to overrule her father's wisdom and lost herself in self-doubt.

Never again.

Dana. Nick. Paige. Rhys. All of them believed in her, and she couldn't doubt the overwhelming trust they'd given her. Most important of all, she had to believe in herself because Rhys needed her.

"Thank you for sharing that story." He stroked a thumb across her cheek. "I wish I could have met your dad."

"He would have liked you." She wiped the remaining dampness from her face. "I needed to get that out. I'm sorry I had to ruin our date doing that."

"Well, it was your turn." He opened his arms to her.

"Oh, Rhys!" This time, tears mixed with laughter, and she fell into his embrace.

He cupped her neck. She lifted her face. They tumbled onto the rumpled blanket.

From the instant their lips touched, the connection that had sparked when they'd first met erupted into an inferno. If their first kiss had held a sweet promise, this one burned with fiery intent.

His mouth traced across her cheek, to her jaw, down the gentle curve from shoulder to neck. Roughened fingertips glided over the length of her arm. Her body tightened. Her senses burned. The soft cotton of his shirt was cool against her fingers. She slipped her hands under the fabric, sliding them up the hard planes of sinew and muscle.

A low growl followed, and Rhys pulled away long enough to jerk the garment over his head, tossing it aside. She rolled onto her back, and he followed. The coarse denim of his jeans razed along her bare legs as she hooked one ankle around his calf. Tenderness and desire came together, blessing each kiss and every touch. The smell of the ocean dissipated as the scent of his shampoo and soap and her own perfume surrounded them.

She raked her nails across his shoulders and down his neck. His body moved in tandem with hers. A drop of water struck her face, drizzling down her cheek. A tear? Sweat? A second drop, then a third, struck her hands and legs.

Rhys pushed onto his elbows, laughter highlighting his handsome face. His green eyes widened with boyish delight. "Rain!"

The pitter-patter turned into a shower. He rolled up on his knees, arms outstretched, face uplifted to the raindrops glittering in the waning daylight. "I love this!"

His body shimmered with moisture. He was all masculine perfection, but it was the unfettered joy on his face that enraptured her the most. She'd never seen him so uninhibited and free and wished she could capture that moment.

A light breeze brushed over her. The temperature cooled, and she shivered in her dampened clothing.

Rhys lowered his arms, resting his hands on both thighs and watching her for a silent moment. He shifted onto one knee and held out his hand. "Come home with me."

Home. Not "my place" or "stay the night." He wouldn't have used that word so carelessly. Any lingering doubts she had were swept away. She wanted a lifetime with this man, and perhaps this night would be the beginning of finding her way to that home she'd always craved. To the one he deserved as well.

Jamie clasped his hand and rose to stand beside him. His lips curved into a smile, tenderness mixed with a wicked boldness, a touch of feral passion in his dark green eyes.

She felt a little wicked as well. She cupped his face, kissed his mouth. "Take me home."

Chapter Thirteen

The sound of rain on the tin roof fell into second place as Rhys's favorite way to fall asleep. Holding Jamie in his arms as they drifted into a well-earned rest seized the first-place prize. Lingering in that half-stage between asleep and awake, he cast out an arm in search of the woman who'd given him a night he'd never forget.

And would love to repeat.

The space beside him was empty. The sheets were cold. A glance at the clock showed it was almost seven a.m. The faint echo of running water told him Jamie was in the shower.

Not the way he'd planned to start the morning. He rolled to his feet and padded down the hallway. The door was locked, which was no surprise.

He had three choices. He could pop the lock, enter, and suggest water conservation. He could be a gentleman and use the shower in the mudroom. Or he could wait for her in bed and seduce her into playing hooky from work for a half-day.

He decided on option two. Sometimes it wasn't so much a matter of picking your battles as it was picking the right battlefield.

When he returned to the bedroom, he found Jamie, wrapped in a towel, talking on her cell phone. Her hair hung in damp curls around her shoulders. He leaned against the door frame, arms crossed over his chest, and enjoyed the view.

"All my notes from the merchants are in the folder with my

name. I need to transfer them into the project plan, but I haven't had time yet."

She looked up, running a heated gaze from his head to his toes, a slow contemplation that sent his blood racing. Her smile taunted him, letting him know she knew exactly the effect she was having on him.

"That sounds perfect, and I'm holding you to that promise. We'll see you then." Jamie set the phone on the top of the dresser, then turned to him. "Good morning."

Rhys closed the distance between them in two quick steps. He locked an arm around her, slammed his mouth against hers. Rougher than he'd planned, but Jamie didn't seem to mind. She pressed herself against him and returned the kiss with equal passion.

"This is the way I wanted to start our morning." He tucked a wild lock of hair behind her ear. "Ease our way into the day."

"That sounds wonderful. That's why I called Dana to let her know we'd be late." She traced a fingertip across his mouth.

He leaned back, checking her expression. Was she pranking him? "You told Dana we spent the night together?"

Her eyes widened in innocent denial. "No, but she probably guessed it."

Rhys glanced at the clock on the nightstand. They had a good hour to celebrate their first morning together and not be *too* late.

"We'll need to stop by Paige's so I can change clothes. Can I borrow a T-shirt to wear? My clothes are still damp."

He subtracted twenty minutes from his estimate.

"I told her we'd meet her at the office at nine."

Cool. An extra hour to…. Suspicion tingled his senses. "Which office?"

"Dana's office. The cleaning company released it."

His hands dropped, and he whirled toward the closet. "Get dressed. We have to get to the office."

"She's meeting us at nine."

"Dana doesn't need to walk into that building by herself and see the aftermath of the cleanup."

He threw a pair of jeans on the bed, then pulled open a dresser drawer. Two T-shirts landed on the bed. "I'll get a pair of gym shorts for you. They'll be big, but…"

"Will you stop for a moment?"

Rhys whirled around. How could Jamie be so casual about the situation? Dana wasn't going to wait around to check on her office.

"We have to go."

Jamie stopped him with two firm hands on his bare chest. "We don't. I told Dana I wanted to take notes as we do the walk-through. She promised she would wait." Her eyes narrowed. "Are you suggesting Dana would break her word?"

Rhys bit back a grunt of exasperation. Why didn't she understand? They had to leave *now*. He had to get to the office before Dana did. He needed to fix...

Oh.

The teasing expression left Jamie's face. "I panicked when I woke up this morning. While I was in the shower, I worried about not having work clothes here. That we were going to be late and Dana was counting on me. Then I heard a shower start in another room."

He nodded. "Mud room."

"I thought 'what am I doing'? I didn't stop to think how you must have felt, and that was wrong. So I called Dana to tell her we would be late." Her lips curved in a brief smile. "She was fine with it. I worried about a problem that existed in my mind alone. I even added an extra hour to when we would meet. Time for you and me." She took a step forward, resting her palms on his shoulders. "And during this time, you are going learn what it's like to let someone take care of you."

A grin eased its way onto his lips. "I like the sound of that."

"Good. Now, drop the towel."

His gaze traveled from her beautiful blue eyes to the knot between her breasts holding her towel in place. With a quick flick of two fingers, he loosened the tie, sending the material pooling around Jamie's feet.

The fierce stare she aimed at him lost its impact as a smile fought free. "I meant yours."

"I know." His grin widened. "So what are you going to do about it?"

"I'm going to take care of you." A second later, his towel joined hers on the floor. "Just like I promised."

Her kiss claimed him, body and soul. What would it be like

to relinquish the control that guided his life? To surrender to the unknown?

He couldn't wait to find out.

Seated at the table in the "front office" of the restaurant, Paige grumbled when the rapping on the front door wouldn't stop. If she'd been in the kitchen, she wouldn't have heard the knocking. But, Karen had showed up on time today and had the prep work well underway.

Then again, it might be an emergency. Or maybe Sam. He'd gotten into the habit of dropping in before hours for a cup of coffee. She didn't know why she allowed that to continue. She really didn't.

Paige spun out of the chair, rushing to the door with a near skip in her step. She halted as soon as she realized the tall, muscular man outside wasn't Sheriff Sam Wallace.

It was Nick Warden.

She slowed her step, taking her good old time reaching the door. She cheered slightly at the irritation on Mr. Warden's face. Stepping to one side, she pointed to the sign on the door.

We're closed, she mouthed.

"It's for Dana." His voice boomed through the closure.

Damn it. She flipped the lock and opened the door.

"This better be on the level. I'm in the middle of prep and working on delivery orders."

"Let's not waste time." He nodded to the table in the back. "We can sit back there while we talk."

Paige fumed as he strode boldly through the room. As if he were the owner. She plopped down in the chair opposite him, ready to let him know he wasn't the boss of her.

"Mr. Warden—"

"By the way, I owe you for two lunches from the other day."

"Sam paid for them." Another meal Mr. Warden hadn't paid out of his own pocket.

"Both? I'll have to thank him."

"Yeah, you do that. So, about Dana?" She bolted upright. "She's all right, isn't she?"

Mr. Warden held up one hand and made a braking motion,

urging her back into the chair. "She's fine." He pulled a paper from his pocket, unfolded it, and slid it across the table.

Suspicion reared its head. The last time Mr. Warden had approached her with a list, it had taken a day out of her life creating a romantic dinner. Granted, Jamie had helped while he'd arranged a garden bistro setting on Dana's patio, but it irked her that he got the lion's share of credit for that in Dana's eyes.

Not that she was keeping score, but facts were facts.

She glanced over the paper, frowning. "This is a copy of upcoming maintenance for my Jeep." One that Mr. Warden had noted as a courtesy when he'd replaced a dead battery in her car. Along with a warning not to let a garage sell her on unneeded work if she chose to go elsewhere.

"I will fix all these…" He picked up the paper. "…in exchange for your help."

She narrowed her eyes. Deals with Mr. Warden didn't always work out in her favor, and she wasn't a puppet at his calling. A nudge from her conscience forced her to admit that he'd always played fair with her. Getting all the car repairs done before something went majorly wrong would be one less financial burden. Then again, if he was willing to trade that much work for a favor, how much effort was he expecting in return?

"What's the favor?"

"Graduation party for Megan. Saturday afternoon. Dana's house."

"That's two days away!" She frowned. "Hey, I thought you said this was for Dana."

He held up his hand again. "After the graduation celebration, it's an engagement party."

Her mouth dropped open. "You and Dana?"

A slight flush crept across his tanned features. An almost bashful grin erupted. "Yes, ma'am."

"You already proposed? I didn't hear anything about it."

"That's because"—he twitched a forefinger between the two of them—"we're the only ones who know about the engagement part of the evening."

"Do you have a ring? What's it look like? Can I see it?"

"It's on order."

Paige ran a palm over the paper, smoothing the creases. He needed her help. She sensed it, felt it, even tasted it. For once, she was in the catbird seat.

"Parts *and* labor?" He nodded, didn't even argue. A major disappointment, as she'd been looking forward to irritating— um, negotiating. "What do you need me to do?"

Another folded sheet of paper hit the table. "Decorations. Cake. As for guests, I guess you, Rhys, Jamie, Sam."

She rolled her eyes. Lame guest list for a high-school graduation party. "I know some kids graduating this year. They're having a progressive party." When he lifted an eyebrow, she heaved a deep sigh. "They go from house to house for an hour or so. Starts at two p.m. and goes to… well, as long as they have a place to go. I'll get Megan worked into the schedule, and let you know what time."

"I appreciate whatever you can do. If it's just the adults, that's what'll it have to be."

"I'll get some kids there." And she would, even if she had to call in favors. "Decorations shouldn't be hard. I'll get a sheet cake for Megan and a small round cake for you and Dana. What about the food?"

"I'm grilling."

"No, you're not." She smiled in the face of what she'd come to think of as his "dad glare." "Keep it simple. Pizza, lasagna, wraps for the kids." She scowled at the list. "I guess your duties for this party are the same as for a wedding? Just show up with the ring."

"Hardly. I have garden duty ahead."

Manual labor. She felt better, and a little guilty. "Maybe Rhys could help you with that."

"I'll keep that in mind. I need to get back to work." He shifted onto one hip to retrieve his wallet.

She faked a jaw drop. "You *do* have a wallet. It's real. Can I touch it?"

"Cute." He placed five bills on the table. "If this doesn't cover everything, let me how much more you need."

Her eyes widened as she saw the denomination. "This is a lot of money. Look, I won't charge for the food. It'll be my gift."

"Your time is your gift."

"Yeah, well, you're taking time to fix my Jeep."

He shook his head. As usual, he ignored her protests. "Call me when you're ready to schedule the work." Mr. Warden pushed back his chair and stood up, shoving the wallet back into his pocket. "Deal?"

"Deal."

He hesitated, then sat back down. "There's something I need to discuss with you before you hear it from someone else."

The serious expression on Mr. Warden's face meant trouble. She leaned forward in the chair. "Okay. What?"

"You know that vacant building on Towne Square?" He paused for her nod, then continued. "This isn't common news yet, but Rhys wants to buy it to convert into condos. He also wants to buy the lot where my garage sits for parking. I'm looking into buying Glenn Thornton's shop at the Crossroads and relocating my business there."

"But how will get your lunch?" She bit the inside of her mouth, cringing at the stupid remark. It wasn't like she was losing big bucks over his business. She'd comped more meals than he'd paid for. In fact, he hadn't paid for any of his meals so far.

He gave a gentle smile. "I hear you have delivery service now."

Paige snorted. "Maybe we can expand our delivery area if Megan gets a car. In any case, thanks for the news."

"There's more. I'm considering buying the lot next to Thornton's."

For an instant, her vision darkened, her blood stilled, and her breathing paused.

Pop's drive-in. The original Carson's restaurant.

She'd closed the diner when it became too hard to go there day after day. Happy memories of working side by side with Pop couldn't ease the heartache of knowing those days were gone forever.

She knew the property would sell at some point. She just wasn't ready for it to be here and now.

"I'm keeping the original building if it passes inspection."

Some of the darkness seeped out of her. She licked her lips, then asked, "What will you do with it?"

"That will become the office. The interior needs renovating, but I'd like to maintain the exterior as much as possible. I wanted to let you know my plans before April Davis contacts you."

Hard as it was receiving the news, it was easier hearing it from Mr. Warden than a cold call from the realtor. "I appreciate it."

He rose. "We'll talk about it more later. In the meantime..." He nodded to the paper lying on the table. "Get busy on that, will you?"

Paige jumped to her feet, calling after his retreating form. "And you think more about that car for Megan if you want lunches delivered!"

He exited the building with a backward wave over his head.

She watched through the window as he passed Megan on the street. A quick hand slap passed between them, then Megan broke into a trot. Moments later she entered the restaurant.

"Morning, Paige."

"Hey there. No sore feet from yesterday, I hope."

"I'm good. I was used to being on my feet working at Frankie's."

"Good. Karen has most of the prep work finished. Check what else she needs. We're getting more orders, so we have to figure out how much you can carry without having to backtrack constantly."

"Did my dad mention my graduation while he was here?"

"Yes-s-s. He said you knew—"

"About the party, right. He said he'd ask you about helping. Right?" Megan paused only as long as it took Paige to nod. "Great. So anyway, I'm talking about the graduation ceremony. Dad talked to the local principal who agreed to let me walk the stage with the class here. Isn't that the coolest thing?"

Paige's respect for Mr. Warden jumped another level. Leave it to him to find a gift one no one else but a dad would think of. "By the way, I know some kids that are graduating this year. Would you like if I invited some of them to your party?"

"I met Macy Montgomery while running deliveries yesterday. She and her friends are having something called a progressive party. Whatever that is."

"They spend a set amount of time at each person's house, and there's one type of food—taco, burgers, wraps—and games or music. Just a variety of stuff. How about I check with Macy and work out a time slot for everyone to come to Dana's house?"

"I don't know...."

She'd never seen Megan look so uncertain. Inviting strangers to a party? Especially ones who had been friends for years. No wonder she was hesitant.

"I know Macy's friends. They're all cool kids. Cool like you and me."

Megan seized her in a quick hug, almost knocking Paige off her feet. "You are awesome! I'm going to check the orders that are ready and get my change bag."

Megan dashed into the kitchen. Paige stood for a moment watching the door swing until it closed completely.

Mr. Warden once mentioned to Jamie that Paige reminded him of his daughter, saying both were full of life and hardworking. Paige didn't completely agree with that assessment. Megan had a cynical edge that Paige lacked. After hearing about life with her bio-parents, that was understandable.

She and Mr. Warden had bumped heads several times but, to be honest, some of the incidents were of her own making. He was tough, but fair.

Paige stared out the front window, even though he was no longer in sight. A curious loneliness crept in. If it had to be anyone buying the old diner site, she was glad it was Mr. Warden.

Chapter Fourteen

Rhys unlocked the back door at the Canfield building, propping it open to allow fresh air to enter. The scent of antiseptic cleansers wafted out, replacing the odors that had assailed Jamie on her previous visit. He walked to the corner of the building, and saw Jamie and Dana still standing beside her vehicle.

An itch crept across the back of his neck as he considered what they were discussing. The uneasy feeling dissolved when he saw Dana lift one foot and Jamie bend to examine the shoe. Twin laughs drifted to his ears.

Relieved, he leaned against the wall, the heat of the sun-warmed bricks penetrating his cotton shirt. Other than switching Paige's Jeep back for his SUV after dropping Jamie off at Dana's house and a quick trip to Main Street, he'd accomplished nothing on his to-do list for the day. On the other hand, he deserved some slack after having the best night of his life followed by the best morning of his life. Today, work had to take second place to…

Falling in love.

He froze, waiting for lightning. For thunder. Fireworks. There was none of that. When love arrived, it came like the first warm day of spring, sweeping away the remnants of a cold, gray winter. It seeped through his flesh and bones and veins, and when his heart bumped, it was to open up that section he'd kept locked away, waiting for just the right woman.

I'm in love with Jamie Danvers.

For all the honesty and confessions that had passed between them since their date had begun the previous night, he'd never said those words. The feeling had existed for a while, brewing somewhere deep within him since they'd first met. She was the first woman he'd never been able to get out of his mind.

The first to put him and his needs ahead of her own. And the first to deliver some hard truths he needed to recognize about himself.

"Good morning," Dana said as she walked toward him. Dressed in a deep jade summer dress, she hardly looked old enough to be his mother.

"Morning, Mom." He glanced at his watch, then looked down at her feet. "Nice shoes."

She reached up, straightening the collar of his shirt. "Seems someone got dressed in a hurry this morning."

Bam. Just like that, he felt four years old again. "Thank you, Mother," he said to the background of Jamie's giggle.

Dana gave a slight sniff as she looked down the darkened hallway. "Enough stalling. Let's see what we have to deal with."

The motion-detector lights switched on as they traveled the length of the hallway to the waiting area. Rhys stepped aside for his mother to walk through the now-vacant space. Jamie stood silently beside him.

The lobby had been stripped to the bare walls and floor. The furniture removed. The artwork and other décor taken away.

"The cleaners said some of the items in the far corner from the shooting were reclaimable," Dana said. Her heels clicked against the uncovered floor as she examined the area, an ominous echo to the emotionless tone in her voice. "I told them to take them all away. I didn't want any reminders."

Except for one. The cast-iron statue of a hummingbird that had once sat on a table outside Dana's office now waited on the reception desk for a new home.

"Keeping this?" he asked.

Dana walked back to where they stood. The corners of her mouth lifted in a hint of a smile. "You bet. I bought it on an impulse the same day I had my interview with you for the Main Street project. My good luck charm ended up saving my life."

Because his mother was a badass who'd coldcocked the SOB and grabbed his gun. Whoever the person was who'd arrived at that moment and pumped three bullets into Lansing had Rhys's grudging gratitude. At least, Dana didn't have to carry the responsibility of killing the corrupt police detective to save her own life. Even if Lansing had been the man who'd murdered her husband.

"Any ideas for the area?" Jamie asked.

"I want to keep the same color palette, but do something different with it. With everything else going on, I haven't given it much thought."

Inspiration shot a bolt through him. "You don't have to. I'll decide for you." Before Dana could protest, he plunged ahead. "I can paint the room in a couple of hours. Figure out something for the floors. Check out what you have in storage. It'll keep you from using this as an excuse to avoid unpacking the rest of those boxes at your house. Come on, Mom. All those boxes have to offend your designer sensibilities."

Dana rolled her eyes. "I'm bearing up under that burden." The snark lost its bite in the midst of a chuckle. "Do you have the time?"

"I'll find the time."

"I'll help too, Dana," Jamie said, then added in a mock side-whisper, "and keep a rein on any crazy ideas."

"Interesting concept for date nights." A gleam sparkled in Dana's dark brown eyes. "I accept."

"To that, let me say…." He wiped a hand across his brow. "Whew!"

"So, brilliant son of mine, that means we're back in business here as far as our offices. I'm heading home to finish out the day there working on redesigns for several of the merchants."

"Unless you need me, I'll be at McCall's the rest of the day. I need to get a handle on the status of the active projects and what's in the pipeline. What about you, Jamie?"

Jamie looked up from her phone. "I planned on working on the website mock-ups. However, Mr. Caine left a voice mail that he had some ideas and wanted to discuss them." Her shoulders sagged. "Except I won't have my car back from the garage until tomorrow. I'll call him back and set up an appointment for another day."

"As much grief as Caine gave Dana and me from the time this project started, let's not spoil the momentum. You've won more cooperation from him than either of us together." He dug a set of keys from his pocket. "Take my car, and you can pick me up after work."

Jamie took the keys. "I will be super careful with your car."

"I'll see you later." He leaned in for a kiss.

Jamie responded at first, then drew back, casting a wide-eyed look in Dana's direction.

Dana smiled and picked up her purse from the reception desk. "Let me know if we need to delay the start time for tomorrow's meeting."

With a wave of one hand, she walked to the back exit. As soon as the door closed, Jamie burst into laughter. "Did you plan that?"

Rhys held up both hands in surrender. "It's not as if she didn't know, thanks to your call this morning. No need to hide it, especially since she gave us permission to sleep in tomorrow morning."

"She did not!"

A deep laugh rolled from his lips. "She certainly did. 'Let me know if we need to delay the start time.' Sounds like the go-ahead to me."

Her smile softened, and she wrapped her arms around his neck. Warm breath brushed across his cheek as she whispered, "I love you."

Those three words froze him in place. Before he could respond, to tell her those same words lived in his heart, she ran a hand down his arm. "I had to say it."

She stepped back, meeting his gaze with eyes filled not with tears, but with a glow that bathed him in the purest love he'd ever known.

"I'm not afraid anymore," she said. "Whether you feel the same now or not yet or ever, it won't change how I feel. And I'll say it to you every day, not to pressure you, but because I can't hold the words inside."

"You don't have to wait a second longer." He cupped her face between his palms, then kissed the lips that had given him the most precious gift of his life. "I love you, Jamie. Now and forever."

Jamie wrapped her hands around his wrists. "Tell me this is real."

"It's very real." He lowered his forehead to rest against hers. "Wanna play hooky?"

Jamie drew back, laughing. "I'm a bad influence on you."

"No, you're the best." Heaving a deep sigh, he nodded to the hallway. "But since you're so eager to go see Bart Caine, I'll go to work too."

"Do you want me to drop you off at McCall's?" Jamie asked as they walked to the back exit.

"I'll walk over, but I need my briefcase."

Jamie waited for him to secure the back door before they walked to the Navigator. He opened the passenger door and retrieved the briefcase from the front seat. In his other hand, he held out a small rectangular box.

"For you."

"This is from Caine Jewelers." She ran a fingertip over the imprinted logo on the black-and-gold-striped lid. "I can't accept this."

"At least look at it... please?"

Her resolve faded in the face of his eager anticipation. She removed the lid, and a soft gasp of admiration escaped her lips.

Gold and silver beads were threaded through a leather wrap bracelet. Suspended in the center, a single gold charm glistened in the sunlight.

Dragonfly.

"When did you...?"

"This morning. When I dropped you off at Dana's house and said I needed to make a quick trip to Main Street. I kept thinking about what you said the dragonfly represented. Your father said it represents joy. I wanted to give you something to signify the joy you've given me." He lifted the bracelet from the box and unhooked the clasp.

Rhys waited, letting her make the decision. With only a second's hesitation, Jamie extended her arm. He held her gaze as he wrapped the bracelet around her wrist, glancing away only long enough to fasten the clasp. "Every time you have doubts, this is a reminder that I believe in us."

"I didn't think I could get any happier...."

Jamie's voice trailed off as Rhys stared over her shoulder.

She looked toward the street where a dark blue sedan idled in front of the entrance to the private parking lot. Rhys stepped around the side of the Navigator, and the driver pulled away.

"He must have thought this was a public lot," Jamie murmured as she swiveled her wrist in either direction.

"The closed gates should have been a clue." Rhys gestured toward the driver's door. "On second thought, why don't you drop me off at McCall's? I want to make sure you're comfortable driving the Nav."

After a quick review of the instruments with Jamie, Rhys settled back for the short ride to the office. Along the way, he kept watch in the side mirror for a dark blue sedan.

Parking wasn't quite as easy driving the Navigator. After one false attempt, Jamie maneuvered the SUV into a space in the temporary Main Street parking lot. She walked down the back alley to the side street where Caine Jeweler's was located.

In the short time since her last visit, the crews had completed sidewalk repairs and replaced street signs on the first two blocks of the retail area. Rhys's original plan for the majority of the construction to take place at night when the businesses were closed and the temperatures were cooler had been struck down by Kevin, a move Rhys intended to reverse. By adding a second shift and reorganizing McCall's project list, Rhys could ensure that Main Street would be completed ahead of schedule.

Jamie opened the door to the jewelry store. The shop was empty, and Bart's worktable behind the back counter was unoccupied.

"Mr. Caine?"

"Be right there!"

Jamie frowned. That deep baritone definitely didn't originate from Bart Caine. Seconds later, a tall man entered from the back room, a friendly smile on his face as he rolled down his sleeves.

"Sorry for the delay. I'm Bryan McAvoy. How may I help you?"

"I'm Jamie Danvers with Canfield Designs. Mr. Caine left a voice mail asking me to meet with him."

The smile left the man's face. "Looks like I have you to thank for sending my grandfather to the hospital."

Jamie's mouth dropped open. Her concern for the gruff old man took precedence over the accusation. "What happened?"

"Possible heart attack." McAvoy's scowl deepened. "All this disruption took a toll on his health."

"I talked with him two days ago. He seemed fine, even excited about the website." She blinked back the rush of moisture to her eyes. "We were going to spotlight the shop and Mr. Caine during the initial launch."

"My grandfather is too old for this nonsense. Thanks to McCall, that Canfield woman, and you, he's the one paying the price."

Heat raced into her cheeks. "Why aren't you with your grandfather?"

"None of your business, but my brother took Granddad to the hospital. I stayed here to close—" He broke off as the front door opened. "Damn it. I meant to lock up before anyone else came in."

Jamie ignored the glare shot in her direction as Bart's grandson approached the three teenagers. She focused on the girls. Stylishly dressed, but no signs of entitled attitude. No giggling or gum chewing.

"Ladies, we're—"

Jamie nudged her way in front of him. "Welcome to Caine Jewelers. Are you looking for something in particular?"

"A birthday gift for my mother." The brunette looked around, then shook her head.

"Hey, Becca. Check out these boxes."

The girls congregated around the keepsake boxes. They picked up one after another, opening lids, turning them over in their hands, then setting them aside. Jamie glanced at Bryan in time to see him wincing at the disarray.

"What are they for?" the blonde girl asked.

"Everything." Jamie listed the suggestions she'd given to Bart on her initial visit to the shop. She took a step back as the girls chattered.

"…a place for all my lip gloss…"

"…my chargers, and my brother better keep his hands…"

"…great for my art supplies…"

"…sewing kit for Aunt Helga…"

"…take one back to Anne since she couldn't come with us…"

The girls eventually migrated to the register. Jamie leaned against the opposite counter, smiling each time McAvoy's gaze traveled to her. After the final purchase was completed, Jamie walked with the girls to the door.

"Courtney is going to be uber-jealous when she sees—"

The door closed, cutting off the rest of Becca's boast.

"Pleased with yourself, Ms. Danvers?"

Jamie walked back to the register. "Helping make a combined two-hundred dollar sale for Mr. Caine? Yes, I am."

"Then you can leave with your head held high." McAvoy nodded toward the door. "This nonsense is over. I'm not allowing you and your associates to put my grandfather in an early grave."

Her stomach churned. Just a bit. Not enough for Jamie to doubt herself. Instead, it spurred her to hold her ground. She tilted her head upward, jaw jutting. "That's not your decision, Mr. McAvoy. Your grandfather was excited about the changes, and I was looking forward to working with him. I hope he recovers quickly and can return to work. In the meantime, Sally Van Kirk is the vice president of the Merchants' Association and will be the one making those decisions."

"Then you have no further need to remain here. The shop is closed until further notice—" He broke off with a grunt as his phone rang. Pulling the phone from his pocket, he turned his back to her. "David? How's Granddad?"

Jamie eased closer, hoping to hear an update on Bart's status. Lifting her face to catch the downdraft from the overhead ceiling fan, she rubbed her thumb over the dragonfly charm.

I did it, Dad. I didn't back down or run. I stood up to him.

"Miss Danvers?"

The sharp tone pulled Jamie's attention to McAvoy waving his cell phone. A scowl decorated his features. Other than the initial smile he'd offered when she'd first arrived, the man's face remained etched with a glower.

"Yes, Mr. McAvoy?"

"My grandfather wishes to speak with you."

She stepped forward, holding out her hand.

McAvoy jerked back the phone. "I'll put it on speaker." He tapped the screen, then said, "Go ahead, Granddad."

"Is Miss Jamie there?"

Jamie smiled at the crochety tone. Somehow grumpy was charming when it came from the irascible old man. "Yes, I'm here."

"Ah, well, good. My apologies for missing our meeting."

"I completely understand. It was something you couldn't help. I hope you're feeling better."

"Indigestion. Told the grandsons that, but nothing would do but hauling me over to have a doctor tell me what I already knew."

"I'm happy to hear you'll be all right."

"Quite kind of you. I told Bryan to give you those ideas I wrote up for the website."

"Wonderful. I'll look those over and make updates to the mock-ups. I'll also leave some sketches for those interior changes we discussed."

"I'll speak to Bryan about those later. They're getting ready to—I *said* I don't need a wheelchair—"

The line went dead.

Jamie reached into her satchel for the folder Dana had provided. She held it out to McAvoy. "May I have the notes Mr. Caine left for me?"

McAvoy walked to the work area, then returned with several sheets of paper filled with handwritten notes.

"Thank you." She tucked them into her bag and turned toward the door.

"Are you free for dinner tonight, Jamie?"

Jamie halted, stunned by the swift change in the man's manner. She half-turned, pausing only long enough to answer. "No, I'm not."

He caught up to her at the door. "You're not holding our disagreement against me, are you?"

"No, Mr. McAvoy—"

"Bryan."

"I'm seeing someone."

He shot a glance at her left hand. "I don't see a ring. Can't be that serious."

Jamie barely held back a laugh. Was that observation supposed to be a dare? Did he think trading a scowl for a smile had the power to sway her?

From the beginning, Rhys McCall had been the one and

only man who held her attention. Who drew her as no one else ever had or could. Their path toward love had started with a simmer, then ignited into a blaze as bright as the future ahead of them.

She caught her breath as snippets of the past twenty-four hours swept over her. Tearful truths in the fading light of an ocean sunset. Carefree joy shimmering in an evening rainfall. Soft laughter in the dark. Tangled limbs beneath a cool cotton sheet. Whispered passion and unspoken promises.

I believe in us.

"It's very serious, and the answer is still no."

The blunt reply wiped the half-smile from McAvoy's lips. Jamie exited the shop, leaving him standing with his mouth dropped open. She walked toward the parking area, never looking back. Whether he closed the door behind her or watched, she wasn't interested.

Once back in the Navigator, Jamie heaved a sigh of relief. She started the engine, waiting a few moments for the A/C to cool the interior. Traffic was light along the Old Main route. Feeling more comfortable driving the vehicle, she settled back to enjoy the spacious luxury.

Movement in the side mirror caught her attention. The car that had been behind her had pulled into the oncoming lane. Jamie glanced at the speedometer. She was just under the speed limit, but apparently that wasn't fast enough for the other driver.

Fine. Let him go around her.

The window behind her exploded. A scream flew from her lips, and her hands squeezed the steering wheel.

Who…? She darted a frantic look in the side mirror, but could only see the bumper of the vehicle coming up beside her.

The car pulled even with her window, and a hand extended toward her with a gun. Jamie jammed her foot on the brake, fighting the pull of the SUV as it fishtailed. The second bullet screeched across the windshield, and she winced.

A horn blared from a truck in the oncoming lane. The shooter swerved in front of the Navigator and sped away. In those few seconds, Jamie saw the car.

A dark blue sedan.

The sign for Crossroad's Body Shop came into view. She had to hold herself together for a few more moments.

The Navigator spanned two parking spaces when she rolled onto the lot, and she didn't care. Her knees buckled as she stepped out of the SUV. Somehow she managed to remain upright and stumble into the office. The adrenaline pulsing in her blood faded. Her breathing slowed to shallow pants. A chill shook her body when a blast of cold air from a nearby vent swept over her.

"Call the sheriff." Spots danced in front of her eyes as she clutched the counter. Her knees buckled again. "Someone shot at my car."

She heard a shout, then fell into darkness.

Rhys raced through the emergency entrance at Rollison Memorial Hospital toward the information desk. He changed direction when Sam exited the triage area.

"Jamie?" His heart pounded a furious beat.

"She's getting checked." The sheriff jerked his head to the closed door. "Dana's with her."

"I need to see her." Rhys pivoted toward the door to triage.

"Know anything about a blue sedan?"

Rhys halted, stomach plummeting. *I knew it!* He should have listened to his gut and not let Jamie go alone. "There was a dark blue sedan idling in front of the parking lot at Dana's office."

"According to Jamie, the driver was following her, then sped up and pulled into the oncoming lane. The first shot hit the back driver's side window. The second shot was intended for the driver. Jamie slammed on the brakes, and the bullet grazed the windshield instead. A truck was in the oncoming lane, so the shooter was forced to disengage and leave the scene."

Jamie could have been killed. Rhys's mouth went dry, and his insides began to shake.

"We've located the sedan a couple miles from there. It was stolen off the temporary customer parking lot on Main Street. Doubtful anyone paid any attention, but maybe we'll luck out."

Rhys raked his fingers through his hair. The attacks on Dana and his father. The motorcycle trying to run Rhys down. Now someone shooting at Jamie. Why? None of it made sense.

"We also found the motorcycle that tried to run you over abandoned in a ditch on the south side of the Crossroads. Found the helmet too. If we're lucky, there'll be some trace evidence that matches what we collected from the sedan." Sam snapped his fingers. "I have an update on your dad's attack. Turns out the security cameras on both sides of the parking garage had been disabled. I'm arranging to get footage from the cameras on the side of the courthouse that faces the garage." Sam shuffled one foot. "I'm starting to question whether your two incidents are connected to the assault on your father rather than to Dana's situation."

Or were they pieces of a larger puzzle? Either way, today's attack on Jamie had been meant for him. Her life had been put at risk because of her proximity to him.

The door behind him opened again, and Jamie and Dana exited the triage area.

Jamie moved slowly but didn't seem to be in pain. Her face was pale, shadows marking the delicate skin under her eyes. Seeing him, she smiled.

If she knew what he suspected, she would never smile at him again.

"I'm fine." She slid one arm around his waist, leaning into him. "I fainted from the excitement, but Dana wanted me to get checked."

"Dana was right." He managed a small smile in return, then looked to Sam. "Are we done here?"

"We are. Jamie, take care. I'll be in touch as soon as we find out anything." With a nod, Sam departed.

Jamie's arm tightened around him. "I'm so sorry about your car."

The tears brewing in her eyes cut to the core of his heart. "I don't care about the car." He hugged her, savoring the closeness while he could.

"We have a problem with transportation," Dana said, holding up her cell phone. "My car only holds two. I checked with Nick. He's finished with your car, Jamie, but wants to test drive it. How about I drive Jamie to Paige's house? Nick will pick up Rhys here. Rhys can take Nick back to his garage and keep Jamie's car. We'll figure out tomorrow when it gets here."

Rhys repeated the sequence to himself, then nodded. "That works for me. Why don't you go ahead and leave? Jamie needs to rest."

Dana nodded. "Jamie, take the day off tomorrow and rest."

"Absolutely not. Work will keep my mind occupied, and I need to move around."

Rhys brushed Jamie's lips with a light kiss. When he exchanged a quick hug with Dana, her eyes narrowed.

"We'll talk." Her soft words were more a warning than an invitation.

Rhys nodded, fighting to maintain a bland expression. He escorted the women to Dana's car just as Nick turned into the parking lot. He hopped into the passenger seat beside Nick, expecting the ride to be a brief one back to the garage.

Instead, Nick drove across town and turned onto Old Main.

"Car sounds good," Rhys said, stretching out his legs as best he could in the compact. The ride was smooth. The engine purred, and the A/C ran like a dream.

Nick nodded. "How's Jamie?"

Rhys looked out the window at the passing scenery. Had it only been a day since he and Jamie had traveled in this same direction on their date?

"Shook up but not physically hurt."

"Dana told me what happened. Sounds like Jamie kept her wits while all of that was going on."

Only her quick thinking had saved her life. Acid boiled up his throat, and he had to swallow hard. "She could have been killed." He clamped his mouth shut and kept his gaze fixed on the window.

"Did you tell Dana about the motorcycle incident?"

"I told Jamie and Paige." Silence from the other man forced him to turn his head. "Dana has too much to deal with now without worrying about me."

"Not a good idea to keep secrets from her."

Not like Mom didn't suspect something already. Warden was right. Better to fess up before Jamie or Paige mentioned it.

Nick turned onto a side street, traveled a few blocks, then made another turn to take them back to the downtown area.

"Dana told me about the meeting with this Toddy fellow."

"Strange guy. He's like a chameleon. One moment, he's the gracious host, then the sad old guy who lost his family, then a sarcastic SOB. After Dana left the room, he didn't hold back taking shots at me."

"I've known some old guys like that. They like to push buttons to get something started, then sit back and laugh while watching the fireworks."

"Not the same with him. It's a possessiveness." At Nick's heated glare, Rhys shook his head. "Not in the sense you're thinking. It was all about *his* family, about him. No acknowledgment of what Dana lost. I wish I could chalk it up to loneliness, but it seems to be something more."

Nick parked in the lot behind his garage. Both men stepped out of the car, pausing in front of the vehicle.

"The car shouldn't give her any trouble as long as she keeps up with the maintenance. I'll include a recommended schedule with the other paperwork when I see her."

Rhys reached for his wallet. "How much for the repairs?"

Nick's mouth quirked to one side. "I'll settle up with Jamie when she's able to come by."

"I can take of the bill now and take the papers to her."

The smirk turned into a chuckle. "Son, your heart's in the right place, but your head needs to think again."

Warden's expression made it clear he wasn't budging. Further arguing would only give him more excuse to laugh at Rhys's expense. Why did it matter to Warden who paid him? Jamie wouldn't mind…

I don't need you to fix me.

"Got it."

"Thought you would." Nick tossed the keys to him.

Rhys rounded the car and opened the driver's door.

Nick leaned one hip against the front fender. "One thing that never sat right with me in all this is why Joshua Canfield left without a word to Dana."

"Some sort of falling out with his father." Easy to understand. As much as Rhys had missed PI and his father during those years he'd lived on the mainland, the distance had allowed him a certain peace of mind.

"What if accidents started happening to Joshua? Maybe Canfield *sent* Joshua away to keep him safe." Nick straightened, paced a few steps, then turned. "Or maybe someone killed him, and Canfield just thought his son was safe."

Rhys ran a hand along the back of his neck. "Who? Lansing?"

"Maybe. But somebody else had to be pulling Lansing's

strings. Probably the same person who ordered the hit on Keg."

"Which means Canfield's story about a falling out between him and his son might not have been true."

Nick shrugged. "If Canfield was protecting his son, the lie might have been to protect Dana from knowing Joshua was in danger." His brow furrowed for a second. "Seems like each of us knows bits and pieces. We need to all sit down together, compare thoughts, and see if we can make sense of all this."

Proactive. Stop waiting for another clue to come to light or a new danger to erupt. Rhys nodded. "Sounds like a good plan. You, me, and Sam."

Nick chuckled. "All of us. Including Dana."

"No way. She's been through enough—"

Nick held up one hand. "Take some advice from a guy who knows from experience. I did some investigating without Dana's knowledge and had my ass handed to me when she found out."

Rhys bit back a snicker. Better Warden than him to have learned that lesson. He didn't like putting Dana through any additional stress, but Nick's suggestion made sense. "Agreed. Sometime this weekend, then?"

"Early next week would be better. Megan has graduation on Saturday." Nick scuffed a foot along the pavement. "Which leads me to another subject we need to discuss."

Rhys tensed. What else…?

"I asked Dana to marry me, and she said yes. She planned on telling you, but I'm jumping the gun here because I want to give her the ring during the party. Before that"—another scuff of the foot—"I wanted to get your blessing."

Rhys rubbed the back of his neck. The news didn't hit as hard as he'd expected. He couldn't fault Nick for falling for Dana. His mother was an incredible woman, and she deserved someone to cherish her.

He jerked his attention back to the man in front of him and extended his hand. "You got it, and congratulations. I'm not totally surprised, other than it seems quick."

"Love sometimes happens like that."

Yeah, it does.

"Last bombshell of the evening. Megan and I are moving into Dana's house on Sunday."

"You want my blessing on that too?"

"No, I want your help moving furniture."

"You got it."

Nick glanced at the car, then back to Rhys. "Need me to follow you where you're going?"

"No, I'm sure the car is fine. I'm heading home."

"Wasn't talking about the car."

Rhys hesitated, then shook his head. "I'll be fine."

With a nod, Nick stepped back. Rhys started the car and drove off the lot.

The drive home usually relaxed him, but not tonight. During the entire trip, his senses stayed on alert, his nerves jangling. Each car on the road could be a potential weapon, each pedestrian a possible assailant.

When he caught sight of the house, he released a slow breath of relief. He'd arrived safely at home with no incidents. He turned into the driveway, and his headlights illuminated the side door to the house standing wide open.

What the…?

Rhys's heart thumped a heavy beat as he exited the vehicle. Something was wrong. Very wrong. A low roar echoed from inside. He jerked the phone from his pocket.

"Sam, it's Rhys. Someone broke into my house." He mounted the steps, glancing through the screen door.

"I'm heading out now. Do not *enter the house."*

"I hear you." He cocked his head. Somewhere in the house, water was running.

"I'm dead serious, McCall. You enter that house, and I will arrest you for tampering with a crime scene."

"Then get here quick because I'm not waiting long."

Chapter Fifteen

Rhys waited less than ten minutes, the maximum he was allowing the sheriff before entering the house. A flashing light bar announced Sam's arrival, followed by Deputy Mike Winslow's.

The two approached with guns drawn. "Any activity from inside?" Sam asked, sparing no time for pleasantries.

"Not so far."

"Front door locked?"

"Didn't try it."

Mike mounted the steps and checked the door. "Locked."

A third vehicle drew to a halt at the side of the road. Deputy Tom Hunter jogged across the road, joining them.

"Mike, guard the front. Tom, you go with me. Rhys, you wait here until we make sure it's safe."

"No one's inside. I've been here ten minutes, and there's been no sign of movement. If they had been here, they would have taken off when they heard me call you."

"I said 'wait.'" Sam shot a glance at Winslow as he strode toward the back entrance. "Mike, cuff him if he gives you any problem."

Mike grinned, tapping the handcuffs attached to his belt. "You got it, boss."

Son of a... Rhys bit back the curse and paced to the end of the driveway. So much for playing by the rules. He should have gone in when he had the chance, *then* called Sam.

His temper grew as each moment passed. Finally, the front door opened, and Tom motioned to him.

"Sam says it's okay for you to come in the back door."

After a scowl at both men, Rhys jogged to the rear of the house. Sam stood in the doorway, waiting.

"No one's here—"

"I told you—"

Sam cut off the interruption with one of his own. "You can come in, but don't touch anything."

They entered through the mud room. The door to the bathroom was open.

"The shower and sink were running full-force," Sam said. "Take it you didn't leave them on."

Rhys glared at him. "No."

They moved on to the kitchen. The doors to the refrigerator and freezer were open. "Faucet was on here too. The fridge was unplugged. At least, the intruder didn't smear food all over the kitchen."

"You tick off a lady friend?" Tom asked. "This sure seems like something a woman would do."

Sam cocked an eyebrow at the deputy. "You would know this because…?"

"Heard talk. Seen movies." Tom nodded down the hallway. "In case you're wondering, same thing in the bathroom. Faucets on in both the shower and sink."

Rhys glanced through the open doorway. Not to mention that someone had strewn the contents of the medicine cabinet and linen closet all over the floor. "This doesn't make sense. It's vandalism, but nothing like what happened to Jamie or my dad."

"Not done yet." Sam waved one hand for Rhys to follow.

They bypassed the empty spare bedroom, a quick glance revealing no additional clues or damage, to the main bedroom.

Rhys halted in the doorway. His breath caught as he viewed the chaos. The closet door was open, clothes thrown to the floor. Covers pulled from the bed, sheets and pillows rumpled.

"Someone was in here."

Sam pulled a flashlight from his belt and leaned over the bed.

"You had company lately?" Sam glanced back over one shoulder. "There's a number of red hairs that look similar to the ones we found in the bike helmet."

Rhys's stomach turned. The intruder had rolled around in the same bed where he and Jamie had made love?

"Hold the flashlight, would you?"

Rhys focused the beam on the head of the bed while Sam drew on a pair of gloves. Using tweezers, he picked up the long strands of hair and dropped them into an evidence bag. He handed the sealed bag to Tom when he entered.

Sam picked up the pillow, sniffed it, and held it out to Rhys. "Recognize it?"

Rhys sniffed, jerking back at the strong musky scent. "I've smelled that perfume somewhere before." He struggled to recall the elusive memory of when and where.

"You could have smelled it anywhere. Even in one of those inserts in a magazine. I'll have Tom bag the linens for evidence." Sam nodded to the clothes on the floor. "While he takes care of the linens, I'll clean out the spoiled food, and you pack what you need for now."

"I'm not leaving my house unattended."

"You going to stay here all day tomorrow? And all the following days until we catch this perp?" He jerked a thumb toward the bed. "You plan on sleeping there?"

Rhys glanced at the rumpled sheets. "I'll sleep on the couch."

"What if they return, and you're asleep? You're not going to get any rest here." Sam planted his feet, a fierce scowl on his face. "Here's what I think. Someone has you in their sights. Don't know if it's connected to your dad's attack, but I'll bet money it is connected to the shooting at Jamie. That person didn't shoot at your truck because she thought it was you. She did it because it *was* Jamie. And all this"—he twirled a forefinger in a circle—"is to let you know how close she can get to you."

Ice crept through his veins. "So you're saying…"

"I'm saying it looks like you have a stalker."

He slammed a fist against the door frame. "And that's the very reason I can't go somewhere else! I can't put anyone else at risk."

Frowning, Sam tapped a hand against his thigh, then said, "Dana has an alarm system at her house, doesn't she?"

Rhys heaved a deep sigh. Like Mom needed another load of trouble dropped on her doorstep, but what other choice did he have? Dad's place was out. He didn't even have a key to get in.

He gave a short nod. "I'll head over to Dana's."

Sam clapped a hand to his shoulder as he passed. "I'll follow you to her house."

Sam sent Mike on his way, and within minutes, Tom had collected the remainder of the evidence, Sam had cleared out the spoiled food, and Rhys had packed up what he needed.

While he waited for the other cars to clear his driveway, Rhys called Dana.

"Hey, Mom. I'll fill you in when I get there, but can I bunk at your house tonight?"

"Of course. Are you—"

"I'm fine. I should be there in about twenty minutes."

"I'll be waiting. Love you."

"Love you too."

As he drove to his mother's house, Rhys glanced in the rear view mirror several times, irrationally comforted by the official escort following him.

The porch light was on when he pulled into Dana's driveway. The front door opened seconds after he parked, and Dana stepped outside. When the sheriff's vehicle arrived, her mouth dropped open, a hand flew to her chest, and she raced down the steps.

Rhys caught her in his tight embrace. His stomach churned for causing her further distress. "I'm okay, Mom."

She stepped back, scanning his face. "What happened?"

"A break-in at my house. Sam thought it would be better if I stayed somewhere else tonight." He shot a glare at Sam as he joined them, a silent command to not worry Dana with the specifics.

"Any problems here, Mrs. Canfield?" As he spoke, Sam's gaze traveled over the surroundings. "I can take a look around if you'd like."

"Everything's been quiet." She looked from one man to the other. "What am I not being told?"

"I'll let him fill you in." Sam tipped two fingers to his forehead. "Call the dispatcher if there's any sign of trouble."

Rhys picked up his bag, catching Dana's hand with his free one. "Ready to call it a night?"

Her eyebrow lifted, freezing him in place. "Do you really think you're going to get out of telling me what's going on?"

Nick had warned him about keeping secrets, and he had only himself to blame when his stupidity came back to bite him.

Rhys settled on the couch, eyeing the tray Dana set on the table in front of him. He'd made sure everything was secure—doors locked, alarm system activated—before allowing himself to relax. His declining an offer of food hadn't stopped her from fixing a snack.

He coated a cracker with a liberal amount of cream cheese spread and popped it into his mouth. No need to waste good food.

She wouldn't take her eyes off him. He motioned to the tray, trying to distract her. "Good. Crab and red pepper?"

"And a few other things. Try the spinach dip."

His appetite kicked in, and he took full advantage of the food. He recognized Dana's intentions to feed more than just his stomach. The meal helped calm him as he relayed the incidents of the last two days, starting with the motorcycle near hit-and-run. That part was easy. The story about what happened to Jamie wasn't.

"Sam thinks Jamie was the intended target all along." His voice cracked, and he had to take a deep breath.

"What if Sam is wrong? What if this is just another layer to what we're already dealing with?" Dana's protest broke off in a choked cry. "I brought this trouble with me. If I'd stayed away—"

The pain in her dark eyes hurt him more than any gunshot could have done. "If you'd stayed away, I wouldn't have you in my life. No one is more innocent in all this than you." He closed his hand around hers. "You're not to blame, Mom."

She stared at him with tear-filled eyes. "Then neither are you."

He gave a short nod, acknowledging, but not accepting, that excuse.

"There's a couple things I need to tell you. I meant to tell you sooner, but we haven't had time with everything else. It's not the best time, but I want you know." She tucked one leg under the other. "Nick proposed, and I accepted. We haven't set a date yet, but Nick and Megan are moving in."

"Nick told me while we test-drove Jamie's car. He asked for my blessing."

Her lips parted, then curved into a smile. "That was sweet."

More of a strategic move on Nick's part. Sincere, but also assuring Rhys that he was still a part of this new chapter in Dana's life.

"Nick's a good guy. We butted heads at first, but we're okay now."

"We're having a graduation party for Megan on Saturday. I'd love for you to be there."

"Nick mentioned that too." He fought the smile that was threatening to erupt as he pictured Dana's reaction when Nick presented a ring to her.

"Quite a talk the two of you had." Her dark eyes narrowed, suspicion dripping into her tone.

"Just thinking how I'm finally going to have the little sister I always wanted."

She jammed an elbow into his ribs. "Hardly. You told me more than once you liked having it be just you and me."

"As I recall, I also said *if* I had to have one or the other, I would take a brother."

"You may get your wish on that one."

His jaw dropped. His gaze flew to her stomach. "Holy shit! Are you—?"

"Oh, God, no!" Dana fanned a hand in front of her face. "I was talking about your father."

His life had become totally, utterly, completely insane. He massaged the bridge of his nose. "I wasn't aware Dad was seeing anyone."

"I found out by accident. She's someone he knew before we met. They've reconnected since she moved back to PI. Along with her son… Kevin."

"April Davis?" He sank back into the couch. "That explains how Kevin snagged a job so quickly. Figure she's told him?"

"I wouldn't doubt it. It's all so bizarre. April and I have been friends since I bought this house. Then I find out about her and Erik." A shadow dashed across her features. "She wasn't happy to find out I'm his ex and your mother."

"Too bad for her." In the big scheme of things, April being upset was the least of his concerns.

"April's offered to see what she could find out from Erik about that day at the hospital. He may be more willing to talk to her." Dana took a deep breath. "Do you have it in you for one more piece of news?"

He groaned. "How either of us can top what's happened tonight, I don't know. But give it a try."

She opened a drawer in the table next to the couch and pulled out two sheets of paper. "Remember my birth certificate you found?"

"Sure." He took the paper and glanced over it. "Did you see something we missed before?"

"No. What occurred to me is that I have another birth certificate. The one that belonged to the other Dana." She held it out to him. "Check the names of the parents."

"Christopher Dennison. Carolyn Avery. Those are your parents. The others are Robert Colby and Anna... Avery?"

She nodded. "Good chance that Carolyn and Anna are related."

"Do you remember an Anna Avery or Anna Colby?"

Her face twisted in frustration. "No, and you'd think I would after living this other life for so long. All I can remember is a nickname for the other Dana. Dee Dee. I certainly should have more memories of her, especially if we did look so similar." Her frown deepened. "I need to go through the rest of the papers. At least whatever birth, death, and marriage certificates I can find and see if anything sparks my memory."

"Nick had a good suggestion. That we all sit down and compare what we know."

"You two had quite the bonding session."

"We have something in common." He winked, then held up the certificates. "The switch no longer seems like the product of a random opportunity, does it?"

"Opportunity...." The words came out as a whisper. "The blue car. It *wasn't* an accident. Dee was trying to run my car off the road." Her dark eyes glittered in a face washed of all color. "She wanted to kill me."

He stiffened and leaned toward her. "You remember what happened that day? You remember her?"

"No. Yes, partly." She threaded her fingers through her hair, the heels of her hands massaging both temples.

"The two of you argued?"

"We did... but why?" She jerked upright, dropping her

hands into her lap. "I can't remember."

They needed answers, but nothing further could be accomplished tonight by pressuring her.

"It's late," Rhys said. "Let's call it a night."

"You need to rest, and I've kept you up too long." Dana stood and reached for the tray on the nearby table.

"Go on up. I'll put the food in the fridge and turn off the lights." He hesitated for a moment, then said, "If you want to call Nick—"

Her wan smile, devoid of its usual vibrancy, still warmed his heart.

"No need to call Nick." She cupped a palm to the side of his face. "I have you here with me."

He returned the smile because she expected it. Kissed her cheek and hugged her because *he* needed it.

Returning to the living room, Rhys picked up the birth certificates. He stopped to reread the topmost one.

Dana Denise Colby. The woman who'd almost killed his mother. The woman buried under his own mother's name. Which meant there had to be a death certificate. One that identified where she was buried.

I never knew where she was buried.

Rhys sank down on the couch. What if "Dana" never died? A death certificate could have been faked. Had she survived the crash? Was *she* the one directing everything that had happened to his mom over the past two decades?

Nick was right. They needed to pool all their information together. Next step after that would be hiring a private investigator. One vetted by Sam. Right now, they couldn't take anyone on trust alone.

He returned the certificates to the drawer and pushed it shut. After he put away the leftovers, he walked through the downstairs again, rechecking the windows and doors, then the alarm. The house was secure.

As much as any place could be.

"Mommy! Don't leave me!"
He ran as fast as he could, but he couldn't catch up. His legs were too

short. He could still see the red car in the far, far distance. As long as he could see her, she wasn't lost.

Why didn't she hear him?

His legs ached, his chest hurt, but he wouldn't quit. He couldn't quit. Something bad was going to happen. He knew it. He felt it.

He needed to fix it before someone got hurt.

If he could just grow…

He did! He was tall and strong and could run faster than ever.

Mom!

His legs pumped, his chest expanding as he drew in sweet oxygen. The world around him passed in a blur. He drew close enough to see the car wasn't red. It was white, washed in the bloody red of a setting sun.

A roar sounded behind him. A car drew beside him, keeping pace. The window rolled down. A man with gray hair called to him. His teeth gleamed in his tanned face.

"Try harder. Joshua would have caught that car miles ago."

He ignored the taunts and pushed himself to go faster, leaving the luxury car in the dust. He drew closer and closer. Close enough to see two cars.

A dark blue sedan. A white BMW.

That wasn't right. Mom said, "…my car was red… another car, blue like the sky…."

He ran so fast, he passed both cars. He turned, just as they sped by him on either side. Dark blue faded to cerulean. White ignited into scarlet.

Metal screamed, a woman screamed. His heart screamed the loudest. The blue car landed upside down in a ditch. He didn't care about the driver. She'd endangered his mother and deserved her fate.

He raced to the other car, also in a ditch but still on all four tires. The front was crushed, the windshield shattered.

"Hang on, Mom. Don't give up. Don't leave me!" He jerked the car door open.

Ocean-blue eyes stared sightlessly up at him. Blonde hair stained with blood tumbled around lifeless shoulders. He fell to his knees, grasping for a hand that could no longer hold his.

Jamie!

Rhys bolted up in bed, gasping. He sucked in several deep breaths while waves of cool air drifted down from the ceiling fan, drying the sweat on his skin.

Just a dream.

He didn't believe that lie for a minute. Ghosts from the past were haunting him, and specters of the future were daring him to intervene. He might not be responsible for what was happening now, but he had a duty to stop it from hurting anyone else.

Until he could fix things, everyone he loved was in danger.

Vicky Towers eyed the bar on the Lighthouse Cantina's pavilion. She'd scored several drinks so far. The turnover of men, along with the free drinks, had ceased once that flippant little redhead arrived, making an absolute fool out of herself. Everyone seemed to know her name.

Stacy. Stacy. Stacy.

Vicky wasn't going to let the bimbo spoil what had been a marvelous day. The fun had actually started the night before when she'd followed the very handsome Mr. McCall and his Barbie doll companion to the beach.

Vicky had waited outside, curled up in the rocking chair on the side porch, listening until they'd worn themselves out. The man's stamina was impressive and, from what she could hear, so was his technique. When it became quiet, she picked the lock and made her way through the house to the bedroom.

Her target that night wasn't the man. It was the woman. She'd toyed with killing her in her sleep. An ice pick through the ear would be quick and silent.

I like to play with my prey.

How delicious to think what McCall's reaction would have been if he'd woken to find Beach Barbie had bit the big one. However, he could have been arrested for murder and no longer available for pursuit. Which meant lucky, lucky Barbie got to live.

She giggled and took another sip from the pretty drink with a cute umbrella.

She'd napped in her car, hidden on a dirt road, until the lovebirds had finally departed. Then she'd reentered the house and stretched out on the bed for a couple hours of sleep. On his side, of course. When she woke, she'd left a trail of mayhem for McCall when he returned.

Just to mess with his mind. To show him nowhere was safe.

She'd driven to town and caught the trolley to what passed

for a shopping center in this burg. Swiped a car and went a-huntin'. She could have popped off a shot or two when she'd seen the two of them on that private lot downtown, but that was too public, too risky. Especially with a POS car with not much go-power.

She'd followed the blonde, until realizing the woman was headed back to the shopping area. Patience paid off when Barbie made a return trip.

Bang! Bang!

She still couldn't believe she'd missed.

Vicky took another sip and studied the framed poster of a blue-collar man posted on the exterior wall of the restaurant. Rugged and handsome, but no McCall.

Mr. Man-of-the-Month, you have serious competition.

She traced her fingertips over the envelope in front of her, still fuming over how Barbie had kept her cool and hadn't run off the road. What a waste of time and two good bullets…

She really should have gone with the ice pick when she'd had the chance.

Chapter Sixteen

"That covers everything as far as Main Street," Dana said, checking the itinerary. "As for Towne Square, Nick should have asking prices for the Thornton and Carson properties sometime today. Rhys, do you have a bid ready for his property?"

Gathered around the breakfast nook table at Dana's house, Jamie sensed an unspoken tension weaving its way to the surface over the course of the meeting. Less so with Dana, but not with Rhys. His laid-back demeanor had disintegrated. He sat, leg jiggling. He stood and paced. He leaned against the island, tapping a finger on the countertop. He barely ate, and when he spoke, his usual animation was missing.

Did Dana know what was wrong? Maybe not, as Jamie caught her casting curious looks of her own at Rhys.

The early morning text from Dana rescheduling the location of their meeting seemed odd. Even more was the request to have Paige drive her to Dana's house. Why couldn't Rhys have picked her up on his way, especially since he had her car?

None of this made sense.

Jamie jerked her attention back to the discussion when Rhys replied to Dana's question about the bid on Nick Warden's property.

"I know what it's worth, but we'll need to sweeten the deal. Otherwise, he can tear the building down and rent out spaces to the condo owners."

"Do you think he'll move his business?" Jamie asked.

"He was firmly against it at first," Dana said. "Now, he seems excited about the prospect. Rhys, have you heard from Mr. Marcum?"

Rhys shook his head. "He said he'd have a firm asking price to me within the next few days."

"That's all I have." Dana closed her tablet, a note of relief in her voice. "I'll be on Main Street most of the day. What do you have today, Jamie?"

"I'll be here working on the website and setting up project files for Towne Square."

"Rhys?"

"I'm headed over to McCall's."

They all stood for a moment, silent and frozen, until Dana acted. "I'm taking off. Jamie, call if you need anything."

She nodded. "I'll set the alarm if I need to go out."

With a quick goodbye, Dana left. As soon as the front door clicked shut, Jamie rushed to Rhys's side.

"What's wrong? I can tell something—"

"We need to talk." He looked around the kitchen, then gestured toward the living room.

She sat down on the couch, expecting him to do the same. Instead, he took one of the armchairs.

"Is it your father?" A horrible thought struck her. "Something about Dana? Is she in danger?"

The emotion missing from him finally appeared. A crease in his brow deepened, his lips quivered, a sheen glistened in his eyes.

"I need you to understand what I'm about to say."

"Understand what? Whatever it is, we'll handle it together."

He bolted from the chair, pacing in front of the couch and back. "That's the problem. There is no *we*."

Her heart shuddered. A faintness much like the one she experienced yesterday washed over her. She lifted her palms to her face and forced the nausea away.

Believe.

Jamie took a deep breath. After what they'd shared, he wouldn't say what he had without reason. She patted the cushion next to her, relieved when he complied.

He took a deep breath. "The person who shot at you yesterday... that was because of me."

"That was road rage. Someone who didn't think I was traveling fast enough."

"It was that same sedan we saw outside the parking lot at Dana's office."

"There are a lot of dark cars. It was a coincidence."

"It wasn't a coincidence. The near hit-and-run with the motorcycle, then the shooting. Sam thinks there's a connection between the two incidents. He's going to compare some trace evidence found on the bike helmet and the car to...."

"They found the car? When did you find this out?"

"Last night. Sam told me while he and a couple deputies were checking out a break-in at my house."

"A break-in? Oh, honey...." She reached for his hand. He didn't pull away, but he didn't respond. Her stomach quivered as he listed the damages and disarray.

"Sam found some evidence there to compare with the motorcycle helmet." He sucked in a deep breath. "Hairs on my pillow along with a strong smell of perfume."

"Someone was in your bed?"

"On the side where I'd slept the night before."

Her stomach lurched. No wonder Rhys seemed so stunned. Finding his home had been entered would have been shocking, but for the intruder to invade his most private space was chilling.

"Where did you stay last night?"

"Here. With the alarm system installed now, it seemed safer than elsewhere."

"We have to take precautions. Whoever this is—"

Rhys shook his head. "Jamie, you can't be involved in this. Yesterday proved that. Someone is willing to hurt you because of an obsession with me."

"All the more reason we should stay close. Together, we're stronger and safer. I'm not letting you go through this alone."

"You don't have a choice."

Hot anger replaced the chill inside her. "Excuse me? There are two of us in this relationship."

He pushed off the couch with an irritated grunt. "I'm not putting you at risk." The tenderness she'd missed all morning shone in his eyes as he gazed down at her. "I can't bear the thought of something happening to you. I *won't* let it happen. If walking away is what it takes to keep you safe, that's what I'll do."

Fire burned in her belly as she walked to him and took his hands in hers. *I love you, but I'll never allow anyone to control me.* "Is this the way it'll be whenever decisions are to be made? You decide, and I'm to go along with you? I know you want to protect me, but we can't let this person control our lives."

His jaw tightened. "This is the way it has to be."

"End of discussion, in other words." She dropped his hands as if they were some loathsome thing.

"Jamie, don't feel…."

"You might think you can tell me what to do. But don't you dare tell me how I should feel." With a quick flick of her thumb, she unclasped the bracelet from her wrist. She held it in front of her, the dragonfly dangling from the leather cord. "I guess this was a lie."

"Jamie…."

"Go fix something," she said, shooting a glare that should have seared him on the spot.

She walked back to the kitchen, tossing the bracelet to one side as she sat down. She waited, listening. He didn't follow her, didn't call out to her.

Did he expect I'd just roll over and wait while he risks his own life? She dropped her head onto her crossed arms. Hot, bitter tears streamed from her eyes. *I'm tired of being shoved aside as if I don't matter. I thought you were different. I thought you believed in us.*

The only sound she heard was the beep of the security system as he set the alarm, followed by the closing of the door. The beep continued for several seconds, taunting her with his promise to keep her safe.

Rhys turned the chair sideways from the desk. He stretched out his legs, rested his head back on laced fingers. Since his conversation with Jamie, the day had continued to deteriorate.

His self-righteous glow had taken an immediate hit as he'd descended the front steps. He'd been stuck without transportation. The only car in the driveway was Jamie's. No help there, and he certainly wouldn't ask. Dana was well on her way to Main Street. By this time, Paige would be deep in prep work at the restaurant.

A call to Sam resulted in him sending Mike Winslow. A trip

that ended with the deputy announcing Rhys's arrival at McCall's with a flash of the light bar and a quick squawk of the siren.

Since then, even Stacy had taken him at his word that he didn't want to be disturbed. Whether she believed his explanation that he needed uninterrupted time to refamiliarize himself with ongoing projects, he didn't care.

Go fix something.

The bitter taunt had burned him all day. What did Jamie think he was doing? If he didn't take this step, then she could be the one paying for it with her life. And that was one thing he couldn't fix and certainly couldn't live with.

I'm doing this for us! For a future someone wants to take away.

A sharp tap sounded on the door. Before Rhys could respond, Stacy entered, closing the door behind her.

"Sorry to interrupt your"—she gazed over his outstretched form—"cerebral planning session, but you wanted me to remind you to call about your car."

He sat up and reached for his cell. "Thanks."

"I already called. It's ready." She perched on the edge of the chair opposite his desk, forearms resting on the surface. Pink lace and a hint of cleavage peeked out as she leaned forward. "Thought I'd check if you need a ride there."

The unexpected offer trumped his irritation over the interruption. "I'd appreciate it. Thank you."

"Good. Pack up your stuff and let's go."

He checked his watch. "It's three o'clock."

"I want to go before traffic gets heavy on that road. I have things to do this evening. You must also."

His gaze shot to the first-date photo from Jamie. "Not really."

Stacy stretched out her arm and nabbed the frame, gave the photo a quick look, then replaced it. "Hmm, okay. Meet me at the elevator." She winked. "I'll tell Kevin we're both leaving and won't be back."

Rhys shook his head. Stacy never stopped being Stacy.

Settled in the sleek sports car, he expected her to grill him about the photo during the drive. She didn't disappoint.

"You and Jamie? Problems?"

"None of your concern."

"That bad?"

"I'm not discussing it."

"I just need to know if this clears the path for the two of us."

The saucy tone and side smile didn't amuse him. "Never going to happen."

"Not even for revenge? A little something to pay her back for whatever she did."

"Jamie didn't do anything."

For a moment, blessed silence followed. An all-too-brief respite as suspicion took root. Someone with red hair had slept in his bed. He turned his head, giving a quick sniff. Nope, not the same perfume, and he would have noticed sooner if she had worn that particular scent.

Keeping his tone as casual as possible, he asked. "Did you do anything in particular last night?"

She shot a cynical look in his direction. "You want to talk about my evening? Really?" When he didn't respond, she shrugged. "Okay. Yes, I hung out at the Lighthouse Cantina. Half-price margarita night." She giggled. "There was this one woman. Thought she was hot stuff. Kept trying to get the men to dance with her. She was one or two shots short of totally plastered when I left. That was almost as bad as last week when the PI kids from college came home. Derek—he's the bartender—caught every one of their fake IDs."

Stacy couldn't have been the shooter. At that time, the two of them had been working at McCall's. Still, just in case….

"Are you out by yourself late at night? You don't carry a gun, do you?"

"And risk breaking a nail? Hardly. I've taken self-defense classes." She winked. "Plus, I carry mace and a siren-alert."

"Ever ride a motorcycle?"

She quirked a brow at the question. "Please, if I want something hot and throbbing between my legs, it won't smell like gasoline." She flipped on the turn signal. "Here we are."

Thank God.

She grabbed his wrist as he reached for the door handle. "I hope you and Jamie work out whatever's wrong. Until then, please come in with a better attitude. Today was like having Erik back in the office."

Ouch. "That bad?"

"For him, no. For you, terrible."

Scolded by Stacy, and he deserved it. Jamie's safety came

first, but others didn't need to pay for his attitude. "I apologize. Tomorrow will be different."

Her gaze softened, her smile fading as she loosened her grip. "Jamie and I aren't best buds, but we had some bonding moments in college. She's one of the few females I can say is a genuinely nice person. You're making a big mistake if you don't make things right with her."

"I'll keep that in mind." He exited the car, stopping to retrieve his briefcase from the backseat. "Thanks again."

"Anytime." She gave him a once-over with a flutter of eyelashes and a tah-tah wave of her fingertips. "Remember that revenge offer if you change your mind."

Shaking his head, he walked away. He stopped to inspect the repairs to the Navigator, then proceeded to the office. Deductible paid and keys in hand, he settled in his car.

Now where? He had cleanup to do at home. No food though. He glanced at the vacant lot next to the body shop.

The silver bullet diner sat among weeds, but it was still beautiful. The Carsons had been his family, opening their home to a child when they'd had no reason to do so. How would the rift with Jamie affect Paige? She'd been his best friend since childhood, but Jamie was her friend now too.

Was this lost feeling what Dana had experienced when her world had crashed down around her? What she'd gone through prior to relocating to PI would have crushed most people. By her own admission, she'd faltered. But she'd picked herself up and soldiered on. With help from Toddy.

It galled Rhys to credit the man with any positive motives. Just because he didn't like the old man didn't mean Toddy's concern for Dana wasn't legitimate.

He reached for the ignition, his hand stalling as his phone rang.

Dana.

Please, no more bad news!

He took a deep breath. "Hi, Mom. What's up?"

"I was wondering what plans you had for tonight."

"I'm picking up my car now and getting ready to head home. You need something?"

"Your company at dinner. Nick and Megan are coming over. I'd like you to meet Nick's daughter before the party tomorrow. I noticed you left

your bag here. If you'd like to spend the night again, I'd love the company."

Great. A family dinner. Exactly…

…what he needed.

"I'd like that too, Mom. I'm on my way."

Dinner gave him a weird sense of déjà vu. When staying at the Carsons', dinnertime was the four of them. Pop, Mrs. C, a chatterbox named Paige, and him. Now it was Dana and Nick, a chatterbox named Megan, and him.

He glanced at Megan. Dana would have been the same age as Megan when she was pregnant with him. Too young to be single and responsible for a baby. Still he couldn't recall his mother being anything less than happy when he was a child. Except when Dad came around. Even then, she'd shuffled Rhys to another room so he couldn't see them argue. But he remembered hearing angry words and seeing tears his mother tried to hide.

A nudge to his foot pulled his attention back to the table.

"Mom asked you a question," Megan said.

He raised one eyebrow at her reference to Dana as "Mom."

Megan slapped a hand over her mouth as she burst out laughing. "Did you see that? He does that same thing with the eyebrow that Dana does."

Nick smirked. "Needs some work, but you're getting there."

Rhys looked to Dana. "Really?"

Her dark eyes sparkled. "You had it down pat as a child. I haven't seen it for a while, but… good job."

"You two really do look alike," Megan said. She tilted her head, studying him. "Did anyone ever call you pretty?"

He glared at her. "Only once." He paused. "Brat."

She rolled her eyes. "Like I haven't heard that before. Besides, irritating you is part of the little sister job description."

He considered what all that might entail. "Have you seen the big brother job description?"

"No-o-o." She sounded less sure.

He leaned toward her, lowering his voice into a hard whisper. "Be afraid. Be very afraid."

Megan slapped both hands to her cheeks, eyes wide, mouth open in a silent scream.

Nick and Dana broke into laughter. Megan shot a thumbs-up of approval at him as he joined in.

For the first time today, the tension inside him relaxed, replaced by a comforting warmth. This could have been his life. Two parents, a sibling.

What a power couple his parents could have been if they'd overcome their differences and stayed married. Or if Dad could have let go of his bitterness over the past and found happiness. If it'd come down it, Rhys would have settled for having two sets of parents/stepparents if it had meant having a real family.

I can have that with Jamie. But that couldn't happen until he stopped the person who threatened all their futures. Not even then, if Jamie refused to forgive him. She *had* to forgive him. To lose the heaven he'd found with Jamie was unimaginable.

Another nudge to the foot pulled his attention back to the conversation. He offered a silent apology to Dana as their gazes met.

"How's your father?" she asked.

"They're getting him up to walk around the ward twice a day. They'll probably release him in the next day or so. Between his housekeeper and visits from the home nurse and April, he's covered for care. I offered to stay and help out, but he refused." The rejection still stung. "Told me keeping the business running was best way I could help."

"Look on it as a sign that Erik trusts you."

Megan's head swiveled from Dana to Rhys. "Erik's your father? And he had an accident?"

"He was attacked in the downtown parking garage. A guy hit him with a crowbar, and Dad fell down a flight of concrete steps."

Megan's gasp was so soft, he almost missed it. Fear shadowed her hazel eyes as she met his gaze. "I heard some guy bragging about beating up a guy named Erik. I thought it was a street fight or something."

Nick frowned, his fork clattering against the plate. "Where were you?"

"Making deliveries on the street where the bookstore is."

"Trenton and Federal," Rhys said. "McCall has a work crew there. The city subcontracted us to repair the sidewalk."

Megan's head bobbed. "Right. There were three guys with McCall T-shirts. They must have had their lunches with them because they only ordered drinks. I heard them talking while the guy named Rob got money from the truck."

"Didn't they notice you listening?" Dana asked.

Megan shook her head. "I looped the cords to my earbuds over the top of my ears while I waited. To this guy, it must have looked like I had them in my ears."

Rhys shifted in his chair. "One of the McCall workers said something about attacking my dad?"

"It was another guy who came by. He asked if any of them knew how to contact Mitch, that he wanted to share the good news about Erik going ass over teakettle down the garage steps." She shot a quick glance at Dana. "Language, sorry. Anyhow, one of the McCall guys said it was nothing to joke about."

Rhys looked at Nick. "I don't know anyone named Mitch. Sound familiar to you?"

Dana spoke before Nick could answer. "Mitch Davis is April's ex-husband. He and your father had a rivalry over her. Supposedly Mitch and some of his friends beat up Erik to prevent him from seeing April before she left PI for college. He was in the hospital for some time after that recovering."

Rhys shook his head. "I never knew that."

If Dad and April hadn't been kept apart, would that have stopped the chain of events that had manipulated all their lives over the past twenty-plus years? A chill shot through him. If that long-ago attack hadn't occurred, his own parents wouldn't have met, and he would never have existed.

"Whatever the history between the two men, it doesn't sound as if Davis ordered the attack if this fellow was asking for his location."

Nick had a point. There was more to the story. He switched his attention back to Megan. "What did the guy look like?"

"Older guy. Gray hair with a reddish tint, no-neck, beer belly." She tapped her fingertips on the table. "Rob called him something with a 'D.' Denton? Dawson?"

Rhys sank back in his chair. He knew the rest of the story. "Chet Dalton. Dad fired him two days before the assault." He pushed back his chair. "I'm calling Sam."

When Rhys returned to the breakfast nook, he found Megan in the process of clearing the dishes from the table.

"Dad and Dana are on the patio." She grinned. "You're

supposed to help clean the kitchen."

"Uh-huh." Rhys moved to the other side of the table. "Sam's on his way over to get your statement and have you view a photo lineup to identify the person who talked with the work crew."

"Then they'll arrest him?"

"Sam pointed out that Dalton's statement doesn't prove he was the attacker, even considering the timing of his firing. However, if he is the person on the security footage from the courthouse camera near the parking garage, that would place him on the scene at the time."

"So I really didn't help then?"

"You definitely helped. Especially if you can identify Dalton in the security footage."

Megan sucked in a deep breath that hissed back out through her teeth. "Will I have to testify in court?"

"I don't know. Depends how Dalton pleads if he is the one who attacked Dad."

She met his gaze full-on. "I'm sorry about your dad. I'll do whatever's needed."

"Thanks. I haven't seen the security footage yet to know if an ID could be determined. With what you heard, it could make a difference in getting an arrest."

"I also owe you an apology for earlier. For the big brother comments."

He took the dishes from her hands and carried them to the sink. "You made me laugh. I needed that."

"It was presumptuous. I don't know how much your mom has told you so far…."

"I know Nick proposed and that you two are moving in this weekend." He chuckled. "Nick asked for my blessing."

A laugh spluttered from Megan's lips. "Did you give it?"

"Yeah, I did. Nick and I, we're good." He leaned an elbow on the island. "The news took me by surprise, especially since they haven't known each other very long. But I'm more than okay with it. Dana deserves happiness, and I'm not going to stand in her way. I know Nick loves her, and she loves him."

She propped both elbows on the island, hazel eyes gazing across the counter. "Do you believe in love at first sight?"

"Uh…." He hadn't expected that question, especially from a teenage girl he'd met only hours ago.

Megan burst into a series of from-the-gut laughs. "Get over yourself! I didn't mean you. I meant Dana."

"And Nick?"

"No, I meant me." Her chuckles subsided. "It wasn't really at first sight. I liked her from the beginning. I could tell she cared about Dad, but she didn't try to force an instant relationship with me. I know she must have hoped for one, but it felt natural." She cast a wistful glance toward the patio area. "My mother has no maternal skills. Her primary interest is men and having fun. The first time I came here, it hit me that this is what a family and a home should be like."

Been there too.

She leaned forward. "I want that. Not just for myself for now, but to have that experience to pass on when I have a family of my own. I want to have a normal family for whatever time I can, and I went overboard with expecting everyone to fall in with my plans. I'm sorry."

It wasn't a bad dream to have. Maybe… just maybe, he could share that slice of normality to smooth the way into his own future.

"We made a good start tonight." He pointed to the sink. "You wash, I'll dry."

"Hey, what about the dishwasher?"

"China. Silver. All hand-wash only."

Megan's smile offered more than a hint of mischief. "Plenty of time for more bonding, big brother."

"Let's get busy, Sis. Sam'll be here soon, and you are not sticking me with the dishes."

Chapter Seventeen

Rhys dashed through the doors at Carson's. A busy morning meant a late lunch. He could sit at the table in the back of the room. Eat in the quiet and decompress. All in all, not a bad day so far.

Jamie had been quiet at the morning meeting at Dana's house. She'd denied him the camaraderie they'd had from the beginning, shutting down every effort he'd made to convince her that he wasn't abandoning their relationship.

On the positive side, he, Kevin, and Stacy had fallen into a productive rhythm at McCall. The job lists were prioritized, crews rescheduled. Best of all, he'd assigned two crews to Main Street, working separate shifts between six in the evening to ten in the morning. The crews would avoid working in the worst heat of the day, and the shops could operate without construction dust and noise.

That should make Bart Caine a happy man. He couldn't wait to tell Jamie so she could pass on the news. If she'd grant him the time to talk to her.

The door to the kitchen swung open, and Paige walked to the counter. She slapped his sandwich onto the countertop, and he winced. Seems Jamie's mood had infected Paige too.

"Mind if I eat at the back table?" he asked, grabbing a bottle of water from the refrigerator case.

"As a matter of fact, I do."

He set the bottle on the counter, staring at her. Throughout all the quarrels they'd ever had, he'd never heard her tone so cold and dismissive. "Why?"

"Because I'm mad at you. I can't believe you're treating Jamie this way."

"I'm doing this to keep her safe."

"You could do that without cutting her out of your life."

"It's only until we find out who's behind these attacks." His temper flared at the unfair accusation. "Besides, this is between Jamie and me. You and I are supposed to be friends."

"Not when you're wrong." She picked up the sub, pointing it at him like a sword of vengeance. "You know what? You can get your food somewhere else."

The swelling inside him grew not out of anger, but hurt. He didn't begrudge Paige supporting Jamie, but was it too much to expect her to consider his side? To recognize that he was trying to protect the people he loved?

A cold chill ran through him. Paige was one of those people, possibly the next one on that psycho's list.

He stared at her for one long moment. Long enough that the burst of anger faded from her face. Long enough that regret crept into her eyes. Long enough for him to make the decision that would protect his dearest friend.

Forgive me, Paige.

He walked back to the beverage case and replaced the bottle, then headed for the door. He paused, looking around the room. "I'll do that."

When he returned home that evening, a white pasteboard card was stuck in the crease between the frame and the door.

His business card with the credentials crossed out and replaced with three letters: D O A.

His stomach clenched. Whoever this psycho was, she wasn't giving up. At least the focus was back on him. For now, Jamie and Paige were safe. He'd made the right decision, and when this was over, he'd make things right between them.

He pulled out his phone and called Sam.

Rhys scrubbed his hands through his hair. Yesterday's

successes had turned into today's disasters.

A lost shipment of lamp posts, resulting in having to reassign work crews. Electrical fixtures received with incorrect fittings. Insurance issues with equipment repairs. Snafus in home healthcare arrangements for Dad's release from the hospital.

Never thought he'd say it, but thank God for Kevin and Stacy. Both of them had jumped into action, calling for information or advice when needed, but otherwise handling the issues. Between Kevin's keen intellect and Stacy's "take no BS" attitude, every snag had been handled.

Except the one in front of him.

Sitting on the floor in the waiting room of the Canfield building, Rhys eyed the swatches of fabric and paint attached to the wall.

"Face it, McCall. You are not a designer."

Dana made it look so effortless. She always had. From his earliest memories, she'd instilled a love of art in him. Drawing. Crayons. Even finger painting. She saw magic in every color just as he discovered possibilities in every line and shape.

"We all have our strengths." He scowled at the evidence of his mishaps. It didn't look horrible, but it certainly lacked the spirit and flare of Dana's touch. "And our weaknesses."

So much for knocking this room out in a night or two.

He gathered up the samples, packing everything in his backpack. Just as he finished, his phone rang. A glance at the display showed the caller as Mike Winslow. A call from a deputy could only mean more bad news.

"Hey, Mike, it's Rhys."

"Just checked on your house."

His heart pounded. "What did you find?" There was no longer a question of "if," just "what."

"Flag was up on the mailbox. I checked in case your stalker left a nasty surprise."

"And?" He flipped off the lights and headed down the hallway.

"Found a straight razor. Blade was painted red. You still at your office?"

"I'm working late at the Canfield building. I'm getting ready to walk out now." The back door lock clicked behind him. The glow from the alarm system confirmed it was active. His gaze swept over the area as he walked to his vehicle.

"Up to you, but I recommend you find somewhere else to sleep tonight."

Back to Dana's it was. Rhys headed to the Navigator, but slowed his steps. Something wasn't right.

Large silver rings dangling from the door handle glittered in the glow from the security lights.

Not silver rings. Handcuffs.

His breath froze in his throat. He swallowed hard. "Mike, get someone to the parking lot at Canfield's."

"What is it?

"Handcuffs. Soldered to the door handle of my SUV."

"Hang on."

Mike's voice crackled and echoed in Rhys's ear as the deputy relayed the information to the dispatcher. With the sheriff's office across the street from Dana's building, less than a minute passed before a deputy arrived.

It was enough time for Rhys to think. Enough time to make a decision. If these ongoing incidents were meant to unnerve him, they'd done more than succeed. They'd made him furious.

Risking a future with Jamie. Destroying his friendship with Paige. Because of this psycho? No more. It was time to take the offensive.

He just needed to figure out how to do that.

Jamie didn't recognize the number displayed on her cell phone, but since she'd forwarded the Canfield office lines to her phone, there were plenty of reasons why the number wasn't familiar. She wasn't going to let Rhys's dire predictions run her scared.

"Canfield Designs. Jamie Danvers speaking."

"Ms. Danvers. I was hoping to speak with Mr. McCall. Or perhaps Mrs. Canfield if she's available."

The soft Virginia cadence along with the man's elegant manner immediately charmed her.

"Mrs. Canfield is at a client site at the moment. Mr. McCall is at another office. Have you tried his number?"

"I did, but it went to voice mail. My hope was to speak to someone in person."

"If you'd like to leave a message with me, I can try to reach one of them to return your call. Could I have your name, sir?"

"John Marcum. I own a sizeable piece of property in downtown PI. I've had several discussions with Rhys regarding its sale."

John Marcum. The man who could make or break the Towne Square project. If only Dana was… No, she could handle it.

She took a deep breath. "I've been involved in some of the conversations on our side. I handle marketing and communications for Canfield Designs, and please, call me Jamie."

"I gave Rhys permission to inspect the building. Is it still his intent to turn the old mercantile into a condo building?"

"Yes, it is."

"Tell me about them. How big? How many?"

She couldn't give square footage or list support beams the way Rhys could. She couldn't discuss nickel-plated fixtures or crown molding in the manner Dana would. Instead, she told him about the flow of the various floor plans, how a building closed for years would be home to couples and families. She described the view from the condos that would face the ocean, the scenic park that would be visible from the other side.

"Of course, you're familiar with the views, Mr. Marcum."

"True, but it's been a while since I've seen them. I'm certain things have changed during that time. Good to picture it again through new eyes. You've helped me make my decision, Miss Jamie."

Jamie held her breath.

"I want one of those units. Top floor, facing the ocean, and including any upgrades I want."

"Certainly. I'll make sure you're the first on the purchase list."

"No, dear. That's my asking price for the building. I've been away from PI for too many years. I don't want a fixer-upper. Don't want a lawn to take care of. Just a spanking new home where I can sit in the fresh air and watch the waves." His voice wavered. A cough followed. "I'm ready to come home. Can you make this deal happen for me?"

"Rhys will have the final word on the decision, but I feel positive he'll accept. I'll get in touch with him immediately to return your call."

"Thank you very much. I look forward to meeting you."

The call ended just as the beep of the security system announced someone entering the front door. From the sound of the footsteps and the echoes of voices, both Dana and Rhys had returned.

"Jamie," Dana called from the living room. "Are you free to join us? I want to catch up."

Jamie saved the file and picked up the message. She walked into the living room and took one of the armchairs. Dana was seated on the couch, massaging her bare feet.

"Remind me to wear flats next time. I didn't expect to walk as much as I did. Oh, and Rhys, I felt like such a fraud."

"What did you do?" he asked.

Jamie bit her lip, fighting back envy at their easy banter. She missed being a part of that. Another thing Rhys had taken away from her. Without meeting his gaze, she held out the message, releasing it when she felt the tension of his grasp.

"I made so many people happy today when I explained to them why there was no construction going on during their shop hours. I gave you due credit, but as the messenger, I got the praise."

"I will bask in the reflected glor—" He held up the message. "John Marcum called?"

"You didn't answer his call so he tried Dana's number."

Dana frowned, and Jamie flinched inside, sensing the unspoken disapproval for her clipped tone.

"There was a lot going on this afternoon, and I hadn't had a chance to look at my phone. Did he leave a message?"

"He's decided to sell." She couldn't hold back a smile any longer. "He wants a condo on the top floor, designed to his specifications."

Dana and Rhys exchanged curious glances.

"Seems fitting he would be our first buyer," Rhys said. "Did he indicate if he'd decided on an asking price?"

"That *is* the asking price. He wants to move back to PI and wants a view of the ocean and no maintenance." A nervous laugh escaped her lips. "He asked so many questions I couldn't answer about square footage or design specs. So, I talked to him about the view and how this vacant building would become homes for families and couples."

A triumph shout escaped as Rhys jumped to his feet. "This is amazing. Sorry, Mom, but Jamie's news beats yours by a mile." A grin gleamed in his tanned, handsome face as he looked at her. "You are incredible!"

The happiness on his face captivated her, urging her to share the triumph. Until she saw the expectant look on his face. Rhys McCall was getting exactly what he'd asked for. What he'd demanded. He had no right to expect her to forget everything and rush into his arms as if nothing had happened.

She shrugged. "I took a phone message. Nothing incredible about that. I was doing my job."

The words, once spoken, shocked even her. She couldn't even look at Dana to see the disappointment that would be on her employer's face. Instead, she had to witness the utter destruction of joy inside the man who, despite all, still owned her heart.

In the frozen silence of the room, the soft inhale of his breath was thunderous. The kinetic energy that fueled his ever-present enthusiasm extinguished in a blink. In his eyes, she saw the hope that had lingered over the past several days fade into nothing.

Rhys turned to Dana, his movements slow, as if he were suddenly decrepit with age. "I have an inspection scheduled on Main Street. I'll call John on the way and ask for some specifics about his request."

He picked up his briefcase and walked to the foyer. The front door clicked shut behind him. Jamie bolted out of her chair, heading for the kitchen.

"Jamie, come back here, please."

She stopped, dreading Dana's disapproval, but she returned to her original seat, her eyes downcast.

"I've stayed out of this situation because it was between you and Rhys. I can't do that any longer, as it's affecting business."

"I was wrong. I'll apologize." Jamie forced herself to meet Dana's gaze. "You think I'm wrong about the other situation too, don't you?"

Dana leaned back, stretching her arms overhead. Her hands fell into her lap, and she sighed. "After the shooting in my office, I learned Nick had been investigating Lansing with Sam's help. If I'd known this, I would have been on guard when the detective came to my office. That evening, I laid into Nick. He was just one more man who'd kept secrets and tried to control my life."

"But Nick did it to…." Jamie's voice trailed off.

"To protect me. Exactly. What he did was out of love. Not out of selfishness like Erik or for whatever reasons James had. So we agreed no more secrets."

"I understand that Rhys wants to protect me. But that doesn't give him the right to drop me, then expect us to pick back up when he's ready."

"Is that what he said?"

"It's what he meant." Her tone sharpened. This situation wasn't her fault. "He told me this was the way it was going to be and had to be. I had no say in the matter."

Dana's expression softened. "Oh, honey. I don't blame you for being upset. Both of you should always have a say in matters and consider each other's view. This is something you have to work out between you. However, I have one question for you."

Jamie ran a tongue over her dry lips and nodded.

"Why are you accepting his decision?"

Her mouth opened, but no words came out. "I… I didn't have a choice."

Dana smiled. "You do. I don't want either of you hurt by this psycho. But being apart isn't the answer, is it?"

Believe.

"No, it's not." She stood. "Would you mind if I made a visit to Main Street?"

"I'd be disappointed if you didn't."

Rhys walked to the edge of the construction site at the head of Main Street. His inspection of the work had turned into getting his own hands dirty. Rivulets of sweat rolled down his face. He pulled off his hard hat and swiped a forearm across his face. A thick layer of dust, dirt, and concrete debris covered his clothing and exposed skin. His body ached, his muscles protested, but it was a good kind of tired. The kind that wiped away thoughts that were best left at bay.

He was brushing the top layer of dirt off his hands when a motion across the street caught his attention.

Jamie. She must have had a marketing meeting with Bart's grandson.

Longing shot straight to his gut. He couldn't look away as she stood next to Bryan McAvoy. Irrational jealousy swept through him when McAvoy cupped Jamie's elbow as she stepped through the open doorway. Tall and blond, wearing a suit that cost more than every stitch of clothing that Rhys owned combined, McAvoy was every inch the successful businessman.

When he glanced that way again, McAvoy had returned inside the store. Jamie stood on the sidewalk, watching him. Her beauty burned his eyes. A breeze swirled the skirt of her powder-blue sundress, and her golden hair and tawny skin glistened in the late afternoon sun. Their gazes met, held, until Jamie began walking toward the wooden planks that ran across the street. She stopped in front of him, less than a half-foot away. A whisper of honeysuckle drifted between them.

"I've missed you." Those weren't the first words he'd intended to say, but they pushed their way from his heart to his lips.

A single step closed all but the briefest distance between them. She leveled a steady gaze at him. "I didn't say everything I needed to say at Dana's."

A chill crept in despite the heat of the day. He nodded for her to continue.

"We're not losing another day by being apart. If that means barricading your house at night, living at Paige's or with Dana, we're together. *That's* the way it's going to be."

Those words warmed the cold corners of his soul. But the risk.... He shook his head.

"When I heard someone had shot at you, all I could think of was that day at Dana's office. There was blood on the floor, splattered on the walls. Lansing had been shot three times, once in the head." His gaze traveled over her shoulder as if he were viewing that scene again. "I can't risk that happening to you."

Jamie's eyes widened, then she straightened her shoulders and took a deep breath. "*You* are not responsible for any of that." She poked a finger into the center of his chest. "You are a good man, but you can't control or fix everything that happens in life."

"So I've been told."

His muttered admission won a small smile.

"I love that you want to keep me safe, but I don't need a

knight in shining armor who expects me to wait on the sidelines. Don't take away my need to give to you. If there's to be an us, it has to be all or nothing."

All. Everything. Forever. God, how he wanted that.

She pushed a lock of hair behind one ear, and his heart soared at the sight of the beaded leather band encircling her wrist. The golden dragonfly swayed with the motion, giving him hope where he'd had none moments ago.

"I want us. No doubts." He gave her a half-smile. "As for the other, I'll try. But fixing things is what I do."

"It's who you are. I don't want to change that, just temper it."

He grinned. "You can be my pressure-release valve."

She wrapped both arms around his neck, giving a slight wiggle. "I know *exactly* where to find that!"

He drew back slightly. "Honey, I'm filthy."

She cupped his face, then brushed a soft kiss against his lips. "Why don't you take advantage of being the boss and quit early? I'll meet you at Dana's…" Another kiss. A nip of his bottom lip. A whisper. "…and we can get filthy together."

Dust and dirt be damned. He wrapped an arm around her waist and pulled her close. His hard hat tumbled to the ground. He was dirty and sweaty, but Jamie didn't seem to mind as she pressed herself against him. Her hand slipped into the back pocket of his jeans, squeezing.

He lifted his head, fighting a grin.

Her blue eyes widened in mock apology. "I was looking for a key to Dana's house."

"Don't you have one?"

"Oh, that's right. I do. I'll see you in your bedroom at Dana's." She threw a teasing glance over one shoulder. "Did I mention I'll be naked?"

His gaze stayed fixed to her swaying hips and gorgeous legs. Applause broke out behind him, pulling his attention back to the job site. Foreman Jake Matthews and several other workers stood in a semicircle several feet away. All their expressions were in the category of "you lucky dog."

"Guess you're ready to call it a day." Jake held out the fallen hard hat to him. "Have a good evening, boss."

The comment was repeated several times as he tipped a

salute on the way past them.

He planned to have a very good evening getting naked with Jamie Danvers.

Moonlight flickered through the window, washing across the bed to puddle on the floor. Rhys stretched, then rolled over, wrapping one arm across Jamie's middle.

She stirred at his touch, snuggling in closer. "I have the most wonderful idea."

Ideas. He had ideas too. More ideas than they could possibly cover in one night. With Jamie's clever mind, maybe enough ideas for a lifetime.

He gave her a gentle nudge. "What's your idea?"

Her breathing slowed into a rhythmic pattern.

"Jamie?"

"Main Street." The words came out in a mumble.

Huh? She couldn't be thinking about work? Could she? He nudged her again.

As she shifted her head onto his chest, Rhys struggled to hear her final words before she sank into a deep sleep.

"Legacy bricks."

His body shook with silent laughter. He wrapped his arms around Jamie, holding her close.

"Oh, baby. What a life we're going have!"

Chapter Eighteen

Nick strolled across the patio at Dana's house, stopping midway. A broad grin broke across his face as he watched the activity. The so-called progressive party had shifted into a one-stop gala in Dana's backyard with more than a dozen teens.

Volleyball. Croquet. Horseshoes. Ring toss. Relay races with water balloons. Best of all, a piñata. Paige hadn't missed a step in combining simple games with music blaring over rented speakers, no doubt spending every dime of the money he'd fronted for the party. If a two-hour party for a half dozen had turned into an all-afternoon-heading-into-evening celebration with twice that number of guests, it was worth every cent and more to see the glowing expression on Megan's face.

Even though the day had started with Megan going through a follow-up interview at the sheriff's office, she'd quickly lost her nervousness and engaged in the process with more enthusiasm than Nick preferred. He crossed his fingers and hoped her sudden interest in a law-enforcement career faded with the rush to the graduation ceremony and preparing for the party.

All that worry had disappeared when he'd watched his daughter walk across the stage at the local high school. The diploma might have been a placeholder for the one yet to be sent from the school in Denver, but the joy on her face had been real. He hadn't been able to hold back a grin of his own. He was so damn proud of his girl.

God, where had the time gone? Holding her hand for her first steps seemed like just yesterday. Now she was taking that leap into adulthood, and she was here on PI to start that journey.

He moved to the buffet, filling a plate with burritos, both chicken and beef, along with chips and salsa.

"Dad!"

Nick turned just in time to see Megan barreling toward him. He shifted the plate out of the way of a collision as she hugged him. Judging from her wet hair and damp clothing, she must have been one of the losers of the balloon race.

"Having fun?"

"The best." She cast a minx-like look up at him. "What about you?"

"Seeing you walk the stage was my highlight. I'm proud of you, Miss Summa Cum Laude."

"Part of my exit strategy."

He tipped a knuckle under her chin. "I need a promise from you."

The smile faded, her eyes growing wide. "What is it, Dad?"

"You've gone through a lot over the years, and Callie didn't provide the best home life or parenting. But that's the past. You have your entire future ahead of you. Get rid of the bitterness and baggage. Promise?"

"I promise I'll try. I'm still getting used to the idea that it *is* over." The perky grin reappeared. "Speaking of the future, and by that I mean the immediate future, is it okay if the party goes on longer?" She leaned forward, whispering. "The first two stops were lame. Videos, chips and dip. The moms didn't want a mess in the house. Some of the other parents cancelled because—can you believe this—they're having a formal party at the yacht club?"

No way was he presenting Dana with her engagement ring in front of a group of teenagers. Then again, it might cement their reputation as the coolest parents on PI.

"I checked with Dana," Megan said, bouncing on her toes. "She's fine with it if you are as long as it doesn't run too late."

"Here's the deal. Everyone out by eight p.m. or when the food runs out. Pass the word. Remember we have a big day tomorrow."

Megan fist-punched the air. "Moving day!" She dashed away, yelling over one shoulder. "You're the best!"

Go with the flow. Of course Dana had agreed, not knowing his agenda. He couldn't wait to see her face when he gave her that ring. It would just be a little later than he'd planned.

Nick carried his plate to a table in the corner of the patio and settled down to eat. The first bite was in his mouth when Jamie joined him.

"Nick, can I talk—Oh, I'm interrupting your meal."

He waved her toward the chair opposite him as he chewed and swallowed. "Not at all. How's the car running?"

"Better than it has in years. I wanted to speak to you about the bill. Thank you for crediting off part of the charges for my helping set up the dinner for you and Dana."

"I didn't realize at the time that you were helping with Megan's party too. So I need to take a little more off the bill."

A flush colored Jamie's cheeks. "Only if you take that off the labor. I insist on paying for the parts. That's money out of your pocket, and I won't take advantage of your kindness. I have the down payment you noted on the invoice, and I can pay off the balance in… three payments?"

"You know I'm buying Crossroads Body Shop and combining it with my business, don't you?"

Jamie frowned at the change of subject. "Yes, Dana mentioned it."

"I've done bodywork before. It's nothing new, but as far as PI is concerned, my reputation is engine work and maintenance."

Her mouth curved in a smile. "So we need to rebrand Warden's as a full-service automotive center."

Nick shook his head, grinning. "Damn, you're good."

She laughed. "It just popped into my head."

"What else you got?"

Before she could answer, Rhys arrived. He dropped a kiss on Jamie's cheek then pulled out the chair between the two of them. "Mind if I join you? I need to ask Nick a couple of questions when you're finished."

"Go ahead," she said, standing. "Nick, you need something to drink. I'll get that while you two talk."

"What's on your mind, Rhys?" he asked as the other man's gaze continued to follow Jamie's path.

With a start, Rhys turned back to the table. "What time do you want meet at your apartment to move your furniture?"

"How about one p.m.? Megan, Dana, and I are going over in the morning to move clothes and household stuff. Not a lot of furniture to move, but what's there are large pieces. Sam said he could help."

"I heard about the huge leather sofa. Tom and Mike said they could spare an hour or two to help. Does Dana have somewhere available to put everything?"

Nick grunted. "She does. She's calling it the "overflow room." It's where all the boxes she hasn't unpacked have gone to live."

A moment of shared understanding passed between them.

"We need to move those before tomorrow," Rhys said.

"Garage would work for now."

"I'll take of care it." He nodded toward the yard. "Plenty of volunteers available."

Nick chuckled. "If you're going to ask for volunteers, take Dana. No way they can turn down those big brown eyes."

"I hadn't considered pimping my mom, but if it gets the job done, I'll give it a try."

Jamie arrived on the heels of Rhys's departure. Nick chuckled as the two flirted and exchanged several sets of kisses before Jamie returned to the table. She set a chilled bottle of water in front of him.

Nick twisted the cap off the bottle. "Thanks. I was getting mighty thirsty."

"Sorry. I—" She laughed at the comical look he shot in her direction. "Anyway, back to your question."

"I don't expect you to come up with a full-blown marketing campaign right this minute. If you can get some ideas together over the next couple days, we can talk again. I do expect you to track your hours and bill me for your work. That can go against your repair bills. Win-win for both of us." He tapped a forefinger on the tabletop. "I know you. I know your work through Dana. You have great ideas, and I need your help to transition my business."

The glow washing across Jamie's features satisfied him as much as any he'd witnessed on his daughter's face.

"It's a deal." She held out her hand, and he gave it a quick shake. "I should let you know that according to some of the talk I've overheard, most of the girls out there think Megan's father is—and I quote—super hot."

He threw back his head and laughed. "Not to sound conceited, but so did her friends back in Denver. What can I say?"

Paige rushed to the table. "It's almost time. Want me to start kicking people out?"

"We extended the party until eight, but Phase II can proceed as planned."

"Phase II?" Jamie asked.

"Surprise for Dana."

"The ring?"

Paige bristled. "You *know* about the ring?" She whirled on Nick. "Did you let her see it before me?"

"No one is seeing it before Dana." His phone buzzed. He pulled it from his pocket, and his stomach plummeted.

Dispatch. He tapped the screen harder than was necessary.

"Warden here."

"Hi, Nick. It's Molly. Three-car pileup on Old Main. Sam needs your assistance with a wrecker."

"Anyone else available? I'm at my daughter's graduation party."

"Sorry. I tried everyone else before calling you."

He rubbed his forehead. "Tell Sam I'm heading to the garage to pick up the truck. I'll be there as soon as I can."

Jamie and Paige's commiserations followed him as he located Dana and Megan.

"It's okay, Dad. I want you here, but you have to go. People need you."

"We'll be here when you get home." Dana brushed his lips with a kiss, no less precious for its brevity. "I love you."

Needed. Wanted. Loved.

A man couldn't ask for more in his life.

The sound of footsteps outside the bedroom door broke the light slumber Dana had managed to achieve.

Nick was home. A smile mixed with a yawn as she snuggled deeper under the sheet. No doubt he was trying to be quiet, but—

The bedroom door opened, light spilling in from the hallway. Footsteps trekked to the bathroom. More light washed into the room. Footsteps, this time accompanied by a baritone humming some nameless song, crossed to the nightstand next to where he slept.

Clink. Clatter. Clunk.

Watch, keys, and... something? And why there, when the gorgeous walnut caddy she'd provided sat on the bureau for that very purpose?

He padded back to the bathroom, no doubt deliberately leaving the door open to serenade her with a duet of running water and whistling.

Really, Nick?

She sat up and switched on the lamp next to the bed.

Minutes later, Nick reentered the bedroom. He halted, eyebrows raised and with a grin that almost made her laugh. "Ah, gee, honey. Did I wake you?"

Arms wrapped around bent knees, Dana tossed several wayward curls from her face. "One would think you were *trying* to wake me up."

"One would be right." He slid into bed, leaning in for a quick kiss before rolling onto his back. Arms bent under his head, he asked, "What time did the party end?"

"About nine-thirty. Paige rounded up everyone to help clean up." She stretched out, scooting closer. "How bad was the wreck?"

"Some idiot played brake check with a pickup. He lost, went sailing into the other lane and hit an oncoming car. The idiot and the guy in the truck were shook up. A young couple in the other car were taken to the hospital. Minor injuries, according to the paramedics."

Dana shuddered. "I'm glad Megan and the other kids weren't out on the roads."

A deep breath rushed out between Nick's lips. "You and me both. Which reminds me, I want to take Megan out driving so she gets familiar with the roads and learns her way around."

She nestled her head against his shoulder. "You must be exhausted."

"Not so tired..." One arm snaked out toward the nightstand. He grabbed an item off the tabletop. "...I can't give you this."

Dana sat up, a deep breath filling her lungs as she gazed at the small sapphire-blue velvet box. Just the right size to hold....

"My ring?"

"Let's open it and find out." Back propped against the headboard, Nick lifted the lid.

Dana's breath caught at the center diamond nestled in a halo setting with pavé diamonds lining the split shank. Leave it to Nick to find the unimaginable, the unexpected, the most incredible ring in the world.

Nick slipped the ring free from the case and reached for her hand. The band glided easily over her knuckle.

"Oh, Nick. I love it!" She rolled onto her knees. Planting her palms on his chest for balance, she seared his mouth with a wicked kiss. "It's perfect. You're perfect."

"I try my best, especially when it brings a glow to my girl's pretty face."

"How did you know…?"

"The art-deco style was a no-brainer. The rest was easy. Feminine with just the right amount of flash. I'd planned to give it to you at the party, but this worked out even better." He chuckled. "Paige even had a special cake for us."

Dana frowned. "Is that the box in the refrigerator marked 'Dana, do not open?'"

"Probably."

"Let's celebrate!" She bounced out of bed, waving to him. "Come on! I'll wake the kids."

"Wait! What kids?" Nick rolled to his feet, catching her by the wrist.

"Rhys and Jamie. It's not safe at his house, so they stayed over. Plus it was late when the party broke up. I didn't want Paige to go home alone, so she's bunking with Megan in the other twin bed." Lifting onto her toes, she kissed his chin. "I'll wake them while you get dressed."

Nick shook his head. "Not how I expected this night to play out."

She pulled on a robe on her way to the door. Pausing in the half-opened doorway, she tossed her curls and teased him with a flirtatious smile. "Oh, it will."

Dana dashed across the hallway, tapping on the door, then easing it open a few inches. "Megan, wake up."

"What… Dana?" A note of alarm crept into her voice. "Is Dad okay?"

"He's wonderful. Paige, are you wake?"

"Yeah. What's going on?"

"I want to show off the ring Nick gave me. Plus dig into that cake downstairs."

She left them scrambling and squealing as she moved to the next bedroom. Another tap, another easing open of the door.

"Rhys, Jamie?"

Rhys answered immediately. "Mom, what's—"

"Cake. Ring. Downstairs."

Jamie's squeal matched the ones from the other room as Dana drew the door closed.

Leaning against the wall outside their bedroom, Nick grinned. "I'm holding you to that promise."

She threw both arms around his neck. "I'll make it up to you."

Tired and rumpled, he gazed down at her. The warmth brewing in his eyes left no doubt of his love for her. "Looking forward to hearing you brag about what a wonderful guy you have."

"I plan to do exactly that." She grabbed his hand. "Let's get downstairs before the rush."

They reached the bottom of the stairs when both bedroom doors opened, following by the pounding of feet.

"You're loving this, aren't you?"

The noise, the clamor, the mess. For a woman who thrived on order and organization, she couldn't have been more thrilled.

"You bet I do. Let's get some cake."

Rhys stretched out in the lounge chair on the patio. The night air was cool and the new French doors Dana recently had installed blocked the conversation still going on in the kitchen. Nick had already headed back to bed. Poor guy probably hadn't gotten any sleep at all since arriving home.

Rhys could have gone upstairs as well, but there was something soothing about gazing up at the stars and listening to the crickets. His body relaxed, his mind beginning to doze, when a hand touched his shoulder.

He looked up to see Paige standing beside the chair.

"Can we talk?"

He dropped his feet to either side of the chair. "Sure. Have a seat."

She straddled the lounge chair and sat down, their knees touching. "Awkward in there, wasn't it?"

"Yeah, it was." He took a deep breath. "Paige, I need to apologize—"

"Yes, you do. But I need to do it first. I'm sorry for the way I talked to you at the restaurant. I shouldn't have taken sides, and I was sorry as soon as I said what I did. I just didn't expect you to walk away."

"I was wrong to shut you out, but I couldn't trust that this person wasn't targeting everyone close to me." He shook his head. "I couldn't put you in danger."

Paige caught his hands in hers. "We've been friends for as long as I can remember. We've always had each other's backs. But you didn't have my back by not telling me what was going on. I love you, and I say this with love—"

Rhys groaned.

"—sometimes you're an idiot. A good-hearted one, but still an idiot. People *care* about you, and it's wrong for you shut us out. Don't you get it? The more people watching out for you, the safer you are. Plus, it keeps us on alert too."

"I've seen the light, Paige." Between Jamie, Nick, Dana, and now Paige, the message was imprinted in his brain.

"Good. I don't like when we argue."

"Me either."

"Then we're good?" Her firm tone emphasized they'd stay here all tonight until that happened.

"Good enough that I'll stop by Monday morning and fix the overhead fan."

"And I'll fix breakfast."

A piece of his world shifted back into balance. Love for Paige fell into a special category. They knew secrets about one another that no one else in the world suspected. Without a doubt, they'd argue again in the future, but they'd always make up. Their bond was eternal and unbreakable.

He nudged her knee with his. "You're my best friend."

She nudged him back. "Always will be."

Jamie set a tray of glasses filled with orange juice on the front-office table in Carson's along with a small take-out box. Paige followed with a platter of mini breakfast burritos. They sat down in their usual seats, joining Megan.

"Sorry you had to come in early, Megan," Paige said. "Karen didn't have to take the day off after all. She just didn't let me know beforehand."

"No problem. Dad dropped me off on the way to work. With everything moved out of the apartment, I would have had to hang out in the garage anyway." She set a burrito on her plate. "Thanks again for the party. It was super cool. All the kids you invited were great. I think I can be friends with a couple of the girls."

Jamie smiled. "Any of the guys strike a spark, or is there a boyfriend back in Denver?"

"I didn't date many guys at my old high school." Megan nodded toward the front of the restaurant. "Maybe I would have if they'd looked like him."

Rhys stood on the third step of the ladder. One foot rested on the fourth rung, his stance stretching his jeans snugly over a well-defined male backside.

"Eh." Paige shrugged and returned her attention to her breakfast.

"No secret that Jamie likes his butt." Megan laughed, wagging her eyebrows. "She got a handful of it on Main Street."

Her face flaming, Jamie whirled around in her seat. "Where did you hear that?"

"Got it straight from Macy Montgomery at the flower shop. She got it from Lia Kincaid, whose older sister Molly works at the sheriff's department. Who got it from their brother Brandon at the job site, where pretty much most of the construction guys saw it."

"I can't believe I did that," Jamie muttered, shaking her head.

Grabbing Rhys's butt in the middle of the construction zone on Main Street had to have been the most impulsive thing she'd ever done. The only thing on her mind at that moment had been putting things right between them. She'd totally blocked out anything but the man standing in front her. It had just seemed *so natural* to slide her hand into his back pocket and…

"You're drooling," Paige said, nudging her with one elbow.

"I am not!" Jamie retorted, dabbing a napkin to the corners of her mouth. Just in case.

"Paige, question to you," Megan said. "What's with the 'eh'?"

Paige shrugged again. "It's hard to get excited after seeing a guy in his Underoos."

"Underoos?" Megan looked from Paige to Jamie then back. "Is that like boxer briefs?"

"Superhero underwear."

Her gaze shot back to Rhys. "Really?"

Jamie shook her head. "They're for children."

Megan's frown deepened. "When did you see the Underoos?"

Paige grinned at the memory. "Last time I remember he was six. It was winter break from school. Mr. McCall was off somewhere right after Christmas, so Rhys was staying with us. It was after bath time, and he came running in to show my dad. Flexing his—ha-ha—muscles."

While Paige and Megan laughed, Jamie's thoughts toyed with the dream of baby McCalls. "That's adorable."

"Eh," Paige said again.

"I have to know which superhero." Megan bounced in her chair as Rhys descended the ladder. "Superman, right?"

Paige turned her gaze to Jamie. "What's your guess?"

Jamie huffed. For Rhys's sake, she should stop this silly conversation. On the other hand… she did want to know. "I'll say Batman."

Paige giggled. "Sp-Sp-Spiderman!"

All three burst into laughter that continued until Jamie waved one hand in warning. "Okay, stop. He's heading this way."

"Sounds like everyone is having a good time," Rhys said, reaching for one of the mini burritos.

Paige reddened as she struggled with barely suppressed laughter. "Super."

"Great job there, big brother. Guess you have a head for heights," Megan said. "You climbed that ladder like a *spider*."

His eyes narrowed, his gaze circling the table to discern the reason for all the amusement. Suspicion flickered across his tanned features. "Paige, the fan is fixed."

A woman standing at the front counter cleared her throat, and Paige scrambled to her feet.

"Oops, left the front door unlocked. Rhys, there's plenty if you have time to eat. If not, I prepared a take-out box for you. Thanks for fixing the fan. I'll let you know if it gives me any more problems."

"I'm sure you will." He shifted his attention to Jamie as Paige scurried to the front counter. "I need to head over to McCall's."

"I'll see you at Dana's tonight." Jamie handed the to-go box to him. The dragonfly charm swung from the band around her wrist.

"Hey, Rhys." Megan lifted her wrist. "My birthday was a couple weeks ago."

"Sorry I missed it. Catch you next year. Ladies, later." He gave a half-salute and turned.

"See you at Mom and Dad's for dinner!" Megan called.

A half-step pause broke his stride as he walked to the door. Jamie stood, swinging her purse onto her shoulder. "I need to get going too."

"Wait!" Megan shifted in her chair to see around Jamie. "What's wrong with Paige?"

Jamie whirled to see Paige at the front counter talking with Abby Wyatt from the Lighthouse Cantina. Paige looked stricken. Abby handed Paige a large envelope, then departed. Paige trekked back to the table, sinking into one of the chairs.

Jamie sat down again. "What happened?"

Paige stared at the envelope. She pressed both palms against the flat surface as if to contain the contents. Her brown eyes were wide with shock. "I just unsaw the Underoos."

All three stared at the package on the table.

"Abby runs the M-O-M contest at the Cantina, doesn't she?" Jamie asked, a nervous note creeping into her voice.

"Is that the Man-of-the-Month poster?" Megan asked. "Macy and I went over there so I could get a picture of Dad's poster. So... oh."

"Abby knew Rhys would never agree to enter the contest. His name was scribbled on the entry form, and she suspected it was a fake."

"Why didn't she ask him?"

"She was embarrassed."

Megan eyed the envelope. "How bad?"

Paige opened the package and pulled out a photo. "This one isn't too bad."

Rhys kneeling in the sand, the ocean sunset in the distance behind him. Body shimmering with moisture. Arms outstretched, face uplifted to the raindrops glittering in the waning daylight.

Jamie gasped. Her hands shook. "She was there. Watching us."

Megan frowned. "Was it a woman?"

"The hair samples Sam found on the motorcycle helmet and Rhys's bed were long and dyed red. They also noted a smell in that stolen car that was similar to the perfume on Rhys's pillowcase." Jamie shrugged. "Not proof positive, but likely."

Megan wrinkled her nose. "Creepy."

Paige pulled out a second photo, angling it for Jamie's view only.

He was lying asleep. One arm under his head. One leg stretched, the other bent. Strong, beautiful, masculine perfection. Moonlight bathed his form, bare except for a sliver of sheet concealing that most intimate area. Jamie's hand rested on his stomach, fingertips lingering below the scrap of cloth.

"She was in the house. Watching us sleep." Jamie's hand flew to her mouth. She swallowed, forcing back the bile rising in her throat. "Give that to me. I have to let Rhys know."

She grabbed the envelope and jumped to her feet. Paige and Megan raced behind her to the exit.

"Sam needs to know." Paige insisted, catching Jamie by the door.

"I have to get to Rhys. He can call Sam later."

"Wait!" Megan waved her phone. "I'm calling—hey, Rhys, get back here ASAP. No, we're fine, but there's something you need to see." She lowered the phone. "He's right down the street. He saw Dana's car and stopped to talk with her."

"I'm on my way." Rhys shoved the phone into his pocket and turned to his mother. "Don't go into the building. Drive to Nick's and stay there till you hear from me."

"What happened?" Dana's eyes widened in alarm.

He backpedaled across the parking lot. "Megan called and said they needed me back at Carson's. I don't know what's happened, but please do this for me."

Dana reached for the door handle. "I'll go, but you call me as soon as you can."

He carefully paced his way across the lot until Dana's car turned onto the street, then broke into a run.

The door was pulled open by the time he reached the front window. Paige shoved a bottle of water into his hand and pointed to the back table where Jamie was sitting.

"What—"

"We're fine, but there's something you need to see."

Jamie looked up as he jogged to the table. She waited until he sat down, then pushed an envelope across the counter.

"Abby Wyatt brought this to Paige this morning."

He eyed the envelope, not touching it. "Tell me."

"An entry form to the poster contest with your name scribbled on it."

"And?"

"Two photographs."

He opened the flap and pulled the photographs from the package. Heat rose in his face as he viewed the image on the beach. The second one—

"Damn it. She was in the house while we were sleeping. She could have—"

"I know." Jamie clutched his hand. "But she didn't. And we're here. We need to report this to Sam."

Rhys shoved the photos back into the envelope. "No way."

"Way, yes!" Paige said. "They can get fingerprints off the envelope."

"Along with how many other people's? And don't you think she wore gloves? Besides, if I report this, these photos go into evidence, which means any number of people can see them." He stood, holding up the envelope. "This is one thing out of all this mess I can control."

He turned to Jamie. "I didn't know what was going on and sent Dana over to Nick's garage. I'll walk you back to her office and call to let her know it's safe to return."

Jamie rose and picked up her purse. "Sure. Let's go."

"Paige, I'm serious. Do not call Sam."

"I get it, Rhys. It's something personal and private." Paige nodded and held out her hand, pinky extended.

He rolled his eyes, fighting a grudging smile as he curled his pinky around hers.

Pinky swears were sacred. His secret was safe.

Chapter Nineteen

Lunch on the pavilion at the Lighthouse Cantina should have relaxed Rhys. Blue skies, sun, low humidity, and a light breeze. The food was good. The company was tolerable.

He shoved the cynical attitude aside.

The past three days had been free of any threats. Not knowing how widely the attempts would spread, he'd made Kevin and Stacy aware of the incidents for their own protection. Work was settling into a routine, the three of them transitioning into a cohesive team. Kevin had become less abrasive, challenging Rhys's decisions only when they impinged on the financial side. A lesson for Rhys as well. Having run the company solely on his own at one time, he needed to respect the knowledge that Kevin brought to the table.

Even Stacy had settled down. Other than a minor rant today over not being allowed a margarita.

"Great idea having lunch together, isn't it?" Kevin looked around the table for agreement. "We should do this more often."

Rhys considered the suggestion and gave a nod.

Dad's health was improving, his attitude as well, now that he was recuperating at home. Main Street would be finished ahead of schedule. Prep work on the Dennison would begin as soon as the permits were granted. He'd even carved out time in his schedule to finish work on Dana's lobby—as soon as she told him what needed to be done.

Best of all was the bond with Jamie, which grew stronger every day.

All the good didn't erase the threat that still hung over his head. One of the deputies made a check several times a day, driving by his house. He returned home once on his own. A walk-through showed nothing else had been disturbed or removed. As if the perpetrator weren't interested in that site if Rhys wasn't there to experience the shock of another intrusion.

For now, he intended to enjoy the moment. A strong fragrance wafted by him, shattering his momentary peace.

That scent! The one that had reeked on his pillowcase, that had permeated his house. Easing back in his chair, he scanned the area, looking for a woman with long red hair.

"I'll be just a minute." Stacy pushed out her chair and walked to the nearby bar.

Kevin scowled. "Can't believe her. Sends texts while we're eating. Takes selfies. Uses her camera to check her makeup. Now runs off to flirt with the bartender."

Rhys ignored Kevin's gripes as he searched the surroundings. No one seemed interested in their table, and the only redhead in sight was Stacy.

"If she gets a drink, I'm writing her up. I expect you to back me."

Stacy scampered back to the table, reclaiming her chair.

"Time to leave." Kevin's tone warned that he had no tolerance for any arguments.

"You can go. Rhys and I have to wait for the sheriff." She wiggled her fingers at Rhys. "Give him a call, would you?"

"And tell him what?"

"Tell him I found your stalker."

Rhys grabbed his phone. As he hit the autodial number, he looked at Kevin. "Buy her a drink. Whatever she wants."

Abby Wyatt, the owner of the cantina, offered her office without question upon Sam's request. The woman exited, exchanging one awkward glance with Rhys on her way out. Embarrassment was the least of his concerns at the moment. Sam motioned to the small sofa. Stacy sat down on one end, the sheriff on the other. Kevin and Rhys took the two guest chairs, leaving the chair behind Abby's desk empty.

Despite the gravity of the situation, Rhys fought back a smile. If Sam's intent was to create a casual, trust-me attitude with the seating arrangement, Stacy dealt a trump card by slowly crossing her legs under her short skirt, angling her body toward the lawman.

Sam shifted on the sofa and cleared his throat. "First of all, Ms. Andrews—"

"Call me Stacy."

Sam rubbed his forehead. "Stacy, first of all, how do you know the person you saw is Rhys's stalker?"

Stacy glided a gaze toward Rhys. "Remember the woman I told you I saw at the Lighthouse trying to get the men to dance with her? I saw her today when we arrived for lunch. She was watching Rhys. Not that he isn't watchable, but this was in a creepy sort of way. So I decided to test her and asked Rhys to change seats with me."

Kevin frowned. "Was that when you were complaining about the sun in your eyes?"

"Exactly. After we changed seats, psycho-woman moved to the bar where she had a clear line of sight again."

Sam looked up from his notes. "Can you describe the woman?"

"Better yet. I can show you her picture. *Someone*"—she glared at Kevin as she thumbed the screen of her phone—"accused me of taking selfies at the table. However, I was taking a photo of her."

Stacy handed the phone to Sam. He frowned at the image, shaking his head, then handed the phone to Rhys.

"I've seen her before." He wiped a hand over his face as he stared at the picture of the woman who'd nearly killed Jamie, who'd stalked him, who'd put his family at risk. "She stopped me on the street several days ago. Asked for directions to the nearest trolley stop."

She'd been that close to him. How many others times had she been near, and he'd not known? If it hadn't been for the perfume she always wore, he wouldn't have known it today.

A hand landed on his back. "Are you okay, buddy?" Kevin asked.

For once, the term didn't irritate him. He nodded and handed the phone back to Stacy.

Sam gave a business card to Stacy. "Forward any pictures you have of her to me." He turned to Rhys. "We'll get copies made and distributed to—"

"Her name's Vicky," Stacy said as she tapped on her cell phone. "She's staying at Maisie Porter's B&B."

Sam grunted in exasperation. "When did you find this out?"

"A few minutes ago. Just before I told Rhys to call you."

He gritted his teeth. "*How* did you find this out?"

"After she went to the bar, I texted Derek, the bartender on duty, to chat her up. She talked with him, but kept watching Rhys. Then it looked like she got a text from someone. On her way out, she made a pass by our table, right behind you."

"That's when I smelled her perfume." Rhys exchanged a glance with Sam. "The same scent that was on my pillows."

A choked cough erupted from Kevin's mouth.

"After she left, I checked with Derek on what he found out. I'm guessing it's Mrs. Porter's B&B. The woman said it was 'some antiquated wedding cake of a house run by an old woman who rambles on about her garden and dead husband Clyde.'"

Sam nodded. "That's Maisie Porter."

Rhys jumped to his feet. "Maisie could be in danger from this woman."

Sam held up a hand. "This woman has no clue we're onto her. I don't want you racing out there and tipping her off. I'll radio Tom and meet him at the B&B." His phone chimed. After a quick glance, he nodded to Stacy. "Thanks for the photos. Good work."

They were walking back to the pavilion toward the parking lot when Stacy tugged on Rhys's arm.

"We need to stop by the bar so you can pay for the free drinks Derek served psycho-woman. Oh, and you owe him fifty dollars for helping."

He didn't argue. Small amount to pay if it led to the woman's arrest.

Ben waited out of sight until Vicky arrived. She parked off the side of the road. His own car was hidden, well away from the site. She arrived, bitching as usual.

Ben smirked. "Bad timing?"

"The worst. I had a cute bartender on the line, just waiting for him to finish his shift. This better be good, or I swear I'll cut your throat in your sleep."

"Better than good. I found a place you can keep Rhys McCall while you do… whatever you plan on doing."

Vicky broke off mid-curse. Her head swiveled, looking in all directions, a fevered gleam in her eyes. "Show me."

He led the way through a thick maze of trees and tall grass to a large structure seated on a brick foundation. A dozen steps led to the main level. The surface was a mix of stone and brick, patched in places with tar or cement, depending on what decade—or century—the repairs had been made. Stone posts stood sentry at each corner.

"Welcome to Ye Olde Towne Square," Ben said. "The former center of PI. Where the town crier called out the daily news. Where banns were announced and miscreants were punished." He leaned over her shoulder, lips close to her ear. "Can you picture it, Vic? The pillory… stocks… whipping posts. The good and gentle folks gathered around to watch and taunt?"

Vicky whirled around. "What good does this do me? Out in the open where—"

"Patience, Vic. No one can see this from the road." He pointed to the post behind her. "Twist the knob on the top to the left."

With a grunt and another curse, she complied.

A section of stone trembled, then slid open, revealing a set of steps. "There's a sequence that has to be followed in positioning the knobs. I turned them all but this last one. Wanted to give you the honors." He pulled a flashlight from his backpack.

Vicky crossed her arms over her chest. "You first."

Ben turned on the light, illuminating the path as they descended the steps. "Seems some of the staid Colonials preferred to interrogate their prisoners in private."

He held out the flashlight. "Hold this while I light a torch."

"A torch? Really?"

"Left over from a haunted house tour." With a click from a disposable lighter, Ben ignited the torch and set it back in the sconce. He took the flashlight from her and tucked it into his pocket.

Vicky looked around. "Creepy, but not as bad as expected."

"It was cleaned up for the tours." He walked to a stone table in the far corner. Shackles were bolted at the head and foot of the platform.

"Kinky." Vicky spun around. She pressed both hands against the stone surface. "Can't you see McCall chained to the table? Naked and totally helpless."

"I'd rather not."

Her eyes narrowed. "How did you find this place?"

"Sources. I listen, talk, ask questions. Make friends." He leaned against the wall next to the staircase, ankles crossed, hands in his pockets. "You'd do much better being nicer to people, Vicky."

"Ah, Ben, my life coach… not." She moved to the far wall to examine a set of shackles bolted to it. In the flickering light, her features grew hard, her hair shining with a demonic hue.

Ben shifted a few steps to the left to stand in front of the open stairway.

"So many possibilities."

He eased backward up the first step.

"Still it would be risky moving McCall from the wall to the slab."

Another step, then another.

"Can't take a chance of him escaping. I'll need your help—"

The last of her words faded away as he dashed up the remaining steps. He moved to the center of the platform.

And waited.

A screech broke the silence. Seconds later, Vicky burst out of the staircase. Chest heaving, fists clenched at her side, she glared across the platform at him.

"What was your plan, Ben? Lock me down there?"

"The question you should be asking yourself is why did I bring you here?" He nodded toward the opening to the dungeon. As her gaze shifted to the staircase, he eased one hand into his jacket pocket. "Why did I let you see that potential playground for your games?"

She tossed her head, a snarl creeping across her lips. "Before I take McCall prisoner, maybe I should test my knives. Make sure they're nice and sharp. In case you're wondering, I'm talking about old lady Porter—"

"Like I'd let you get away with harming that woman."

"Oh, please. Once you finish your business here, you'll take her out with your boring trifecta, and she can join her precious Clyde in the afterlife."

Trifecta. His signature. Two shots center mass and one to the head.

"I told Nathan what I was planning. He laughed and said just don't get caught."

Ben fumed. What was Stoddard thinking to put his own plan at risk for the momentary amusement of a psycho? Whatever the fallout, he'd expect Ben to clean up the mess. No problem with that scenario other than moving up the timetable.

"He's not happy with you, Vicky. Especially after I explained how you stole a car and waited outside the gates at the Canfield building for Rhys McCall to leave. How you rolled down the window, took a shot at him, and almost hit Mrs. Canfield."

Her eyes bugged out. "I never did that!"

He laughed at Vicky's outraged innocence. "Mr. Stoddard thinks you did, and that's what counts. Your assignment was to eliminate McCall. Quick and clean. But what was it you said? Oh, yeah. *I like to play with my prey.*" He chuckled. "Karma, like you, Vicky, is a bitch."

With the ease of years of experience, Ben slid the gun from his pocket. For the first time, he saw fear on Vicky Towers's face. Fear she attempted to hide behind a pathetic show of bluster. He cherished every moment.

"You can't kill me. I'll tell Nathan the truth. You think he won't believe me?"

Ben shrugged. Small odds, but not like she'd have the opportunity to make that call. Time to end this before Vicky decided to run. He saw her intentions in the frantic darting of her gaze, the shifting of her body.

"I brought you here to let you know what you'll never enjoy."

One. A quick pull of his finger on the trigger sent Vicky to the pavement.

"So your body will be found."

Two.

Blood pumped from her body. Her eyes were glazed. Death was seconds away.

"Wh—why?"

He could have toyed with her. Could have watched her bleed out.

He didn't play. He was a professional. One who did his job, swift and efficient. Just this one time, he delayed long enough to grant her final request.

"So McCall knows he's safe."

Three.

The mark of a professional was a well-constructed plan.

Remove Vicky's cell phone from her purse. Gloves worn to prevent fingerprints.

Gun broken down. Each piece carefully wiped, then buried in separate spots as he returned to his car.

Shower at the athletic club. Change of clothes. Other garments bagged and disposed of in trash bin.

Car wash.

Text for roadside assistance. Don't want to leave Vicky's body too long to the elements. Cell phone dropped into trash can. Memory card into sewer.

A stop at Carson's for coffee. He deserved it.

And now a call to Mr. Stoddard.

Ben took a deep breath as the line rang.

"Hello, Benjamin. You have something to report?"

"Slight change in plans. I had to eliminate a stumbling block."

"Explain."

Nathan definitely didn't sound happy. Too bad. What was done was done, and as usual, Ben had to clean up the mess.

"Your emissary decided to stalk Mr. McCall—"

"I'm aware of that. It seems harmless, and the result will be the same in the end."

Vicky had definitely worked her wiles on Stoddard. Riding high on whatever liberty their employer had allowed, she'd grown too bold, too careless. One thing was for sure: Ben Hampshire wasn't taking the fall for Vicky Towers's screwups.

"Did she mention almost killing Mrs. Canfield when she took a shot at Rhys McCall?"

Ben could almost feel the heat across the line as the lie worked its magic.

"No, she omitted that piece of information."

Ben swallowed back a snicker. "I handled the situation."

A brief silence followed before Stoddard continued. *"Well, it seems you had no choice. As for McCall—"*

Ben slowed his car as a sheriff's vehicle exited the driveway to the B&B. Another cruiser remained parked at the far end of the lot.

Just as he'd suspected. Vicky had overplayed her hand, and the law had come calling. He glanced at the clock on the console. Doubtful roadside assistance had found the body yet.

"Mr. Stoddard, I recommend we put that action on hold for the immediate time."

"For what reason?"

"Damage control. I just returned to the B&B. Two deputies are here, talking to the landlady."

Are here. Were here. Semantics.

"Take care of it." The line went dead.

He shifted his features into a worried look as he stepped from the car. Pulling off his sunglasses, he jogged across the parking area and up the front steps. Mrs. P sat on the front porch swing, the lines on her face relaxing at his arrival.

"Are you all right? Was there a break-in?"

"They were here about that woman." She patted the seat next to her. "I knew something was up with that one."

He eased onto the swing. "Did they say why they were looking for her?"

"No, but I have my suspicions." She pressed her lips together, then nodded. "Bank robbery is my guess. Or one of those online scams. Came here to hide out."

Ben hid a smile. "You might be right." He glanced toward the road. "I guess she's not here. Is that why the one deputy stayed?"

"It's been quite an upheaval here. First the sheriff and one of his deputies showed up. Tom Hunter—I've known him since he was a pup—was the one who just left. Michael—the one parked out there—has only been here a couple years. My suspicion is Tom went to get a warrant to search Miss Snooty's room."

Ben laughed.

When Vicky had demanded he dispose of the gun she'd used to shoot at McCall's girlfriend in return for her silence to the local law enforcement about his reasons for being on PI, he'd agreed immediately. She never realized the location he'd selected to leave the weapon was behind the dresser in her room. Almost made him wish she was still around so he could see the look on her face when the gun was discovered.

Her supreme ego never suspected that he was one step ahead of her game.

Always.

"I say, good riddance!" Maisie slapped a hand on her leg. "Ben, I'm sorry, but dinner is going to be late. With all this commotion, I don't have a thing cooked."

"Why don't I treat you to dinner?" Why not? The old lady deserved an evening out.

She peered over the top of her glasses. "If it wasn't for not knowing what's going to happen here, I'd take you up on that offer. What I can do is rustle up something simple. How does bacon and eggs sound? Hash browns on the side if I can get you to peel the potatoes."

"I'm your huckleberry."

He stood, holding out a hand to help Mrs. P to her feet. Keeping time with her slower step, he followed her inside.

All in all, not a bad day. Vicky Towers was no longer a threat to his own plans, and Mr. Stoddard was no wiser to Ben's interference. And Rhys McCall escaped from a fate worse than he might have ever imagined.

One question though remained unanswered. What to do about Dana Canfield?

Nick slowed his truck as he spotted a vehicle parked on the shoulder of the road. Ford Mustang, yellow. Hard to miss.

What was missing was the driver.

Something about the situation didn't sit right. Nothing but a paved road for several miles either way. Perfect place for a robbery or an ambush. Nothing to suggest he might not be the next target.

Nick unlocked the dash compartment and retrieved his gun and magazine. He loaded the gun, then placed a call to Sam.

"What's up, Nick?"

"I'm on a roadside call on Bradford. Car's here but no driver."

"Maybe they took a walk while they waited."

"Doubtful. Nothing but trees."

"So they stepped away to take a leak." A short pause followed. *"I don't have anyone free at the moment."*

"I'll wait and see if anyone shows up."

"Call me back either way."

Nick tucked the phone into his pocket. Gun in hand, he exited the truck and walked to the car. A glance in the back seat showed no one had taken refuge there for a nap. A quick look at the front seat showed a purse in plain sight.

He looked around and listened. Birds were chirping, and a squirrel skittered across the road. Something about this place was familiar. He walked a few steps farther and saw the overgrown path to one side.

Halloween Haunted House. He'd driven one of the wagons to this drop-off point.

He looked closer and saw the heel prints in the dirt. Trampled grass formed a parallel path to the one in the dirt.

Walking several feet away from either path, he followed the trail, knowing it would lead to Olde Towne Square. He circled the structure, mounting the steps on the far side.

Nick reached the top of the pavilion and halted, his breath catching. A red-haired woman was lying motionless in a pool of blood. Left-handed, he pulled his phone out again and called Sam.

"Find the driver?"

"Found her body." The answering silence lasted long enough for Nick to ask, "You still there?"

"What's she look like?"

"Haven't gotten that close, but I can see red hair."

"I think you just found McCall's stalker. Where are you?"

"Olde Towne Square pavilion." He walked around the perimeter, stopping again. "The staircase to those underground rooms is open. I can see a flickering light. Maybe a torch."

"You armed?"

"You bet I am."

"I'm on my way. Stay on the line with Molly."

The line crackled, then Molly spoke. *"Hi, Nick. I'll keep listening in."*

"Thanks, Molly, but I should be okay. Whoever shot this woman is long gone."

"How do you know?"

"Because she didn't call roadside assistance herself."

The house was quiet. Ben stood by the bedroom window, reviewing the events of the day. He and Mrs. P had just made it to the front door when the deputy arrived at the steps, requesting an interview with Ben.

Interview. Interrogation. Semantics.

No, he didn't know Vicky Towers other than to speak to her once or twice.

His impression? Rude.

His reason for being on PI? Vacation. Computer consultant. He'd reserved two months at the B&B in case a client needed onsite assistance and he had to leave, wanting to be sure the suite would be available when he returned.

Why was his car so clean? A youth group from one of the local churches was holding a car wash. Mrs. P asked him to take her car this morning. They did such a good job, he took his in the afternoon. Ben didn't bother to add that he'd brought the car wash to Mrs. P's attention while reading the morning newspaper.

The deputy left with a page full of notes and nothing to pin on Ben Hampshire. Credit given to Mrs. P for her staunch defense of him.

There was nothing—nothing at all—to link him with Vicky Towers. Nor to Lansing or Buzz Grainger, that pathetic goofball the detective had hired to eliminate Mrs. Canfield. What a loser. Grainger couldn't even pull off a simple hit-and-run.

Ben walked to the dresser and picked up his cell phone. He tapped in the additional digits that allowed him access to Stoddard's phone. As soon as the man answered, all recent texts and phone records downloaded to Ben's device.

"You have more to report?"

"The authorities are investigating the shooting. Of course, they've connected it with Lansing and Grainger."

"They're not total idiots, in other words."

Ben grinned. The sarcasm was strong in Mr. Stoddard tonight.

"Not totally, sir."

"I want this matter finished. The clock is ticking, and we have a small window of time remaining. You are correct in what you said, Ben. It might be wise to delay killing Mr. McCall until things calm down."

"And Mrs. Canfield?"

"I'll handle that personally."

Ben glanced at the screen. *Download complete.*

"Until then, continue as you're doing. I'll let you know when to expect my arrival. At that time, you can proceed with eliminating Mr. McCall."

"I'll keep you updated if there's any changes here."

"I can always count on you, Benjamin. Have a good evening."

"You too, sir."

Ben disconnected the call and settled on the bed to review the new entries. Nothing of interest in the texts. Several numbers he recognized, a few he'd need to research. He searched through the saved recordings, locating the call that had confirmed the nagging suspicions he'd had over the past several weeks. He connected the earbuds and tapped the *Play* icon.

"I hope to you see soon, Nathan."

"Things are falling into place here as well, Rebecca. I look forward to joining you."

"I'm in the process of obtaining staff. Ones that are discreet and trustworthy as you requested. What about your current staff? I presume there are some that cannot be let go with a simple recommendation?"

"Unfortunately for them, that's true. Can't allow any loose ends."

"The one you mentioned before. Benjamin? Will he handle those loose ends?"

"Quite effectively."

"And what about Benjamin?"

"As I said, no loose ends."

"Excellent. I'll have everything perfect when you're ready to join me."

"I wouldn't expect anything less, darling. I can always count on you."

Ben shut off the recording and pulled the buds from his ears.

"Good luck, Rebecca. You'll find out the only thing you can count on from Stoddard is betrayal."

Ben hadn't survived as long as he had without listening to his inner voice. The one that niggled at him to notice things that didn't add up. Promises that didn't pan out. Discrepancies that couldn't be explained.

Had Stoddard intended to have Vicky eliminate both Ben and McCall? If so, he'd made a poor choice.

Ben sat up, shaken by a sudden suspicion. What had Vicky told Stoddard between the time she'd arrived and her meeting with Ben at Olde Towne Square? There was nothing Vicky knew as fact that could hurt him, but what about something she'd chosen to make up?

Stay alert but don't burn that bridge just yet. Until he had to do otherwise, he'd do the job he was paid to, and he wouldn't leave any loose ends.

Chapter Twenty

Standing in the bucket lift, Rhys stared out at the crowd gathered below in Towne Square and beyond. Behind him, scaffolding and building tarps were in place. One sheet of canvas proudly proclaimed *Future site of the Dennison*.

Several hundred people had already gathered in Towne Square. Side streets were shut down. Temporary seating had been set up in one area. Some folks had brought their own folding chairs. Popcorn, snow cone, and other food carts, along with a BBQ truck, lined one of the side streets.

If only Dad could be here.

He'd made a point of stopping by his father's house, sharing time with him before leaving for the celebration. Not that Dad had been alone. April was there to keep him company. A slight shake of her head had confirmed she hadn't questioned his father yet about Dana's accident.

"Good to be home," John Marcum said, clapping a hand on Rhys's shoulder.

Rhys shot a grin at the man standing next to him. When offered the opportunity to ride up with him in the bucket, John had immediately agreed. The man's love for life belied his age. His silver hair glistened in the sunshine, and his blue eyes shone with excitement.

"It's thanks to you, John. Things wouldn't have progressed this quickly without your generosity."

Two weeks ago, the Dennison had been a dream on paper. Today, the road to reality had been set into motion.

"Giving back. Paying forward, son."

On the opposite side of the square, the DJ cut the music as Mayor Wolfe joined him on the platform. With his usual good humor, he limited his remarks, then gestured toward the bucket lift.

At the signal, Rhys lifted the bullhorn. "Thank you all for joining us today. Is everyone having a good time?" The volume and length of the cheers gratified him. "First, thank you to everyone for your support of the project we're wrapping up on Main Street. Especially to the shop owners who had to contend with disruptions in their business along with dust... lots of dust."

He paused again, his throat swelling as he viewed the upturned faces, the gathering of those he knew by name or by sight. Those he'd yet to meet. The weight of responsibility lifted, replaced by a mantle of thanks.

Giving back. Paying forward.

"Many of you know the man beside me. Thanks to him, the next project for McCall Construction and Canfield Designs is the Dennison, formerly Marcum's Mercantile. Please welcome John Marcum."

John rested his hands on the rim of the basket. He turned his head, scanning the crowd. "I'd like to say I see a lot of familiar faces, but it's a bit too much distance for these old eyes. It's good to be back on PI. Since I came back, I had a number of people ask me 'John, why condos?' Short answer is this young fellow next to me offered." Palms out, he shrugged. "As you know, a number of business and professional offices moved in and out over the years. Flat out wasn't financially feasible to keep the building operating under those circumstances."

He paused for a deep breath. "Condos. That's another word for homes. Homes for a young couple starting out. A small family. Or a retiree who wants to spend his remaining years surrounded by memories and friends. People who'll become part of our community." His voice broke with a quaver. "I'm happy to be home, folks."

He handed the bullhorn back to Rhys.

"Thank you, John. I have one more acknowledgement. Jamie Danvers, head of marketing and communication for Canfield

Designs—Jamie, can you step out front, please?"

Below, Jamie stepped out of the crowd. Her cheeks blushing a bright pink, she smiled and waved graciously.

"Jamie has worked tirelessly with the Chamber of Commerce and the Main Street merchants on promoting the renovations and planning for their grand reopening. She'll also be applying her talents on the Dennison to ensure we fill the space."

John leaned over, speaking into the bullhorn. "If I'd only met Miss Jamie sooner…."

Rhys grinned and returned the horn to its original position as he clapped the man's back. "Too late, John."

As Rhys stood high above the crowd, his heart soared even higher. Like that moment just before the roller coaster tops the highest track, he was pitched on the edge of the greatest adventure of his life.

Believe.

"Jamie, I want you stay where you are. I have an important question to ask you as soon I get down."

He couldn't mean… Could he?

Jamie vaguely registered the murmurs around her. Dana and Nick were close by. Paige's excited squeal came from somewhere to her left. Frozen in place, Jamie couldn't look away from Rhys's face as the bucket descended.

She'd changed since her arrival on PI. Dana, Paige, Nick—all of them had helped her in that journey. Greatest of all was Rhys and his love. She'd grown from a timid, insecure newcomer to a confident, accomplished woman.

She owned it.

Rhys had grown as well. Her love had taught him to receive as well as to give. Each day, the bond between them became stronger.

The bucket landed, and Rhys removed the hard hat, handing it along with the bullhorn to John. A hand, a foot, on the rim of the bucket, he leaped to the ground. His long legs ate the distance between them, that slow, easy stride that captured the attention of more than one woman. He dropped to one knee long enough to kiss her palm, then stood. A courtly gesture from a modern man.

"I love you with all my heart, Jamie Danvers. I want to start a family with you. To make a home and live the rest of my days with you. Side by side. I promise to spend those days making you happy."

He paused, took a deep breath. Not due to nerves or doubt, Jamie realized. It was respect for the monumental step he was about to take.

"Will you marry me, Jamie?"

Tears birthed from joy brimmed in her eyes. When she answered, her voice was strong and sure. "I love you with all my heart, Rhys. A thousand times yes, I'll marry you."

He caught her when she bolted into his embrace. Her arms wrapped around his neck as he swung her in a circle.

"For those of you who couldn't hear," John bellowed through the bullhorn, "she said yes!"

Applause and cheers. Laughter and hollers. Noise filled Towne Square and beyond with celebration.

Mayor Wolfe's voice was broadcast over the din. "I can't say a thing to beat that, other than let's get the party started!"

They made their way through the crowd to a small area with a table and chairs that Paige had corralled for their use, their arrival a slow process, with friends and neighbors stopping them to express their congratulations.

Dana was the first to embrace her. "I'm so happy."

Jamie returned the hug. She loved this woman with all her being, and her heart sung at the thought they soon would be family. She'd have the mother she'd always wanted.

Rhys stepped forward, his turn to embrace his mother. "I feel like the luckiest guy in the world." He dipped his head for a moment. "I haven't forgotten about my promise to find your past."

"It's my fault. I need to go through those papers and boxes, and I can't make myself do it."

"They may have the answers we need."

"I know, but once I open that door.... I don't know if I'm ready for those answers. I'm starting to remember more things about my life. In those memories, I have my family. They're there, waiting for me." She blinked back tears. "I'm not ready to find out that they're gone, and I never had a chance to say goodbye."

"Or they still could be there."

"You're right, and I need to get myself ready." Dana drew a deep breath. "Tomorrow. I'll be ready tomorrow."

"Let me know what time."

Nick arrived, setting a hand on Dana's shoulder. "Has anyone seen Megan?"

Rhys gestured toward the concession area. "She mentioned something about the hot dog cart."

Jamie laughed. "More like checking out the guy running the cart!"

Nick frowned. "Donnie Bishop?"

"No, his summer helper. College kid named Cole."

"Really?" Nick turned, glaring in the direction of the carts. "I might wander over and check that out for myself."

Dana caught his arm. "No, you're not. We're going to put that music to good use."

Nick smiled down at her. "I suppose I could put that off long enough for a dance or two with my best girl."

"She's happy," Rhys said, watching as Dana and Nick melded into the crowd of other dancers.

Jamie rested her head against his shoulder. "She's not the only one."

They had just a moment alone before Sam ambled to their table. He was dressed in jeans and boots, his badge shiny and bright on a soft blue cotton shirt.

"Congratulations, you two. Got some news for you, Rhys. Dalton pleaded guilty. Sentencing comes up next week."

"At least that won't be dragged out. Did you find out anything about the Towers woman?"

"Multiple IDs. Wanted in several states for embezzlement, fraud, assault. My guess is Towers came to PI to hide out and became fixated on you. There's no indication that she's connected to anything in Dana's past. As for Dalton, that was bad blood between him and your father over getting fired."

"What about Towers getting shot three times? Just like with Lansing?"

"As I said then, someone was willing to kill to keep Dana safe. Maybe that extended to protecting you." Sam lifted a hand. "I'll let you know when I find out more. Until then, I intend to enjoy this party."

Without waiting for a reply, he looked around, then turned

back to them with a frown. "Where did Paige go?"

Jamie pointed to the dance area. "She's dancing with Ben."

Sam scowled in the direction of the blond-haired man and walked away.

"Snooze, you lose!" Jamie shouted at his retreating back. She turned to see Rhys's curious expression. "Oh, no, you don't!"

"Don't what?"

"Don't go over there and interfere with Paige's fun."

"What do you know about him?"

"He's some sort of computer consultant here on vacation. He stops in at Carson's for coffee every day. Sometimes for takeout. Oh, and he's staying at Maisie Porter's B&B."

His eyes narrowed. "That's where Vicky Towers was staying."

"Yes, and Mike questioned him. So did Sam. He didn't know anything more than Maisie did." She tugged his hand. "So let it go."

"Yes, ma'am." Rhys gestured to the roped-off area around them. "Dance with me. Just the two of us."

"I want to dance with you forever."

Jamie slid an arm around his neck and whispered a secret in his ear. One that made his eyes grow wide and swing her around in a circle. She lifted her arm, smiling at the bracelet around her wrist.

Sparkling in the sunlight, the golden dragonfly danced in joy.

THE END

ABOUT THE AUTHOR

Dianna Wilkes is an award-winning contemporary romance author, known for the Providence Island mystery series.

Reading has always been an important part of her life. "I learned to read when I was four years old," she said. "Writing my own stories seemed a natural progression."

Dianna holds a B.A. in Visual Communication and a M.Ed. in Instructional Technology. She worked as an Education Consultant for a medical technology company before leaving the corporate world to write full time. Despite all that nerdy stuff, she loves creating stories of romance and mystery with touches of humor.

When she isn't writing, Dianna is deep in researching various twigs and branches on her family tree or fulfilling entries on her travel bucket list.

Facebook: www.facebook.com/DiannaWilkesAuthor/
Website: www.diannawilkes.com

MORE BY THIS AUTHOR

The story continues in *South Pointe* (Providence Island Book 3):

Paige Carson never expected that both a handsome sheriff and a charismatic newcomer would be vying for her affections. The choice isn't an easy one, as she's now responsible for raising her orphaned goddaughter, Jess.

Sheriff Sam Wallace didn't lose at love. He got kicked to the curb. Hopeful that courting the feisty Paige will end differently, he can't help but feel suspicious about his romantic rival. Is Ben Hampshire the man he seems—or is Sam's jealousy clouding his perspective?

Sam's determined to win Paige's and Jess's love, but he also has to keep Providence Island safe. More than just Sam's heart is at risk if he fails to find the killer who walks the streets of PI—a killer with more than one agenda.

Turn the page to read a short excerpt from *South Pointe*.

EXCERPT FROM
SOUTH POINTE

Paige Carson stepped through the door of the diner, stopping halfway to the front counter. The early morning sunshine cut a swath through the windows, and dust motes floated in the stale air. Except for the rumble of an occasional car passing outside, silence surrounded her. A year ago, Carson's, better known as Pop's, had been the most popular family restaurant on Providence Island. Today, it was a vacant building. Tomorrow, it would belong to someone else.

She closed her eyes and went back to that time when bright lights overhead filled the room with energy. The click and clatter of tableware mixed with the chatter of family and friends, and mouthwatering scents teased the waiting patrons. Paige and Rhys McCall, her brother in every way but blood, waited on the customers and bussed the tables. Mom worked the register while Pop manned the main grill in the kitchen.

Then Mom passed away, a mere three months after her diagnosis. Soon after that, Rhys left for college, then stayed on the mainland to work in upstate Virginia. Paige and Pop continued with the rest of the staff for the next seven years until a heart attack had taken him away.

She'd put the property up for sale and opened a pizza and sandwich shop in downtown PI. And never told anyone about the times she'd visited the old site. Walking through the kitchen, stripped of the appliances she'd repurposed at the new location. Sitting in one of the booths, sipping a soft drink and nibbling on chips. Sweeping a floor that no one else cared about.

The visit this morning was her last chance to stroll through the past. Tomorrow, she would sign the papers transferring ownership of the property to Nick Warden.

Heavy footsteps echoed from the kitchen, and Paige's heart started pounding. The back door was locked; she knew it. Taking a half-step back, she tugged her cell phone from the pocket of her jeans, thumb hovering over the emergency button.

The door swung open. Mr. Warden strolled into the room,

and her rapid heartbeat eased. If he didn't irritate her so much, Paige would admit he wasn't bad looking. Even handsome for being on the shady side of his forties. He stopped midstride, flashing a quick grin in her direction, before continuing to the front counter.

"Thought I heard someone out here." He nodded to the phone in her hand. "Hope I didn't startle you. I parked out back."

Paige slipped the phone into her pocket. "Heck, no. I was checking for messages."

A slight uptick at one corner of his mouth hinted that he didn't quite believe her. "Thanks for the extra set of keys. Gives me a chance to get some ideas before meeting with Rhys to reconfigure the interior."

Paige slid onto one of the barstools. "No problem. I decided to make a last walk-through before—" Her throat closed, and she waved one hand in a circle.

No doubt Mr. Warden had big plans to convert the building into offices for the body shop he'd also purchased next door. Tear out the counter where she'd first learned to wait on customers. Throw away the tables where families had gathered to eat Sunday meals after church services. Rip out the booths where high-school kids had met after games to celebrate. Everything Pop had worked for would be gone.

Nick wrapped his hands around the rim of the counter and leaned forward. "If you're having second thoughts, now's the time to say so."

Second thoughts? How about third or fourth or thousandth?

She spun on the stool, turning her back on his too-perceptive gaze. "This is Pop's legacy...."

She waited for the explosion. Mr. Warden would be furious if she backed out now. Especially after he'd made plans to move his repair shop from downtown to the body shop next door. It wasn't as if he needed her property. He could keep the office where it was now and forgo the extra parking.

"Paige."

No explosion. Just one softly spoken word.

Don't say my name. Not like that. She couldn't handle kindness or, even worse, his pity.

"You and I have butted heads from the beginning—"

Shoulders stiff, chin set, she spun around. "You think?"

He smiled. A slow and easy grin. The kind she'd seen him give his daughter Megan. "I know so. But this"—he twirled a forefinger in a broad circle—"isn't your dad's legacy."

Heat shot up her neck. *How dare—*

"*You* are. You live his legacy every day. You're a hard worker and always on the spot when someone needs a hand." A brief silence filled the space between them. "Any man would be proud to have a woman like you for his daughter."

Paige swallowed back the lump crowding her throat. "It was hard coming here every day after Pop died. Pretending things were the same when they never would be again."

"You moved on, and that's a healthy thing to do." He straightened, thumping one fist against his chest. "I'll probably shed a tear or two when that wrecking ball takes a chunk out of my old garage."

Paige choked back an unexpected giggle. Darn him for *almost* making her laugh. A quick glance revealed the concern in his dark brown eyes. Not for a deal that might fall through, but for her. She'd never admit it to anyone else, especially not to the man standing in front of her.

Nick Warden was such a dad.

She swiveled side to side on the stool to break the mood. "What are your plans for the place?"

"I'm keeping the counter. Customers on one side, computer stations on the other." He snapped his fingers. "Which reminds me. Eddie Roberts wants to buy the booths. Since the place technically isn't mine until we sign off tomorrow, I told him I'd check with you."

Paige frowned, trying to picture the booths in Eddie's Sea-Shack. "How did he know you're buying the restaurant?"

"Glenn Thornton told him. They're fishing buddies."

Paige glanced through the window at Crossroad's Body Shop on the next lot. "PI gossip chain."

"Gotta love it." He shrugged. "It occurred to me that you might want to use the booths at the new place."

"No." She pushed away another wave of memories. "Time to let those go too. Besides, if I sell them to Eddie, I can buy tables and chairs for the restaurant. Dana said that tables instead of booths would give me more flexibility for seating once I open up the dining room."

"Would you mind if I kept a few of the bench seats for the waiting area here?"

Paige smirked. "I can add those in with the cost of the property."

"Next question. What did you do with the tabletop jukeboxes? I want one for my den at home."

Her mouth dropped open. "Dana let you have a man cave at her house?"

Mr. Warden's scowl lifted her mood an extra notch. "It's not a man cave."

"Leather sofa. Big-screen TV. Now, a jukebox. Sounds like a man cave to me."

His toe tapping behind the counter gave her spirits another boost.

"For sale or not?"

"Not. However, as bartering is the basis of our relationship..."

He shook his head, grunting. "What do you want?"

"There's a baker's rack in the kitchen. Load it in your truck and take it to my house, and I'll trade that favor for one of the boxes."

More than a fair deal in her opinion. Not much effort on his part, and she didn't have to continue waiting for Rhys's convenience.

"Deal." He extended one hand, closed into a fist. "Let's get the rack loaded."

Paige bumped her fist against his. Sliding off the stool, she halted at the sound of Abba's "Dancing Queen" blasting from the back pocket of Mr. Warden's jeans.

A laugh snorted through her nose. "Maybe you don't need a jukebox after all."

"Damn it, Megan." He clawed the cell phone from his pocket. "She reset all my ringtones."

Curious as to what ringtone had been assigned to her, Paige thumbed through the call list on her own phone, looking for his number. When he muttered another curse, her head shot up.

"Paige, we'll have to do this another day."

At his grave tone, her heart spiked into double-time. Not like she didn't have ample reason to worry. Three attempted murders in the past month, two aimed at Mr. Warden's fiancée, Dana Canfield, and the third one at Dana's son Rhys. Three *failed* attempts, thanks to a shooter whose motives remained unknown. A stranger who even now could be walking the streets of PI.

"What is it? What happened?"

Mr. Warden strode toward the swinging doors into the kitchen. "Megan's text said I need to come home. I texted her back, but she's not answering."

Paige flipped the lock on the front door and jogged after him. "I'm going with you."

"No, you're not. I don't know what's going on, and you don't need to be there."

He pushed open the back door, and she caught it a split-second before it slammed shut in her face.

Paige dashed to the passenger side of his Expedition, hooking her hand around the handle. "Megan works for me, and that makes it my business. If you don't take me with you, I'll go in my Jeep, and I *will* beat you to Dana's house."

Mumbling something she couldn't hear, he jerked the driver's door open. A second later, the lock clicked open on her side. She hopped onto the seat and grabbed the seat belt. In less than a minute, they were headed toward the Crossroads.

"You'll stay in the truck until I see what's going on. Understand?"

"Sure."

He shot a warning look in her direction. She ignored it, just like she intended to do with his order to stay in the vehicle.

Paige sank back in the seat, tapping out a message to Megan.
What's going on? R U OK?

A few seconds later, the phone vibrated in her palm.
Sorry. Txtg R. Need u here 2.

"Is that Megan?"

"Yeah, she wants me and Rhys there too," she said, continuing to text. "Maybe nothing's wrong? Maybe some news about that shooter? Or do you think that old man showed up?"

Mr. Warden darted a frown at her, then returned his attention to the road. "Old man? You mean Toddy?"

Paige dropped the phone onto her lap. "I never got it straight who he is."

"Officially, he was James Canfield's godfather. Grandfather figure to Joshua. Rhys didn't have anything good to say about him, but Dana says he was her rock after James was killed. I'd like to meet the guy and find out for myself."

"Or maybe Joshua finally showed up." Paige glanced across the cab. "If it is him, he's going to get an earful from Rhys and from me. Walking away from his family. Not even returning to attend his father's funeral. Dana didn't deserve that."

"Dana didn't deserve any of the things that happened to her. But for over twenty years, she believed that boy was her son, and she loved him. Loves him still."

Paige stared out at the passing scenery. So many places on PI held fragments of her past. Rhys had taught her and her best friend Claire how to drive on these country roads and showed them how to fill the tank at Red's Gas Station. Paige swallowed back a snicker, remembering how sorely they'd tested Rhys's patience. They'd made up for it by treating him to a movie at the Palace Theater, followed by a hot fudge sundae at Dottie's Dairy Bar.

Those memories were a part of who Paige was and who she became. What if she'd been told her history had never existed, and what if she'd had no memory of the life everyone claimed was hers?

Dana had lived that lie for over twenty years. A car accident and switched identities at the hospital, both of which had been deliberate, had ripped her from her life as a married college student and mom and flung her into another world, where she became wife and mother to another man and his child. James Canfield, the man she'd believed to be her husband, had been murdered a year ago and had taken his secrets to his grave. Based on the recent attempts on Dana's and Rhys's lives, the cover-up behind the identity switch continued.

As for whatever reason Joshua Canfield had chosen to separate himself from Dana, it didn't matter to Paige. She was firmly on Team Rhys.

"Joshua could have called or emailed. Anything to let Dana know he was safe. Remember how you felt when Megan was living in Denver with her mother? When you didn't hear from her for over a month?"

Mr. Warden's jaw tightened. "I do, which gives me some insight into how Dana feels. Just like Megan had her reasons for not communicating, Joshua has his reasons as well." He braked at the intersection, then turned left onto Magnolia. "What if

Canfield sent his son away to keep him safe?"

"From what?"

"From the same type of threat that came after Rhys a couple weeks ago. Think about it. The attacks on Rhys didn't start until *after* he learned that Dana was his mother."

"That Towers woman was a stalker. She wasn't connected to Dana."

"Neither was Buzz Grainger, until Keg Lansing hired him to run Dana over with a stolen truck. Lansing admitted to Dana that he'd killed James Canfield. Towers, on the other hand, might not have had a direct connection to Lansing, but I'll bet good money that she was no random stalker. I think someone sent her here, and that person is the link among those three, especially since all of them were killed the same way."

Three gunshots. Two in the torso and one in the head. By a killer still on the loose.

Paige nodded. "You're right. There has to be a connection. Has Dana remembered anything else?"

"A few things... which reminds me. Rhys and I thought it would be a good idea for all of us to sit down and compare notes. Seems like each of us knows part of the story. We need to put those pieces together, then see what's missing."

"If you're right about that Towers woman, we need to get cracking now. Especially before the person behind all this sends someone else."

Mr. Warden turned into the circular driveway in front of Dana's house, and the SUV jerked to a halt. A dark blue Mercedes-Benz sat in the middle of the drive, blocking him from passing.

"What an idiot." Paige glanced in the side mirror. "I think you're clear of the road."

Mr. Warden snorted. "Vanity plates. Figures." He nodded toward the other vehicle as he shut off the engine.

Paige stretched to look in the direction he'd indicated, and her breath caught in her throat.

EVL.

The social circle in Richmond knew the driver as Evelyn Vogel Lockhart, but as far as Paige was concerned, the license plate said it best.

Evil.

If a Mothers-in-Law from Hell society existed, Evelyn would have a seat on its Board of Directors. Poor Claire. Although having a hubby like Matt Lockhart had seemed to be worth it to her.

Why was Evelyn here? There was no reason, unless…

Paige's stomach rolled, shooting acid into her throat. She fumbled for the handle. Once, twice, then she finally opened the door. She bolted from the truck, knees buckling when her feet hit the ground.

She stumbled across the driveway, the slam of the truck door and the pounding footsteps signaling that Mr. Warden was close behind her. She halted at the top of the porch to stare back at the sleek luxury car.

There was only one reason that would bring Evelyn to PI.

Because Claire was dead.

Made in the USA
Monee, IL
05 June 2024

59460617R00152